TITLES BY KATE CARLISLE

BIBLIOPHILE MYSTERIES

Homicide in Hardcover
If Books Could Kill
The Lies That Bind
Murder Under Cover
Pages of Sin
(an eNovella)
One Book in the Grave
Peril in Paperback
A Cookbook Conspiracy
The Book Stops Here
Ripped from the Pages
Books of a Feather

FIXER-UPPER MYSTERIES

A High-End Finish
This Old Homicide
Crowned and Moldering
Deck the Hallways

DECK THE HALLWAYS

A Fixer-Upper Mystery

Kate Carlisle

BERKLEY PRIME CRIME
New York

BERKLEY PRIME CRIME
Published by Berkley
An imprint of Penguin Random House LLC
375 Hudson Street, New York, New York 10014

Copyright © 2016 by Kathleen Beaver
Penguin Random House supports copyright. Copyright fuels creativity, encourages
diverse voices, promotes free speech, and creates a vibrant culture. Thank you for buying
an authorized edition of this book and for complying with copyright laws by not
reproducing, scanning, or distributing any part of it in any form without permission.
You are supporting writers and allowing Penguin Random House to continue to
publish books for every reader.

BERKLEY is a registered trademark and BERKLEY PRIME CRIME and the B colophon
are trademarks of Penguin Random House LLC.

ISBN: 9780451488220

First Edition: November 2016

Printed in the United States of America
1   3   5   7   9   10   8   6   4   2

Cover art by Robert Crawford

To my wonderful mother, Patricia, who loved to hear who I was murdering each day, and who always did Christmas up right.

Chapter One

Eleven Shopping Days Until Christmas

"Merry Christmas, Shannon!" my elderly neighbor shouted as I backed my truck into the street. Wearing a green-and-red-striped housecoat and a red wool hat with reindeer antlers, she stood in her yard watering her colorful flower beds.

We were two weeks into December and Mrs. Higgins's front yard was festooned with rows of dancing candy canes and shimmery swirling snowflakes. A glow-in-the-dark, six-foot-tall blow-up Santa Claus was surrounded by eight large plastic reindeer. On her wide front porch was a life-sized animatronic Snow White and her seven dwarves frolicking around a twinkling Christmas tree.

Overnight, bright holiday lights had been strung up and down across her roof and around each window and the front door. I suspected her sons-in-law had worked all night and I was touched by their kindness, knowing how much their mother-in-law loved the holiday. I also knew from experience that these lights would remain lit twenty-four hours a day into the New Year.

For the next few weeks, astronauts traveling in space would wonder and worry about a strange, radiant glow emanating from northern California, but we locals knew it was only Mrs. Higgins's holiday lights. The woman knew how to do Christmas right—and at the same time made all her neighbors, including me, look like Ebenezer in comparison.

My lights were always the last in the neighborhood to go up and, while I had many treasured ornaments from childhood, my collection of decorations were, comparatively speaking, sadly lacking. Still, I love Christmas and any day now I would spring into full holiday mode, but I wasn't quite feeling the spirit yet. Nevertheless, I smiled and rolled down my window. "Good morning, Mrs. Higgins. You're out early this morning."

"These roses aren't going to water themselves, little missy."

She had a point.

"You have a good day," I said, and she gave me an absent wave as I raised the window and drove off down the street. Mrs. Higgins grew dottier every year, but she was still a good neighbor despite her tendency toward garish holiday overkill.

Honestly I enjoyed Christmas as much as anyone and always looked forward to buying a tree and decorating my house for the season. But was it too much to ask for a few weeks of quiet calm after struggling through the frenzied overindulgence of Thanksgiving celebrations? Did we have to gear up for the next round of hectic merriment so soon?

"Oh, lighten up," I muttered. I was already sick of my

grouchy, anti-holiday attitude and it was barely eight in the morning. The truth was, I hadn't slept well the night before and now I was late for work. It didn't help that my personal life was in shambles, but that was something I refused to dwell on. But if this cranky mood went unchecked, I was likely to turn into what my crew would call The Boss from, well, you know where. In other words, a really bad boss. And that just wasn't me.

With that thought in mind, I drove to my favorite coffee bar and bought the latte that would magically transform me into a reasonable human being.

By the time I arrived at the job site ten minutes later, I was surprised to hear myself humming along to a Christmas carol on the radio. Thanks to James Taylor's magically mellow version of "Deck the Halls," and the wonders of caffeine and steamed milk, I was feeling better. It was like a mini–Christmas miracle, I thought, as I pulled into the long driveway and parked my truck by the side of the six-car garage behind the old Forester mansion.

"Made it," I said aloud, and breathed a sigh of relief. My humor was still somewhat intact and I was ready to get started. I slid down from the cab, zipped up my quilted vest, reached for my knit cap and my latte, and locked the door.

I walked to the back of the truck and paused for a moment to gaze up at Forester House, officially the biggest Victorian home in Lighthouse Cove. That was saying a lot, because our town was known for its truly grand Victorian mansions. But this one was enormous. I felt a shiver skip down my arms, not from the cold—although it was close to freezing—but from gleeful anticipation. This job promised to be one of the most challenging I'd ever faced, but also one of the most fun. Either way, I was ready for it.

Forester House was a true original. One of the oldest homes in the area, it was built in 1867 in the classic Queen Anne style. But though it followed those traditional lines with its intricately detailed tower rising three stories at the northeast corner, its plethora of gables and mismatched window sizes and shapes, and its four tall chimneys, Forester House was anything but feminine and frilly. Instead, it had a dark, gothic vibe made even more intense by thick, sage green sandstone walls and wildly asymmetrical rooflines covered in dark, heavy tiles instead of the traditional lighter weight composite shingles. Enormous dormers with Tudor detailing rose to encompass three stories. A porte cochere on the east side of the house allowed visitors to be dropped off and step directly onto the veranda that wrapped around three sides of the home and was wide enough to be used as an outdoor room in good weather.

Originally the home had been built to accommodate Mr. Forester's wealthy summer guests who'd driven up from San Francisco and stayed for months at a time, so he had added balconies onto all six of the large bedrooms on the second floor. The attic, too, featured several smaller terraces tucked under the sturdy, tile-shingled eaves.

The stones used to build Forester House had not been cut smoothly but instead had been left rough and uneven. Those details did nothing to make the mansion unsightly; on the contrary, the place was a strapping fortress of a home that exuded raw power and strength. It was imposing and even a bit intimidating (although I would never utter that word out loud).

Any remaining Forester family members had long since died or moved away, and after years of neglect the house had gone into foreclosure. It was now owned by the Lighthouse Cove Bank and Trust, a respected and reliable local institution. Half the people in town had accounts at Lighthouse B&T, including me and my father and most of my friends so everyone was thrilled when the bank decided to donate the home to the town's favorite charity, Holiday Homebuilders, instead of tearing it down and selling off small parcels of the picturesque two-acre lot.

The Holiday Homebuilders charity had been created over twenty years ago to support an annual tradition in Lighthouse Cove. Every December, nearly everyone in town came together to help build a house for a family in need. We furnished it and then decorated it for the season, right down to the bowls of Christmas candy on the tables.

Jason Walsh, who ran the charity, used to work on my dad's construction crew so he knew something about building homes. He was truly excited about refurbishing Forester House, subdividing the huge mansion into apartments in order to provide housing for *fifteen* lucky families. It was an unprecedented donation and the news had caused everyone in town to buzz with delight.

And I was buzzing more than anyone else because the person in charge of the entire project was me!

In addition, twelve local contractors had volunteered their services. After many meetings and discussions, I had assigned each of them a section of the mansion to transform into a separate dwelling for either a small family or a single person. Except for the unfinished third-floor attic, most of the rooms would remain single large spaces with the addition of kitchenettes and closets where needed. Local carpenters, plumbers, electricians, and painters had also volunteered their time to the cause. Six local interior decorators would work with the contractors to furnish the spaces. Since many of the families would bring very little furniture with them, it was up to us to turn these places into comfortable homes. The decorators had been working for weeks, shopping for fine quality used furniture and interesting bargains. A local mattress store was donating brand-new beds for each apartment and a nearby furniture store was filling in with everything that hadn't already been covered.

It was heartwarming to see such generosity flowing from my fellow townspeople this time of year. So with all that wonderfulness surrounding me, why hadn't I gotten into the spirit of the season yet? Why couldn't I suck up the joy and get with the program?

"There you are."

I whipped around and saw Wade Chambers, my head foreman, waving at me from the back veranda. He jogged down the steps and ran over to meet me. "Merry Christmas, Shannon."

"Hey, Wade. How's it going?" As I said the words, I scowled inwardly. What was wrong with me? I couldn't extend a happy holiday greeting to one of my oldest friends? Apparently not. I just wasn't ready. Fine. I slid my tool chest out of the truck and tried not to feel too guilty.

Wade didn't seem to notice as he rubbed his stomach. "We're on day ten of Thanksgiving leftovers. Last night was turkey pot pie."

"That sounds pretty good."

"It was, actually. I keep saying I won't have to eat for a week after eating what I did, but I continue to indulge. Ah, well." He glanced at me. "How about you?"

"About the same." I gazed up at the house. "Are you excited? Ready to finally knock this thing out of the park?"

"You bet I am." But he didn't move, just stared at me with a look of concern.

When he didn't look away, I set my tool chest down on the blacktop surface of the driveway. "You're staring and it's starting to freak me out. What's wrong?"

If anything, his concern deepened as his eyes narrowed in on me. "That was going to be my question. Is everything okay?"

I hedged a little. I guess I wasn't quite as good at hiding my odd mood as I thought I was if my own foreman could tell something was off. "Of course. Why not?"

"Come on, Shannon. First of all, you're never late for work. And second . . . I don't know. Something's going on with you." He picked up my tool chest with no effort and started to walk toward the back of the house.

Scowling, I rushed to keep up with him. "I just hate being late, that's all. I would've called but I was running around."

"Yeah? I tried to call you but there was no answer."

I pulled out my cell phone and noticed an unanswered call. "I didn't hear the phone ring."

He stopped. "Something going on I should know about? Why were you running around?"

"It's nothing." I sighed. I wasn't about to confess what was really going on with me. He wouldn't be able to keep it to himself and I would never live down the embarrassment of everyone in town knowing that my pitiful little heart was breaking. So I simply told him the truth about the morning's main activity. "Robbie ran out of the gate and took off for the beach."

Wade's eyes widened and he stopped and gripped my arm. "But you found him, right?"

"I did, thank goodness." My adorable West Highland terrier, Rob Roy, otherwise known as Robbie, had never wandered off before. I had spent fifteen distressing minutes hunting him down. Luckily all my neighbors knew who the little white dog belonged to and some of them helped me find him. The chase had set me back fifteen minutes, so that was why I was late. And why I was cranky earlier. Well, along with the aforementioned heartbreak silliness, but I was doing my best to ignore that.

"Thank God," he murmured. Wade and his kids were big Robbie fans.

"It's just not like him to run off and disappear like that," I said, moving forward toward the house. "I was terrified. I think Mrs. Higgins's decorations set him off. They blink and light up the sky all night long. Maybe the holidays are getting to him as much as they're getting to me."

He shot me a sideways glance. "But you've always loved the holidays. Especially Christmas."

I waved away his words. "I know, I know. I love Christmas, blah blah blah."

He laughed. "Yeah, you're really full of the old holiday spirit."

"Sorry." I shook my head and shoulders like a wet dog, hoping I could fling away this funky feeling. "Don't worry, I'll get into the swing of things." I hoped so, anyway. With a frown, I pressed my hand to my forehead. "Maybe I'm coming down with something."

"You'd better not be. This job's going to wind up

being a twenty-four-seven gig, so we've all got to stay in top shape."

I grinned. "Yes, boss."

But then he stopped and pointed at me. "Right there."

"What?" I demanded.

"It's like I said." His eyes narrowed as if he were studying a strange life form. "There's something else going on with you."

"No there isn't." I kept walking, nipping that particular conversation thread in the bud.

We reached the house and climbed the steps up to the veranda. As I headed for the door, Wade grabbed my arm. "Shannon, wait. I'm sorry I was being nosy."

"You were being a friend." I smiled at him. "You never have to apologize for that."

"I appreciate it." His own smile faded. "I had a reason for calling you earlier. I wanted to tell you about Frank. He's not going to be here."

"Why not?" I stared up at him. "Is he okay? What happened?" Frank was one of my favorite contractors and a great guy.

Wade scowled. "His wife's company just transferred her to San Diego. Frank is thrilled. He's packing up their house and moving next week."

"Oh no! That's terrible." I winced. "I mean, that's great for them. But now we need another contractor."

"I know."

He set down my tool chest and we both pulled our tablets out of our bags. I swept my finger across the screen. "Shoot. I had him in charge of overseeing all the work on the third floor attic. We'll have to reorganize the team leaders."

"Yeah."

My shoulders slumped as I slid the tablet into its case. "He didn't even call to say good-bye."

"Probably couldn't bear to hear the disappointment in your voice."

I cracked a reluctant smile. "You mean he was too chicken to call."

"That's what I told him." He leaned against the wall. "Seriously, though, it's a real drag to lose him."

"I know. I'll give him a call later to wish him luck." The wind picked up and I shoved my hands into the pockets of my quilted vest. I had to consider the alternatives. Almost every contractor I trusted had already signed up to help out. "We'll all just have to stretch a little more."

Wade stared at his own tablet, then nodded. "We can do it."

"Of course we can." But I was still worried. All the work was being done on a volunteer basis, so I didn't want to overburden anyone.

"We might have to call on Carla earlier than we thought," Wade said.

Carla was my second foreman and I had put her in charge of our other work sites while Wade and I covered the Forester House job. But since she wanted to volunteer as well, the plan was for her and Wade to switch jobs after the first week.

"I'll save her as a last resort." I glanced up at Wade. "I hate to say it, but you know it'll be you and me picking up the slack."

He nudged my arm. "We can handle it, boss."

"Your wife is going to kill me," I muttered.

He grinned. "Sandy's one of our volunteers, so it'll work out just fine for us."

"No wonder you're taking the news so well."

He shrugged boyishly. "I'm a glass-half-full kind of guy."

Nodding, I said, "And you're going to pound that Christmas spirit into me until I grab it with both hands, aren't you?"

"I'm relentless that way."

"I know." I sighed as I pushed the door open and stepped through. "I'm sure I'll thank you for it in a week or so." For the moment though, I felt like a grumpy Grinch. And I really hated that feeling.

Chapter Two

My meeting with the contractors took place in the library on the second floor. There were no books on the shelves just yet, but that was fine because they only would have hidden the splendid Art Nouveau–style bookshelves that lined the room. The curving, twisting woodwork was a masterpiece of carpentry, carved from rich, warm golden oak that swirled and undulated from floor to ceiling, covering three walls.

An equally beautiful library ladder moved on a circular track around the room. Two noble Corinthian columns stood on either side of the door as though welcoming the reader into the room and indicating the way forward. A wall of windows allowed a fabulous view of the expansive front lawn and if you leaned in and looked to the left, you'd catch a hint of blue ocean water a mile away.

We had debated whether or not to rent this room to a single person, but finally decided to leave it as a library because the room was just too beautiful. Why not share it with everyone in the house? We also had all those tricky construction details to consider, like adding a kitchenette, a bathroom, and a closet somewhere close by. We decided to avoid those problems and give the tenants a library they could all enjoy. We already had stacks of books being donated by everyone in town, as well as from the bookstore and the public library.

At our meeting, all of the contractors were on board to help cover for the loss of Frank. I gave a good-natured warning that I would hold them to it, but I knew they would come through for me. The guys were anxious to get started and since we'd already had the group tour last week in which I'd pointed out their assigned areas and the basic work to be done, I let them get to it.

Once they cleared the room, Wade and I worked out a more specific schedule of which contractors would cover Frank's assignment each day. Before leaving the library, he and I scoped out our own assignments for the day. One of the jobs I'd given myself was to examine the eight opulent fireplaces in the house to make sure they were all viable and safe. Luckily, Forester House had central heating and air conditioning, so the apartments without fireplaces would still be warm enough in the winter and cool in the summer. Jason had decided that the families renting the larger apartments would pay nothing extra for those big, grand fireplaces since the amount of wood it would take to warm those rooms would be way too pricey for most of our low-income tenants.

"I'm going to get started on the fireplace in the foyer," I said. "I'll try to be finished by the time the morning volunteers arrive. I'll give them a quick pep talk and then hand out their assignments."

The contractors knew they'd be getting two or three volunteers, and they already had some easy jobs lined up for each of them.

Wade shut down his tablet. "How about if you and I meet around ten o'clock after your pep talk? Just to touch base and make sure everyone's happy."

"Sounds good."

I took the main staircase down to the large foyer, where I'd left my tool chest next to the massive fireplace. The foyer in Forester House was truly dramatic, starting with the front double doors made of heavy iron and thick glass. The wrought-iron design was classic Art Nouveau with lush curves and swirls, lacy flourishes, and delicate fleur-de-lis cascading along the edges. The floor was inlaid marble and the fireplace was made of shimmering blue mosaic tile. Graceful alabaster cherubim fluttered up the pillars that supported each side of the marble mantel and the large mirror in the center.

It was obvious that the generous owners had wanted their guests to stay warm and happy while waiting for their carriages and limousines to pick them up after an elegant evening of dining and dancing. Why else would they install a huge fireplace by the front door? In addition to warming up the spacious room, it gave an immediate impression of grandiosity. In fact, every inch of this home hearkened back to a time when lavish indulgence was the norm.

Call me goofy, but the thought of sprucing up this stunning old grande dame Victorian made me a little giddy. I knew this job—with its dozens of volunteers and hundreds of quirky construction problems and puzzles, along with the fact that we had to have the entire project finished by Christmas Eve in less than two weeks—was going to be a real doozy.

I tied my hair back, wrapped a bandana around my head, and secured it with my baseball cap. Grabbing my flashlight, I crawled into the wide, tiled firebox to make sure the damper was still working. After a few minutes of struggling with the pulley, it loosened up and I averted my face as I pushed it back. The flue and chimney were amazingly clear, allowing me to see a bit of blue sky—once I was sure nothing was going to drop down on top of me. I always shielded my eyes because Lord only knew what might be trapped inside these old chimneys. In the past I'd been doused with rainwater, grimy soot, any number of dead birds, and, more than once, a petrified squirrel.

Seeing blue sky wasn't necessarily a good thing in this case, however, since it meant that there was no chimney cap. I made a mental note to purchase caps for all the chimneys in the house to prevent water and animals from getting inside.

Meanwhile, though, I was happy to report that the foyer fireplace was clean and operational. Of course, with children moving into the house and everyone having access to the foyer, I decided I'd better query Jason Walsh about converting this fireplace to gas and covering it with a glass screen. Alternatively, he might want it closed off completely. In that case, it would be simple enough to place a decorative fire screen and a large potted plant in front of the firebox to block access.

I made another mental note to ask the prospective tenants what they thought of those two choices. My mental note list was getting long enough to start actually writing things down, so I crawled out of the firebox to get my tablet.

"Who's in charge around here?" someone shouted from the front door.

I almost jumped at the sound, but quickly recognized that blustering voice. "Dad!"

"Hiya, sweetheart."

I smiled fondly at him. He looked tanned and healthy after a week of fishing up in Alaska. So why was he wearing a tool belt over his work clothes? And what was with the tool chest he was carrying?

Pulling off the baseball cap and bandana I had used to protect my hair, I brushed the smudges of soot off my shirt and hugged him. "What're you doing here?"

He gave a casual shrug. "I heard you're short a contractor. I'm signing up for the job."

I opened my mouth to comment but no words came out. Maybe because I was in shock. My father had suffered a heart attack six years ago and had turned his successful construction company over to me. Now he was looking for a job? In construction? The thought of him overdoing it and getting sick again terrified me.

"Are you sure that's a good idea?" I asked.

"You need my help."

"Not as badly as I need you to stay healthy."

"Are you saying I can't handle the work?"

"Are you deliberately trying to be obtuse?"

"Aw, come on, sweetheart." He grinned. "Don't worry so much. I'm just going to supervise. Pete's going to help me out and we'll have plenty of crew around to take up the slack. My hands will barely get dirty."

"Why am I not convinced?" Dad and Uncle Pete were best pals and two peas in a pod. Could I possibly depend on my uncle to restrain my father's natural tendency to overdo it? On the other hand, it had been six long years since the doctors had given Dad a clean bill of health— on the condition that he took good care of himself.

Letting out a sigh of frustration, I said, "I don't want to see you get stressed out."

"Who, me? Stressed out?"

"Yes, you." I shook my finger at him. "I don't want you lifting anything."

"I'll have minions around to do that."

"You'll end up doing it yourself and land in the hospital."

"No way." He continued to smile. "I'll be so laid back it's frightening."

"I doubt it. You used to be very competitive on your job sites. You always had to work harder, stay later, lift more." I could feel myself losing the argument so I shook my finger at him again, trying for intimidation. "If I see you lifting something too heavy, I'll smack you."

He patted his heart. "I know that's coming from a place of love."

"Of course." Winding my arm through his, I lowered my voice. "Look, Dad. The bank has Mr. Potter overseeing this project. He'll probably be hanging around here every day. I know how you feel about him."

"Potter." He sneered at the name of the bank's senior vice president. "I can handle that lying blowhard. Trust me, he won't come around much. He's allergic to hard work."

"You're probably right about that," I muttered. Giving up, I threw my arms around him again and squeezed him in a tight hug. "Just be careful, please."

"You have to stop worrying about me. My heart's fine." Serious now, he added, "I'll take every precaution. Promise. The last place I want to be on Christmas Day is in a hospital."

"You and me both."

He glanced around, gazing up at the grand staircase leading to the second floor. "So where do you want me to start?"

I frowned at the question. Here was another quandary. I had already assigned my first-floor contractors, but I didn't want my father to have to climb a lot of stairs every day. I could just see myself insisting that he use the fancy black-and-gold wrought-iron elevator Mr. Forester had proudly installed next to the grand staircase. I knew Dad would do anything to avoid that pokey old rattletrap and sneak up the stairs anyway.

Was it unfair of me to play favorites and consign him to one of the plum downstairs suites? After a momentary argument with myself, I made an executive decision to give up my own assignment to him. That would leave me free to cover Frank's room upstairs. It made sense, I had to admit.

"All right, apartment three is all yours. It's huge. It covers the southwest quadrant of the first floor, which includes the ballroom and the butler's pantry."

He gave a firm nod, then glanced around, gauging directions. Correctly pointing toward southwest, he said, "Let's go check out the space and you can tell me what you want done."

He grabbed his tool chest and followed me across the spacious foyer, past the grand stairway, past the small elevator, and into a wide hall that ran the length of the home. "You'll be working at the back of the house, but it's a fabulous space with a nice view of the side yard. It's got its own entry from the parking area, along with direct access to the back veranda."

"That veranda's a great plus, isn't it?" he said. "It's like having another room to enjoy."

"It's spectacular," I said, obviously impressed with the expansive and elegant outdoor space. It was furnished with vintage wicker patio furniture still intact from the home's glory days. Our team would add to the furniture and also provide several barbecue grills so that all the occupants could enjoy the outdoor space once the remodel was completed.

There was even an old-fashioned porch swing that just needed some sprucing up and a bit of oiling to make it functional again.

"This place will be a dream come true for these folks," Dad remarked.

"I hope so. They're so deserving of a safe place to live." I glanced back at Dad as we reached a door at the end of the long hallway. "You know they've all signed up to work with us on the rehab so you'll probably get a chance to meet them."

"I seem to recall that the charity made that a requirement for anyone who applied for housing."

"That's right." I grabbed the door handle. "Here we are." Pushing it open, I stood to the side. "You go ahead, Dad."

I followed him into the elegant ballroom and watched him gaze around. Stepping down from the small entry space into the main part of the room, he crossed the forty foot expanse of shiny hardwood ballroom floor, shaking his head in amazement. "It's still as spectacular as I remember it."

That was a surprise. "You've been here before?"

"Yeah."

I remained in the entry area where two smooth Ionic columns stood sentry on opposite sides of the space. Staring across the room, I could envision couples in evening gowns and tuxedoes waltzing around the room as others gathered on the sidelines to chitchat and observe.

Every inch of the room was extravagantly decorated to a degree I'd honestly never experienced. The coffered ceiling was an explosion of ornate rosettes and flying cherubs. A froufrou ceiling medallion studded each coffer and crystal chandeliers were hanging from every other square. Instead of wainscoting, the room was ringed in half-height pilasters, each with an angel's head topped by rows of classic dentil molding. As with all of the other fireplaces throughout the house, the one in the ballroom was joyfully excessive with iridescent green tiles lining the firebox and satyrs and angels frolicking along narrow pilasters all the way up to the twelve-foot ceiling.

The heavily sculpted wood mantel supported a beveled mirror framed in foot-wide bas relief grapevines.

Dad pointed toward the far side of the room, where a small, raised section of the floor created a stage of sorts. "That's where the orchestra played."

I tried to picture a big band squeezed into the curving, ten-by-ten-foot space. Along the bowed outer wall of the stage area, three sets of ironwork French doors led outside to the back veranda. I imagined the doors were kept open during a party on warm evenings in the summer.

Looking as though he were a million miles and some forty years away from here, Dad continued to wander the room.

"What are you thinking, Dad?"

"Just remembering that night. It was after our high school graduation." He chuckled. "That was some party."

"You went to school with Dorothy Forester, right?"

"Yes. We called her Dodie. She was dating my buddy

Roy, so she invited his whole gang. A few months after graduation, she broke up with Roy and ran off with Joey Schmidt. They got married and never returned. And then she died, of course. Way too young."

"Did Joey Schmidt ever come back?"

"No, they both died in a car crash in Germany. It was big news at the time. Her mother never recovered from losing her only child and died a year or so later. And her father famously committed suicide."

"I remember hearing about that. I wonder why Dodie moved away in the first place. Did her father disapprove of Joey?"

"I can't say for certain, but frankly, I wouldn't blame him." He ran one hand lovingly across the woodwork. "Joey was never much to write home about, but he was a good-looking kid."

"So maybe Dodie fell in love," I said, irked at the suddenly wistful tone of my voice.

Dad looked dubious. "I always thought she was looking for someone to rescue her from her father. Old Forester was a rough piece of work. He ruled with an iron fist, as we used to say."

Franklin Forester had inherited Sylvan-Forester, the country's largest supplier of lumber and a major source of employment along the north coast for more than 150 years. With the redwood groves dwindling and endangered species standing in the way of the industry gobbling up every tree they could get their hands on, those boom days were long gone.

"Did you know him?" I wondered.

"I met him, but I didn't know him. Some folks said he ran his family like he ran his business. Into the ground."

"That's sad." Gazing around at the ornate ballroom walls, I sighed. "His family built a beautiful home, though."

"They did," Dad said. "And the work you're doing here will go a long way toward polishing the Foresters' tarnished legacy."

"I just hope everyone will be happy with the final results."

He stared up at the baroque-style ceiling decorated with all those ornate moldings. "It seems a shame to break up the home into separate apartments, but it's better than the alternative, I suppose."

"Definitely better than tearing the place down. And we plan to keep most of these big, gorgeous rooms intact. They'll be set up like loft-style apartments, you know? We'll add a dining room table and chairs over in that corner, a living area here in front of the fireplace, and the bedroom will be over there where the band played. The designers will come up with all sorts of creative ways to separate the different spaces. You know, using plants and bookshelves and screens and such."

"It's going to look great." Dad slung his arm across my shoulders and gave me a quick squeeze. "I'm proud of you, honey. You'll do a fantastic job."

"Thanks, Dad."

"Hey," he said with a grin. "Speaking of tearing things down, check out this sweet little demolition ax I picked up in Alaska." He pulled a small, black tool from his tool belt, unwrapped the rectangular sheath, and held it up for me to admire. "Is that a beauty or what?"

"It looks lightweight."

"You'd think so, but the ax head itself weighs almost a pound. It's carbon steel. Try it."

"Wow." I took the ax from him and held it in my hand. It was barely fifteen inches long with a seven-inch head. The blade was seriously sharp and the spike end looked as if it could chop through doors. "Very nice. Solid. I like this thick foam grip."

"Isn't that handy? We met some firefighters in a bar in Homer and they all recommended it."

"Well, they ought to know."

He chuckled. "Darn right."

I handed the ax back to him. "I hope you'll have a chance to use it. Believe it or not, we're going to try to avoid as much demolition as possible."

"That's no fun," he said with a good-natured chuckle.

"Don't worry. You're one of the lucky ones. You'll actually get to do a little demo in the butler's pantry." I pointed to the door on the other side of the fireplace. "We want to turn it into a full-fledged kitchen."

"Sounds good," he said, admiring his new ax. "Nothing like a little demo to get the blood flowing."

I rolled my eyes at his bloodthirsty grin. "Let's go check out the space." But I stopped as the sound of pounding footsteps rang out from down the hall.

Dad and I exchanged curious glances just as the door to the ballroom swung open with a bang and the senior vice president of the Lighthouse Cove Bank and Trust stormed into the room. He didn't look happy at all.

"Hammer," he snarled. "Just as I thought."

I took a step toward him. "Mr. Potter, can I help you?"

Peter Potter looked like the stereotypical prosperous banker—tall and balding with a large belly cloaked in an expensive black suit with a red power tie.

"What do you want, Potter?" Dad asked, his tone instantly hostile.

Potter's pasty complexion was mottled and his red nose made me think he'd just indulged in a three-martini lunch, even though it was early in the morning. His eyes flashed with resentment.

He ignored me and glared at my father. "I knew it was a mistake to put your daughter in charge of this job."

Dad gritted his teeth to contain his irritation. "My daughter is the best person in the country to run this project."

"Not if she allows you to work here."

"Now, wait just a minute," I said, squaring my shoulders. Nobody insulted my father when I was around. "You didn't put me in charge, Mr. Potter, and neither did your bank. The charity did. And the other fifteen contractors working here took a vote and agreed, so it's a done deal. They want me to run this project and they won't be sorry. Neither will you."

His lip curled in a disturbing grin and he took another step closer. "I can change the outcome of that vote in a heartbeat." He snapped his fingers in my face.

"Why, you old gasbag." Dad shoved his way between us, forcing Potter to step back. "You try that and every news station and newspaper in the state will hear about it. I'll bet they'd love to get their hands on the story of how you bullied the crew and interfered with this charity project."

"You wouldn't dare."

"Try me." Dad jabbed his finger for emphasis. "And while I'm talking to reporters, I might just fill them in on some even juicier gossip—and I think you know what I'm talking about. It's your choice, but if I were you, I'd stay out of our way."

Potter's cheeks turned even redder and he huffed in a breath. "I want you off this job site now."

"Tough." My dad snorted derisively. "You're not in charge. I'm working here and you can't stop me."

This conversation was descending rapidly, so I tried to calm them both down. "Mr. Potter, everyone here is working for the good of the families. It's only for a little while. Can't we all get along until Christmas?"

He grunted in dismissal. "Your daughter's as big a simpering fool as you are."

Dad came in closer and shoved him in the chest. The banker stumbled backward. "One more word against Shannon and I'll make you sorry you were ever born." He was as angry as I'd ever seen him and I felt a frisson of fear as I worried about his heart.

"Oh, I'm so scared," Potter whined sarcastically. But in typical coward style, he said it while backing toward the door.

"You should be scared," Dad said through clenched teeth. He was still holding his sharp, new ax and he raised it up to make his point. "If I hear you talking trash about my daughter again, I'll kill you with my bare hands."

Chapter Three

The door opened abruptly and an attractive, well-dressed woman stood on the threshold. Her eyes widened at the sight of my father holding an ax over Mr. Potter's head.

Dad lowered the ax and took a step away from Potter.

Letting go of a breath, she said, "There you are, Peter. Are you finished? I don't want you to miss your nine o'clock meeting."

"This isn't over," Mr. Potter said, pointing at Dad and me.

Dad sheathed the ax and slipped it back into his tool belt like a gunslinger. "Yes it is."

I was more mollifying. "We'll do a good job for you, Mr. Potter. Don't worry."

His gesture was a curt brush-off wave, effectively canceling out my words.

What a jerk.

The woman remained in the doorway for another moment after Potter walked out. She had to be aware of how horrible and obnoxious he was because she gave us both a sheepish smile. "Hello. And, well, good-bye."

Dad raised his hand in greeting. "Good to see you, Patrice."

Flustered, she fiddled with her blonde hair, then seemed to realize what she was doing. Without another word, she turned and disappeared down the hall.

I looked at Dad. "You know her?"

"Yeah, she's Potter's secretary. Has been for years. Nice lady." Wearing a scowl, he shook his head. "Too nice to be working with that scumbag."

"He's awful," I muttered, depressed by the confrontation and Dad's part in it.

"That's one word for him," Dad grumbled.

"Knock knock."

We both whipped around. One of the fancy French doors off the band stage was wide open and Santa Claus was standing there staring at Dad.

Santa Claus?

I opened my mouth to say something and once again no words came out. I hated that things kept happening to shock me into silence. And really, until lately I would have thought it was impossible.

But come on, it was Santa Claus! And not just a fake-looking mall Santa. This was a jolly fat man with a realistic-looking white beard and perky red cheeks. It was Santa! Right here on my job site. Was that bizarre or what?

Unfortunately, there was a crowd of people standing behind him and all of them were craning their necks to get a look at whoever had been yelling a minute ago. Great. So everyone had heard Dad confronting Mr. Potter. I didn't need this the first day on the job.

"Can I help?" Santa said, sounding like a sympathetic guidance counselor. "It looked like you were having a little trouble there."

Uh-oh. Was this where I would confess that my Christmas spirit was nonexistent and Santa would put my name directly on the Naughty List?

I shook my head a few times and tried to focus. This wasn't about me. "Santa Claus? What are you doing here?"

"Oh, ho, ho, ho!" he said, holding his belly as he laughed. "Always on the lookout for naughty and nice behavior."

Dad laughed. "How you doing, Steve?"

Steve?

Grinning, Santa nodded. "Good to see you, Jack."

"Sorry to disturb everyone," Dad said, waving to the group at the door. "I was just having a spirited conversation with Potter."

"I noticed." Santa—Steve?—stepped into the room and closed the door behind him. "Potter's going to find himself in big trouble one of these days. I had a run-in with him earlier myself."

"What for?" I asked.

He shook his head in disgust. "He's annoyed that the Santa Brigade is taking up their own collection for the families moving in here."

"But that sounds lovely," I said, then frowned. "What's the Santa Brigade?"

"We're a group of folks who play Santa Claus every year at Christmas. Some of us have been down on our luck in the past, but we've all found a way to survive and thrive. We believe in passing along the good fortune. We try to help people with fundraising and charitable events. Especially this time of year, when we can take advantage of our Santa personas."

"That's wonderful."

"I think so, too, but Potter doesn't seem to agree."

"But why?"

Steve sighed. "Because I'm going to be one of the new tenants here, so he thinks it's a conflict of interest."

I blinked. "You're one of our new tenants?"

"Yes."

Dad jumped in. "Steve Shore, this is my daughter, Shannon. She's in charge of the rehab project."

"Ah, delightful," he said, walking over to me with his white-gloved hand extended. "Lovely to meet you."

"Nice to meet you, too, Steve."

He bowed his head slightly. "Thank you for your hard work on our behalf."

I gave him a wide, appreciative smile. "Can I just say, you make a terrific Santa?"

"You sure can," Steve said with a wink. "And that just put you on the Nice List."

The French door opened again and—good grief, it was another Santa Claus, poking his head in. "Yo, Steve," Santa Number Two said. "We need you out here. We're discussing Brigade business."

This Santa appeared younger and skinnier, with an olive complexion and a lot of extra padding. Still, with the white beard and the red suit, he looked like Santa Claus to me.

"Be right there, Mitch."

I was blinking again and forced myself to stop. So there was more than one Santa Claus on site. Nothing wrong with that. The world could use a few more Santas, after all.

I glanced at Steve. "Is Mitch a new tenant, too?"

"Yeah. Well, we hope so anyway."

"Wow."

"There are three of us Santas moving in, so I guess Potter thinks we stacked the deck. But we didn't. It was all done by lottery. We just got lucky."

"Luck, and maybe all your good work has come back around to reward you," Dad said.

I nodded. "I'm going with that theory."

"Well, thank you, both," Steve said. "Guess I'd better get back out there." He shook his finger at Dad. "Stay out of trouble, Jack, or you know what will happen."

"What?" I asked, mystified as I glanced back and forth from my father to Santa—or rather, Steve.

Steve wiggled his bushy gray eyebrows. "The Naughty List."

Dad waved him away. "You Santa types really lord it over the rest of us this time of year."

Steve laughed—"Ho ho ho!"—and walked out the door.

We both stared after him for a long moment and then Dad turned to me. "Now, where were we?"

"Oh, no way are we just moving on," I told him. "You don't get to be friends with Santa Claus and not tell your own daughter how you know him."

"He's an old school friend."

I would have bet anything that I already knew all of Dad's friends from school. "I've never met him before."

"No, you wouldn't have," Dad agreed. "After high school, he joined the army and left town. When he returned from the Gulf War, he was a little tweaked and fell on hard times." He sighed as if remembering those days. "Your uncle Pete ran into him a few years back and we hired him for some jobs. After a while, he was able to get a full-time job with Stenson Construction. And obviously, he plays Santa Claus every year. He's got the gig over at the North Star Mall."

The North Star Mall was located outside of Flanders, a small town fifteen miles east of us. And Stenson Construction mainly built apartment houses, so it was no wonder our paths had never crossed.

"Why did Potter go after him? I mean, why would he care that the Santa Brigade is helping out?"

Dad glowered at the mention of the name. "Potter doesn't need a reason to be a—" He broke off, apparently unwilling to curse in front of his little girl. He finished by saying simply, "They're old enemies."

I sighed. "Who isn't Potter's enemy?"

"He has very few friends," Dad acknowledged. "He's a miserable old gizzard and that's a plain fact. Most of us would rather see him dead than—"

He was tense and I could see the glitter of battle in his eyes, which was exactly what I didn't want. I still had the memories of seeing Dad laid up in the hospital and didn't want to paint any new ones.

"Dad." I gripped his arm. "I don't want you tangling with Potter. Your blood pressure probably shot through the roof a minute ago when he stormed in. And so did mine."

He patted the ax handle confidently. "Don't worry, honey. He'll stay out of my way."

As much as he was acting the hard case, I knew very well he'd never use that ax on a living, breathing creature. Even Potter. But it was my father's health I was concerned with now.

"Dad," I said in warning.

"Okay, okay. I'll stay clear of him."

"Thank you." I tried to shake off the residual anxiety and get back to touring the room. That would help us both calm down and drive all thoughts of Potter away. "Now I was about to show you the butler's pantry."

Before I could reach the door leading to the butler's pantry, it opened and Wade looked in. "Everything okay in here? A few of the guys heard someone yelling."

I glanced at Dad and waved my foreman into the room. "Mr. Potter was here."

"And so it begins," Wade muttered. "That man can turn a saint into a rabid dog in seconds flat."

"No kidding."

Wade and I had discussed the Potter issue before. The banker had been a pain in the neck since the first day we began our preliminary work on the mansion, back in August. Even though these last few weeks before Christmas were when the official Holiday Homebuilders event began and all the volunteers showed up to contribute their time and energy, I had spent the previous four months prepping for this day. I'd been lining up contractors and crew, scheduling the volunteer force, working with the architect, purchasing supplies and equipment, and getting painters and their crews out here to spruce up the exterior and the garage. All in anticipation of the big holiday event.

And throughout that entire time, Potter had been doing his best to stick his nose into every aspect of the job. I had asked Jason if he could convince the bank to send someone else to oversee the Forester project, but the bank had insisted they couldn't spare any of the other executives. So we were stuck with Potter. I would catch him haranguing my workers on the dumbest little detail, even down to criticizing the method by which the crew assembled the scaffolding to reach the highest peaks of the house. When a hammer fell off a scaffold and grazed his ear, Potter finally agreed that he should rethink his insistence on making daily visits to the job site.

I still didn't know whether that hammer was dropped on purpose or if it was an accident, but since it resulted in Potter staying away, I couldn't say I was sorry. Not that I would wish something truly awful to happen to him, but the guy was a real pain in the neck.

And now that all the work had moved inside and we had begun the ten-day rush to get the apartments assembled and furnished, I once again had to find a way to bar Potter from showing up. I didn't want him getting in everyone's way, complaining about every little change, insulting my contractors, and disrupting my workers. His presence was bad for morale.

"He's so negative," I said. "We've got to figure out a way to make him stay off the site."

"Good luck with that," Wade said.

"I might be able to do something about it," Dad said.

I shot him a look. "I don't want you threatening him again."

He held up both hands, trying to look innocent. "I promised I would stay away from him, didn't I? But I know someone who might be able to convince him."

I stared at him, trying to read his mind. "Do I want to know about this?"

He wrinkled his brow, thinking about it. "Probably not."

"Fine."

Wade grinned.

I'd worry about whatever my dad was up to later. At the moment, we had some time to make up.

"So." I turned to my foreman. "I guess everyone on the property heard Dad arguing with Potter."

"Just about," Wade said, pointing to a vent in the wall. "Sound carries."

I grimaced. "That's good to know."

"Guess we don't want to be spilling any secrets near those vents," Dad said, wearing a pensive frown as he stared at the vent.

"Good advice," I muttered.

"The volunteers are getting restless," Wade said. "Are you ready to talk to them?"

"Yes. Wait." I grabbed his arm. "Should I say something about Dad and Mr. Potter? I know they heard the argument and I don't want them getting the wrong idea."

"Don't worry. None of them like Potter, either." Wade grinned again. "They'll forget all about it as soon as we get them started on their jobs."

"I suppose." But I wondered. "We really need to get rid of Potter. We could lose some good workers."

"I'm not sorry I yelled at him," Dad said, sounding contrite despite his words. "But I'll be happy to apologize to the whole group if it makes your job easier, honey. Potter has always been a thorn in my side."

"He drives everyone crazy," Wade said, waving away Dad's concern. "Don't worry about it."

"Thanks, Wade," he said. "I just want things to run smoothly for Shannon."

"They will," I assured him, then glanced at Wade. "I want to finish showing Dad around. Could you let the volunteers know I'll be out there in ten minutes?"

"You bet."

Wade took off and I turned to Dad. "Let's take a quick look at the pantry and then I'll leave you to it."

"Let's do it." He followed me through the door and up three steps. "I assume we're going to turn this space into a full-fledged kitchen."

"Yes. A small one, but it'll have everything. We've got kitchenette units we'll be adding to some of the smaller rooms with the usual sink, stove, and fridge. But since the pantry already has a nice sink and cupboards built in, we'll just add a refrigerator and a four-burner stove over here."

We stood in the short hallway that led to the kitchen. I pulled my tape measure from my tool belt to show him exactly where a wall would be added to separate the pantry and ballroom apartment from the large kitchen down the hall. "I'll get you the blueprints when we're finished here."

"That would help."

We walked back into the ballroom. "As I mentioned, we won't be adding walls to most of the rooms, so that one's an exception."

"It's going to be great, kiddo."

"Absolutely." I gazed up at the floor-to-ceiling fireplace. "I mean, who wouldn't want to live in a glorious space like this?" My hand grazed the grape-leaf motif that crept up the pilaster and I marveled again at the touches of grandeur everywhere.

"I know you want to get going, but what about a bathroom?" Dad asked. "And a closet?"

"They're both over here. I'll show you." I walked across the room and opened a door just to the left of the front door. "This short hall leads to a large bathroom and then the old cloakroom at the end."

We walked down the hall and Dad glanced at both doors. "I vaguely remember this space." He opened the bathroom door. "It's big. Everything in working order?"

"The plumbing in this part of the house is pretty good. You'll be putting in a new sink and a modern counter and shower, and we'll upgrade the tile floor. And we'll paint the walls, of course."

Opening my tablet again, I swiped my finger across the screen to access my schedules. When I got to the subcontractors' page, I held the screen up and pointed out the dates. "We'll have plumbers and tile layers available every day in case you need them, but I've specifically scheduled them to work on your kitchen and bathroom here and here." I showed him the calendar that appeared on the screen. "If you need to reschedule, let me know ASAP, okay?"

"Will do," he said. "I'll write those dates down on my paper calendar."

We smiled at each other in complete understanding.

"This old cloakroom is so cool," I said. "It's basically a giant walk-in closet."

"I'm pretty sure I hung my coat in here that night." Dad strolled inside, looked around. "It's bigger than some bedrooms I've seen."

"I know." We took a turn around the cloakroom perimeter, checking the walls and floor for any signs of termites or water damage.

"Walls look healthy enough," Dad murmured with a firm smack against the wall's surface. We walked back into the ballroom, where he opened his tool chest to take out a notepad and pen.

"Do we know who's moving into this apartment?" he asked, flipping to a new page and making some notes.

"Yes. Sophie Gainey is a thirty-year-old widow with a six-year-old daughter named Molly."

Glancing around, he asked, "Are they going to share the bedroom out here?"

"That was the idea."

He tapped his chin with his pen, thinking. "So, listen. What if we turned part of the cloakroom into a kid's bedroom? It's plenty big enough to partition it off and stick a set of bunk beds and a dresser in there. That would still leave room for mom to have a good-sized closet. That way, the little one would have her own space. We can paint it a nice bright color, make it real inviting."

"That's a sweet idea, Dad."

"Kids need a room to call their own," he said with a shrug.

I pictured the cloakroom space and tried to imagine a kid in there. "It doesn't have any windows, though." I stared up at the ceiling, pondering the problem. "It does share an outside wall with the veranda. We could talk to the architect, check the feasibility of tearing through the wall and giving her a nice window—without threatening the integrity of the original exterior design, of course."

"Hmm." He smirked. "You say that like it's some kind of mandate they gave you."

"It is, but I've since been told, very quietly, that I can use my own discretion. And my discretion tells me that because we'll be punching a hole in the back of the house that won't be seen from the street, I'm going to say yes to the window."

He patted my shoulder. "Don't worry. I'll make sure it doesn't threaten the integrity of the design."

"I'd appreciate that," I said, smiling. "I'd like to have some sunshine make it in there. Of course, most of the time she'll be out here in the main room with her mom, eating her meals, watching TV or doing her homework, or playing outside. She'll just use the cloakroom for sleeping."

"We can make it work."

"And you'll be able to do some serious demo," I added.

He rubbed his hands together gleefully. "Life is good."

Still smiling, I tapped out a note on my tablet to remind myself to mention a new window to the architect. Even though we weren't moving any walls, I wanted him in on every decision I made. "It's a good idea, Dad."

"Hey, I've designed a room or two in my time."

That was putting it mildly. Before he retired, my father had designed half of the newer homes in town, including most of the modern Victorian mansions on the Alisal Cliffs.

I checked my watch again. "Yikes, I'd better get out there and talk to the volunteers."

"I'll walk out with you," Dad said. "I want to get my sledgehammer and some more tools out in the truck."

I led the way back into the central hall and toward the front foyer. Remembering an important detail, I turned to Dad. "By the way, we lock our tools up each night."

"Seriously? Don't they lock the house each night?"

"Yes, but I'm taking extra precautions." Ever since my tools were stolen and used to commit some serious crimes, I had made it a firm rule.

He nodded in understanding. "I'll be sure to lock them up."

"Thanks. And I'll talk to Wade about assigning some of my crew to help you."

"That won't be necessary."

Hardhead. That was my father. I could see it in the stubborn lift of his chin and the narrowing of his eyes. I didn't want to baby him and chip away at his pride, but I also wanted to look out for him. "You need a crew, Dad."

"I know." It was his turn to check his watch. "And they should be here any minute."

It took a few seconds to mentally play back his words before I slowed my pace. "Who's *they*?"

"Just Pete and a couple of the guys."

"A couple of the guys?" I repeated with some trepidation.

"Yeah, Phil Chambers and some of the other guys I used to have on my crew. They want to help out."

"Phil Chambers? Wade's father?"

He chuckled at the perplexity in my voice. "Yeah, why not? He used to be my foreman, remember?"

"Of course I remember," I muttered. That was how I knew Wade, after all.

"I would trust my men with any job in town. Turns out they're all chomping at the bit to get involved in this project."

"Oh boy. Great. This should be . . . interesting." And I couldn't wait to share the news with Wade. On the upside, Dad wouldn't be working with an all-new crew. Downside, he and his pals might do more gabbing than actual working.

I walked Dad as far as the front door, where he waved and took off down the driveway and over to his truck to get more tools. Alone, I continued on under the shady veranda toward the back of the house where the volunteers had been asked to assemble. I almost jumped at the sound of someone running up behind me, but let go a sigh of relief when I saw Sean Brogan race to catch up with me.

"I'm glad I found you," he said, huffing from his sprint. "Prepare yourself."

I kept walking. "For what? I'm about to meet the volunteers."

He held his arms out to stop me. "That's what I'm talking about." Sean was one of my best crew members, a big, brawny, freckled, easygoing guy, but right now he wore a look of subdued panic.

"You look frantic, Sean. What's wrong?"

"Have you seen what's happening out there?"

I winced. "I should've been out there fifteen minutes ago. They must be getting antsy."

"You could say that, but that's not the real problem. Did you know you've got a bunch of . . . of Santa Clauses out there?"

"Yeah." I chuckled. "One of them is Steve. He's an old friend of my dad's."

"He's not the only Santa Claus."

"Yeah, I saw the other guy, too. His name is, um, Mitch, I think, but—"

"Shannon, they're not the only . . ." Sean let out an exasperated sigh. "Never mind. It's too bizarre to explain. Just come with me."

"I'm right there with you."

Sean took off at a run and I hurried to follow him. Whatever was making him freak out had to be important. He was usually so calm.

We turned the corner and that's when I saw what he was talking about. Yes, there was Steve and his buddy Mitch, but in addition to those two, there were at least eight or ten more men dressed exactly like them. Like Santa Claus.

They were everywhere.

This wasn't a Santa Brigade. This was a Santa army.

Sean was right. It was bizarre. Was this my punishment for not getting into the holiday spirit quickly enough?

"I didn't know there would be so many."

"They say they're volunteering," Sean murmured, "but I think they're looking for wild women."

"Don't say that," I whispered emphatically. "You're talking about Santa Claus."

He leaned closer, wearing a deep frown. "You do realize that Santa Claus isn't real, right?"

I gave him a sharp look. "Of course I do. It just feels disrespectful to talk about him like that. Especially this time of year."

"Look at those guys, Shannon," Sean insisted, pointing across the yard at the motley group of men in every shape and size and height, wearing the identical red velvet suit, black boots and belt, white beard, and cheerful red hat. "They're just a bunch of weirdos in costume. And like it or not, a few of them have been hitting on the women."

Clearly, Sean wasn't feeling the Christmas spirit quite yet, either. On the other hand, some of the Santas did seem to be behaving out of character for guys who were playing the beloved Old St. Nick. I heard snickering and some mild expletives as I walked the rest of the way over to face the crowd. As soon as I cleared my throat to talk, one of the costumed men let out a tacky wolf whistle.

"Whoa. Is she our boss?" one of them asked his buddy. "Now you're talking!"

His buddy snorted and a few of the civilians in the crowd laughed.

"That's enough!" Steve shouted.

"Aw, come on, Steve," one of the Santas said. "We're just having fun. And she's pretty."

I appreciated a compliment as much as the next woman, but trust me, a construction site was never the place for that kind of talk. I sucked in a breath, stuck two fingers in my mouth, and released a piercing whistle of my own. I'd been taught how to do that years ago by my Dad's crew guys. It came in handy every so often. Like now.

"May I have your attention please?" I shouted to the thirty-some volunteers milling around. I noticed a number of familiar faces in the crowd and felt my disgruntlement fading.

"I'm Shannon Hammer," I began, "and I'm supervising the Forester House rehab. Thank you all so much for volunteering. I'm sure you know how much your work means to the families who will be moving into the house. And speaking of work, we have a lot of it. In just a minute I'll be assigning each of you to a contractor and a crew and I can promise you that, besides the work, it's going to be a lot of fun."

A woman let out an ear-piercing squeal and I smiled at her enthusiasm, until she whirled around and slapped the man behind her—another Santa Claus impersonator— across the face. His white beard actually vibrated from the velocity of the woman's openhanded smack.

What in the world?

I jumped off the veranda and ran over to find out what had happened. "Are you all right?"

"No!" the woman howled. "I've just been assaulted."

I turned to the Santa Claus she had just slapped. "Sir? That's it. You can go home now."

"What? But I didn't do anything."

"Yes, he did," the woman insisted. "He pinched me."

"She's lying!" Santa shouted.

I looked around at the crowd. "Did anyone see what happened?"

"Sorry, Shannon, but I was checking my phone for messages," Mrs. Robertson, one of my neighbors, said. "Didn't see a thing."

Others shrugged and shook their heads. Heather Maxwell, the college-aged daughter of one of our city councilmen, was standing next to the woman and I gave her a pleading look. "Did you see anything, Heather?"

"No, sorry. I was looking at my new charm bracelet." She giggled as she held up her arm and jiggled the bracelet. The charms glittered like starlight in the early morning sun. "Isn't it awesome?"

"Pretty," I said.

"My grandmother just gave it to me for my birthday. It's from Tiffany and those are real diamonds." She turned to the woman who'd slapped Santa Claus. "Don't you love it?"

"Yeah, whatever," the woman said.

"It's real sparkly, Heather," I said, trying to make up for the woman's cold comment. Heather was sweet, if a bit ditzy. I added, "Happy birthday, honey."

"Thanks," Heather said with another giggle.

"Uh, hello?"

I turned back to the woman, who looked even more annoyed that I had taken a moment to talk to Heather instead of getting to the bottom of her problem. I gazed at her steadily, trying to figure out who she was. I thought I knew almost everyone in town and, while she had a vaguely familiar look, I didn't recognize her. She was tall and nice-looking with brown eyes and long dark hair pulled back in a ponytail. I guessed she was in her mid-thirties, making her two or three years older than me.

She curled her hands into fists and stepped up close to me. It was an aggressive gesture and I didn't like it. "I want you to get rid of that man," she said, pointing at Santa.

"You can't make me leave," Santa cried. "My wife and I were chosen to move into this building and we both have to volunteer in order to get it." He blinked and seemed to forget what he was saying. But a moment later, he continued talking. "I—I need this place. And I have every right to be here. And she's wrong. I didn't do whatever she thinks I did."

He sounded so hurt and indignant, I was starting to wonder what really happened here. It didn't help that the crowd suddenly began chanting "Santa! Santa!"

Thankfully Sean yelled, "Quiet, please."

"Let's discuss this after the meeting," I said to the woman. "Is that all right with you?"

She reached up and pulled her ponytail tight before folding her arms across her chest. She was obviously furious and I couldn't blame her.

"Do you want to leave?" I asked quietly. "We can reschedule your volunteer time."

I was taken aback when her eyes shot virtual daggers at me. "No way."

All righty, then. Apparently getting goosed by Santa wasn't enough to kill her volunteering spirit. Not that I was accusing Santa of doing anything—yet. Still, why was she so mad at *me*? I could promise her that Santa was going to get a full talking-to later. And if I had to, I would drag Dad's friend Steve into the thick of it. We weren't going to allow any loose, unstable Santas on the crew. And if he was innocent, I would find out why the woman had been so quick to accuse him.

"Okay." I nodded slowly. "Then we'll talk right after the meeting. It'll just be a few more minutes."

She jerked her shoulder and gave a terse nod. "Fine."

"You're welcome," I muttered, turning away and dashing back to the veranda. Shaken by the unexpected argument with Santa and the unfettered acrimony directed at me by the woman, I felt disoriented and had to take a few long seconds before facing the crowd again. The day had started out weird and it wasn't getting any better. Santa Claus accused of assault? It couldn't be true.

But why not? I didn't know either of those two people, so why was I so quick to believe Santa Claus? Was it simply because he was, you know, Santa Claus?

I might have laughed at myself for being so naive, but as I gazed out at the crowd and made eye contact with the angry woman again, my stomach was too clenched up to laugh at much of anything. In that moment, my brain and my gut joined forces to convince me that it was the ponytailed woman, not the volunteer Santa Claus, who would wind up causing me a whole world of trouble.

Chapter Four

Back on the steps of the veranda, I tried to forget about the unknown woman and give my full attention to the volunteers. I did a quick head count and that was when I spied one of my best pals, Marigold Starling, standing in the crowd with her aunt Daisy. I waved at them, then noticed a teacher I'd had in high school. I'd already recognized the clerk from my local drugstore and a few other folks I knew from around town. Seeing so many of my local friends made it easier to forget the angry pony-tailed lady. I deliberately grinned and waved at each familiar face in the crowd.

Because of the overwhelming response to our request for volunteers, we had been able to schedule twenty people at a time to work four-hour shifts in the mornings and afternoons, seven days a week, from now until Christmas Eve.

This morning we were well over our quota. There were thirty-two volunteers, and good grief, ten of them were Santa Clauses, all in full costume and determined to help out. What was their story? Where had they all come from? Did they expect to work together? In their costumes?

Subtracting the ten Santas left us with twenty-two volunteers instead of twenty. I would have to work out the logistics and their assignments with Sean later.

I checked my wristwatch and scowled. Thanks to the Santa Claus distraction and Dad showing up and, of course, Robbie escaping the backyard earlier, I was still behind schedule. It was time to get back on track.

"I want to thank you all for volunteering for this wonderful cause," I said, trying to make myself heard by everyone. "I'm especially thankful that so many Santa Clauses have decided to join us. Are you all with the Santa Brigade?"

The men in costumes cheered loudly. Most of the others in the group smiled, but I could tell they were starting to get impatient.

"I'd like to ask all of the Santa Clauses to meet me around the front of the house in five minutes and we can talk about your contribution to the project. Thank you."

I glanced at the rest of the crowd. "In just a minute, Sean will be dividing you into small groups and assigning each of the groups to our contractors."

I glanced at Sean behind me. "That's Sean."

He waved to make sure everyone knew who I was talking about.

"Now, this won't be the most glamorous work you've ever done," I continued, "but I think you'll find it gratifying and I promise you'll make a big difference to the project. Over the next week and a half, we'll be asking our volunteers to do things like strip wallpaper, spackle cracks, remove tile from several of the bathroom floors, wash and paint walls, caulk around bathtubs and sinks, and basically do whatever the contractors need you to do."

One of the older ladies in the crowd raised her hand. "I've never done any construction work."

"Don't worry about that," I said. "The crew members will teach you to do everything. We won't ask you to lift anything too heavy or use power tools you're not familiar with. Believe it or not, once in a while we might just ask you to vacuum a room where we've been sanding or drywalling. So, you see what I mean when I say these might not be the most glamorous jobs?"

Most of the crowd chuckled, for which I was grateful.

"But your help is invaluable," I continued, "and the families who are moving in will be very grateful. Thank you again for your help. Any questions?"

"Should I bring my own tools?" an older man asked.

"No, we'll provide you with the tools you'll need for any task you're assigned. All we ask is that you use your own pair of work gloves. Did you all bring gloves with you today?"

Almost everyone responded affirmatively and a few waved their gloves in the air.

"Okay, that's great." I turned to Sean and lowered my voice. "Can you give everyone their assignments while I go talk to the Santa Clauses?"

"Better you than me," he said with a grin.

"Yeah, thanks a lot." As I stepped off the veranda, I glanced up to make sure the Santa Clauses were heading for the front of the house, then made a quick detour to give Marigold and her aunt a quick hug. "I didn't know you were volunteering this morning."

"I'm not," Marigold explained. "I just came along

with Aunt Daisy to make sure she gets settled in all right. I've got to get back to the store."

"She thinks I'm too old to take care of myself," Daisy said, chuckling as she patted her niece's arm.

"No, I don't," Marigold insisted. "You're nowhere near old. I just hate dropping you off and running."

"For heaven's sake, Mari," her aunt said with a grin. "We're not in the wilds of the Amazon. And look around. There are plenty of handsome men to help me out if I need it."

I had to smile. Daisy was in her mid-fifties but sometimes looked young enough to be Marigold's older sister. Today, for instance, she was adorable in worn overalls, a long-sleeved Henley with a checkered cotton scarf wrapped around her neck, and work boots.

The two Starlings owned Crafts and Quilts, a high-end gift shop on the town square. Many of the beautiful quilts and wooden toys and other items in their shop had been handmade by their Amish relatives in rural Pennsylvania. Marigold had left the Amish life years ago to join her free-spirited aunt in Lighthouse Cove, but she maintained close relationships with everyone back home.

"Don't worry," I said, giving Aunt Daisy's hand a squeeze. "We'll take good care of her."

"Thank you, Shannon," Marigold said. "I'm scheduled to volunteer tomorrow afternoon, so I'll see you then."

"Good." I nudged her. "Play your cards right and I'll make sure you're assigned to the best team."

"I hope so," she said, laughing.

I walked with them over to where Sean was handing out tasks. "Before I let you go, I want to know if you saw anything happen between the Santa Claus and the woman who slapped him."

"I didn't see him move at all," Daisy said. "We were standing quite close by."

"And you didn't see him reach out and pinch her?"

"No."

Marigold nodded. "I didn't see anything either. It was a complete shock when she whipped around and smacked him."

"Okay, thanks. Have fun today." Waving good-bye, I took off jogging across the lawn, heading toward the front of the house.

My dad's friend Steve caught up with me before I rounded the side of the house. It was still a shock to see a full-fledged Santa Claus standing in front of me, but I managed to snap out of it. "Hey, Steve. What's up?"

"Shannon, I wanted to talk to you before you spoke to the rest of the Brigade. I know it must be weird having all of us Santa Clauses hanging around here."

"It's weird, but sort of wonderful," I said. After all, who didn't like Santa Claus? "But since you mention it, I do have a few questions."

He held up his hand. "I'll gladly answer any question you have if you'll let me explain a few things first. Before you talk to the whole group."

"Sure. Go ahead."

"Okay, here's the deal. Three of our Santas are working as volunteers because we've applied to live here. One of them is me." He seemed to be choosing his words carefully. "I mentioned that a few members of the group have been through some hard times, but we've all managed to turn things around. Life is beginning to look good. That's why we started the Brigade in the first place. To give back to those who helped us out, and to spread the gratitude around."

"Yes, you told me that and I think it's great."

"Yeah, it really is." He took a deep breath before continuing. "Now, the other two applicants are Slim Daley, the guy you talked to about the incident, and my friend Mitch. You remember seeing Mitch earlier?"

"He's the one who poked his head inside the door, right?"

"That's the guy. So the three of us are working here because it's required as part of the application process. And the rest of the gang are all here to support us."

"They sound like good friends."

"Yeah, they are. I just . . ." He grimaced. "Well, I'm not sure what would happen if one of us lost the chance to get an apartment here."

It was obvious to me that he was referring to Slim, but neither of us said his name. I wondered, would Slim fall off the deep end if he couldn't move in here? But I didn't ask because it was all hypothetical at this point. Until I could figure out what had happened out there on the lawn with the ponytailed woman, I couldn't say much of anything to Steve. "I think I get what you're saying, and I'll be as fair as I can be."

He nodded. "That's all I can ask. I appreciate your honesty."

"But now I've got a few questions."

"Go ahead."

"Do you all expect to work in your costumes?"

"Ho ho ho" he laughed, back to his Santa Claus persona. I liked him better this way.

"No, no," he continued. "We thought it would be a good idea to show up in our Christmas gear initially.

You know, so we could present a united front to the folks in charge of the project. And to tell you the truth, we were hoping there would be some reporters hanging around this morning. We can use all the news coverage we can get."

Figured. I should have thought of that, really. Of course the Santas would want some free publicity. It would advertise their cause and might even help some of them find jobs. And frankly, it would help the Holiday Homebuilders cause, too.

Now that he mentioned it, I was starting to wonder, too. Where were the reporters? This was pretty big news.

"I assume they'll be here at some point today," I said. "This is an important event for our area." I could recall that, in previous years, the local news covered the Holiday Homebuilders project as one of the big human interest stories around Christmas. News crews always came out to interview the volunteers and the contractors. And this year, if they played their cards right, they'd get to talk to Santa Claus, too. A whole brigade of them, in fact.

"I hope you're right," Steve said. "I don't know how you feel about it, but if we can get some free press for the Santa Brigade, we'll be able to let more folks know about the work we do in the community."

Since it was for such a good cause, why would I complain? "I think it's wonderful. As long as it doesn't interfere with the other workers, I don't have a problem."

He grinned. "I'll make sure we don't distract anyone."

"I appreciate it." I wasn't sure whether to bring up the subject or not, but I needed to know. "So tell me the truth, Steve. Did you see your friend Slim touch that woman?"

"Absolutely not." He held up one hand as if he were

swearing in a court of law. "I'll admit most of us do enjoy the ladies, and obviously some of the guys were a little loose with their comments earlier. But Slim isn't one of them. He's not a player or a womanizer. And he's applied to move into this place with his wife. He wouldn't do anything to jeopardize his chances. I don't know what else to tell you, but he's just not that kind of a guy."

It was good to hear Steve reinforce my first impressions of the Santa who got slapped. Slim Daley. I absently wondered where he got the name Slim because he appeared to be as chubby and jolly as Steve.

"Did you recognize that woman who complained?"

Steve frowned. "Never saw her before."

"Me, neither." And I had left the yard without talking to her, I realized. Funny, but I didn't feel too guilty about it because, to tell the truth, I didn't believe her. But now I really wanted to talk to her. Why would she accuse Slim of something he didn't do? What did she gain by it? I walked with Steve around to the front of the house where he formally introduced me to the Brigade. He gave me each man's name—and one woman's, as it turned out—and then told them all to stand up straight and pay attention to me. I got the distinct feeling that not only was Steve the head of the group, but it was also possible that he'd been a drill sergeant at some point in his life.

I was stunned when one of the Santas turned out to be a woman, but then figured, why not? The holiday was meant to be a joyful time and Santa Claus represented the spirit of giving—and of delighting young children, right? So why couldn't a woman play the role? The beard was a little odd, of course, but she handled that peculiarity with good grace. Her name was Claudia and she worked at a women's crisis center up in Pentland, eight miles north of Lighthouse Cove. Since the crisis center doubled as a safe house where abused women and children lived, they didn't allow men to visit. So Claudia had taken on the role of first female Santa.

There was also an African-American Santa named Ronald and a Latino Santa named Mario, and both were just as chubby and jolly as the others. I figured, since kids came in all colors, it made sense that Santa did, too. It was sort of awesome when you thought about it.

I had already met Steve, of course, and his friends Mitch and Slim Daley. The rest of the Santas had real names, too. Parker, Al, Keith, and Herb. I wrote all ten names down so I wouldn't forget. Those last four fellows all looked like your classic jolly Santa types, so I wouldn't be able to tell them apart until they showed up without their costumes.

I started my little speech to the Santa Brigade by setting some ground rules. Namely, no Santa costumes after today, no catcalls, no rude language like I'd heard earlier. After a brief discussion of what, exactly, constituted rude language—it was mostly good-hearted teasing and laughing, thank goodness—I texted Sean and asked him to come around to the front of the house to assign the Santas some work. I knew they didn't want to get their costumes dirty, but I couldn't have them simply standing around waiting for the reporters to show up.

As soon as Sean arrived, I pulled him aside. "I have to find that woman who slapped Santa Claus. Do you remember which team you assigned her to?"

"Blake, upstairs in apartment twelve."

I frowned at the news. Apartment twelve was basically the attic. It wasn't even a real room yet. We had originally conceived of a total of ten apartments on the first and second floors. The attic was unfinished and we weren't sure the subflooring was strong enough to allow us to build on it. After meeting with our engineers and Arnie, the architect, they decided that the space was sound enough to support five mini-apartments. These wouldn't be finished in time for the official Christmas celebration, but they would be ready by mid-January.

We assigned apartment numbers and then numbered each team and contractor according to the apartment they were working on. It seemed like the easiest way to keep everyone organized.

Right now, apartment twelve was the attic. But in a few weeks it would refer to just one of five micro-apartments being built up there.

My contractors and I had decided to reinforce the space by removing the subflooring and adding extra crossbeams underneath. Once new subflooring was laid down, the crew would start framing to create five small apartments and a central hall off the main stairway. Until the framing and drywall was completed, the contractors and their crews were the only ones allowed up there. So what was Ponytail Girl doing up there?

"Was there a particular reason you sent her to twelve?" I asked.

"Yeah." His tone was surly. "Because she refused to work in apartment four or anywhere else in the house. She said she didn't trust the other volunteers. She asked if she could help out in one of the attic rooms, so I checked with Blake, who said it was okay. So I sent her up there. I figure she can organize tools or sweep the floors. Something."

"She's going to be nothing but trouble," I muttered. "We probably should've sent her home."

"She might go on her own." His smile was resolute. "I gave her a hard hat to wear and she balked at that, too, but I told her she couldn't stay if she didn't want to follow the rules."

"Thank you for saying that."

He shook his head. "People are freaking weird."

He didn't know the half of it. I patted his shoulder in comradely sympathy and turned back to the Santa Brigade. I finished up my little speech and explained that Sean would be giving them their assignments. Then I ran off to track down Wade. I was in no hurry to bump into the Santa Slapper, but I figured I'd better find out what she was up to.

I found Wade on the second floor working with the team in apartment six, formerly the billiards room. While waiting for him to finish ripping up a patch of rotten wood flooring, I recognized Charlie, a volunteer who was prying the baseboard from the wall, and pulled him aside to ask if he had seen the incident with Santa Claus and the Ponytail Woman.

"Didn't see a thing," he said.

I needed a clearer answer. "Does that mean you weren't looking? Or you were looking and didn't see him make a move?"

Charlie shrugged. "I admit I wasn't actually looking right at him, but I think I would've noticed him make a move. A guy dressed as Santa Claus is pretty hard to miss. And I didn't see him step forward or move his hand or anything."

"Okay, thanks." I went out into the hall to text Blake up in the attic. "How's your volunteer working out?"

Moments later, I received this message: "No volunteers up here."

Frowning, I texted back. "OK, thanks."

Another minute later, I was still scratching my head over Blake's response when Wade joined me in the hall. He groaned when I gave him my other news. "My dad's working with your father?"

"Yeah. And I have a feeling they had it planned out long before today."

He raked his hand through his hair in frustration. "And Frank's departure played right into their hands."

"That's another thing. Dad seemed to know the news about Frank before I did."

Wade raised his shoulders philosophically. "You know how fast word spreads around here."

I glanced around the hall to make sure we were alone. We were, but I lowered my voice anyway. "I'll deny I ever said this, but I don't want my dad and the others working unsupervised."

"Right there with you."

"I know his doctor signed off on everything. I know he's in great condition. But he hasn't worked like this in years. I'm just worried. And he would kill me if he heard me say that."

"He won't hear it from me," Wade said, and jogged back into the room to get his backpack. I followed him as he pulled out his tablet and held it up so I could view the screen with him. "Okay, look. We already scheduled Sean and Douglas to work the ballroom suite when you were assigned to the space. So how about if we get Billy over here to assist upstairs, and leave Sean and Douglas in the ballroom helping out the old guys. Make sure they don't overdo it."

I smiled at him. "To be fair, those so-called 'old guys' are barely sixty years old. And your dad is still working every day."

"Part-time," he emphasized, and let out an exasperated sigh. "You know how they are, Shannon. They're like kids. They'll egg each other on and try to outdo each other, and the rest of their buddies being around won't help matters."

"I know, I know." Nightmare scenarios began to play in my head and I had to force myself back to the conversation. "Okay, let's you and I make a point of stopping by the ballroom a couple times a day. And we'll alert Sean and Douglas to be extra watchful."

Sean Brogan and Douglas Mulcahy had been part of my crew for as long as I'd been running the company. Sean and I had gone to school together and Douglas was a few years younger. I trusted them both to report any shenanigans to me.

"That's all we can do," Wade concluded.

"Okay. I'll call Carla and have her send Billy over here." Billy was another trusted high school friend of mine and had been working on my crew for years.

"Sounds good."

I sighed. "I'm glad we're in this thing together."

I left Wade and jogged downstairs, intent on checking out what was happening in the big kitchen that would be attached to apartment two. But as I passed the open front door, I was distracted by some movement out on the driveway.

"Now what?" I muttered. I walked out onto the veranda in time to see Mr. Potter storming across the front lawn. Glancing toward the other side of the lawn, I spotted Potter's target: Santa Claus Steve. He stood in front of a picturesque copse of birch trees, where he was being interviewed by a few of our local reporters. The rest of the Santa Brigade stood behind Steve, making for a perfect Christmas backdrop. A cameraman was filming the mini–press conference and occasionally he would pan over to show the beautiful mansion that was being turned into apartments for our needy local residents.

I recognized Palmer Tripley, my buddy who owned the *Lighthouse Standard*, our local newspaper, taking notes. Among several other journalists I spotted Ron Wayne, a reporter for our local news station, asking Steve a question. Ron was the same guy who had interviewed me last week in anticipation of the big event.

I whipped around to watch Potter approach and really didn't like the look on his face. The last thing we needed was a furious bank executive being featured on the nightly news blasting Santa Claus. It wouldn't be good for either the Holiday Homebuilders charity or my workers' morale, not to mention the Santa Brigade and Steve himself. Frankly, I just didn't want any more chaos and controversy attached to our project. Call me Pollyanna, but I wanted this to be a happy work site from start to finish. And Potter was destroying that dream.

I jogged straight across the lawn to head Potter off before he got into camera range. When I was close enough, I grabbed his arm and stopped him in his tracks.

"Not so fast, Mr. Potter." I tried to keep my voice down so as not to interrupt the TV interview, but it wasn't easy. "I've warned you before. If you're planning to start a fight every time you show up here, you're not welcome on this job site."

He scowled at me. "You don't know who you're tangling with, pipsqueak."

Since I was about as tall as he was in my work boots and able to look him in the eye, I ignored the stupid insult. "I'm well aware that your bank is funding this entire project, but this is my job site and it's my responsibility to keep order. I won't have you disrupting our work."

"I'm not going anywhere," Potter said with a snarl.

I jabbed my finger right in his face. "The only way you're staying here is if you leave my workers alone."

He pointed at Santa Steve. "That clown over there isn't working. Get out of my way."

He tried to push me aside, but I circled around and stopped him again. "You're wrong. That interview he's giving will help spread goodwill for the Holiday Homebuilders project. And that will result in a number of new charitable contributions. And that helps everyone in town."

"Now I get it." His smile was hideous. "You're wangling for a little kickback, aren't you? How good would it look to see the head contractor caught stealing money from a charity?"

I gasped. I could feel my face turning red. I had the most overwhelming urge to punch him in the face, but I couldn't. But, oh, I wanted to. Instead, I leaned in close, and said, "You should think long and hard about coming around here again, Mr. Potter. Remember that time someone almost dropped a hammer on your head? Next time they might not miss."

Chapter Five

I left Potter on the lawn gaping at me and went back to work. Of course, I couldn't work. I was fuming. Angry at Potter for being such a horse's ass and daring to imply that I would ever take a kickback of any kind. And furious with myself for losing control and threatening him. I was pretty sure no one had overheard me, but those TV microphones were awfully powerful. They weren't very far away from where we were standing. What if they had picked up my words during the interview?

It was too late to worry about that, but I still managed to do so.

After two hours of moving from room to room, helping where I could and checking in on the volunteers, I jogged back upstairs for another short meeting with Wade. I had tried to put the Potter confrontation behind me and I'd been successful for a little while. But now that I was thinking about problems, I realized I hadn't seen the Santa Slapper since this morning. I just hoped she had changed her mind and gone home. Most of the other morning volunteers were starting to leave for the day and we were anticipating the arrival of the next group of twenty in forty-five minutes.

Other than the aforementioned confrontations that morning, we'd had three minor medical emergencies, all requiring bandages. One volunteer had managed to catch a big, ugly splinter in her hand. Once it was pulled out and the wound was bandaged, she wanted to keep working. I told her she could join my crew anytime.

The other two had been sent home early after they'd gotten into a fight over a nail gun. I was relieved that no one had gotten seriously hurt, but I still wasn't sure how those two had gotten their hands on the gun. My contractors and I had unanimously agreed not to allow any volunteers to use certain power tools, and nail guns were at the top of that list. The guys working that room insisted they'd kept the power tools locked up.

We needed to find out exactly what had happened, because the last thing I wanted was a repeat of the incident. With Potter and Ponytail Girl to deal with, I handed the nail gun mystery over to Wade to investigate.

Apartment six, where Wade worked, was on the east side of the house overlooking the thicket of enormous pine trees that lined the property. It was one of the largest rooms on the second floor, tucked under a dormer between the tower apartment at the front of the house and a smaller, quirky room at the back. It was situated nearby the library and would soon be transformed into a loft-style apartment for a single man. Curious, I looked up the names of the tenants and found that the man scheduled to move into apartment six was Steve Shore, the head of the Santa Brigade and Dad's old friend. Glancing around at the classic lines of the room, I had a feeling he would be very happy here.

As Wade and I were finishing our conversation, I gazed out the window and saw Aunt Daisy walking down the long driveway toward the street. "I'd like to go ask how her morning went," I said.

"We're done here, so go ahead," Wade said. "Let's meet up later this afternoon."

"Right. I'll text you." I dashed downstairs and out the front door to find Daisy.

"Do you need a ride back to the store?" I asked when I caught up with her.

"No, sweetie, but thank you for the offer. Marigold is picking me up any minute now."

"Good. Mind if I wait with you and say hello to her?"

"I would love it."

I stared up at the gray sky and raised the zipper on my down vest. We rarely got snow here, but we did get the occasional icy sea wind that could slice right down to the marrow. "If I didn't say so earlier, I wanted to thank you so much for volunteering."

"Oh, it was such fun. I caulked!" She waved her hands at me and I saw the white patches of dried caulk that stubbornly remained on her skin. She seemed to wear it with pride.

"Oh, Daisy. They gave you one of the few jobs where you can't wear gloves."

"I know! My fingers are a mess, aren't they?"

"I should've warned you. Caulk is made of silicone, so it basically turns to rubber. You can't really wash it off. You'll have to rub it off like rubber glue."

"Oh, I don't mind. I'll wear these splotches like a

badge of honor and tell everyone I was working in construction today."

I couldn't help but smile. She was such a cheery, good-hearted woman.

"And caulking is delightful," she continued. "It's one of those tasks you can do while daydreaming, at which I excel. And it was such a pleasure to be surrounded by all those healthy young men in their tight T-shirts and low-slung tool belts. I must say, they're in excellent condition, aren't they?"

I laughed. "Construction work can be very good for your muscles."

"I never realized." She wagged her finger at me. "And you, young lady, have kept it a secret all these years, never letting on that there was such a marvelous side benefit to this job. I can't wait to come back Thursday."

"I have a feeling my crew will be happy to see you, too."

My laughter faded instantly as Peter Potter screeched to a stop at the curb and jumped out of his big fancy car.

"Good heavens, what is he doing here?" Daisy said under her breath.

"His bank is in charge of the project," I whispered. "He seems duty-bound to show up on a regular basis and ruin everyone's day."

Potter rounded the car and only just noticed Daisy and me when he reached the edge of the driveway. Naturally, he bounded right up to us like a belligerent gorilla. "What the hell do you want?"

"Absolutely nothing from you, you old goat." Daisy swung her leather tote at his head, but she missed her mark and just skimmed his shoulder. "We were here first, remember? And don't you speak to us in that tone again."

Potter grabbed the tote bag and tossed it onto the

lawn. "You crazy old bat. I could have you arrested for assault and battery."

"You try it, you bug-eyed worm." Her voice was a throaty growl. "I'd love the chance to drag you in front of a judge."

"Stupid old crow," Potter muttered.

"Cranky old horny toad."

He stormed away and Daisy clenched her fists together. "I hate that man."

I watched Potter walk all the way up the front stairs and into the house before turning back to Daisy. "I don't blame you. But wow, I never knew you could go head-to-head with someone like him."

"Sometimes a girl's got to do what a girl's got to do." She folded her arms tightly across her chest and sighed heavily. "I apologize for my language, Shannon. I'm sorry you had to be a witness to that."

"Don't worry about me." I walked a few steps across the lawn, picked up her tote and a few small items that had fallen out, and handed it back to her. "Honestly, I enjoyed watching you go after him. But what happened, Daisy? What did he do to you?"

"Oh." She shook her head in disgust. "He asked me out on a date last year and . . . well, he was just a big oaf. I suppose he was trying to make a move on me, but he was so clumsy and obnoxious, there was no way anything like that was going to happen."

She waved the comment away as though it meant nothing, but her tone told me she was still annoyed and maybe a little embarrassed by the incident. I knew exactly how she felt and didn't blame her one bit for lashing out at him.

"I told him to go home, but he refused," she continued.

"I ended up kicking him in the shins and gave him a stern talking-to. He pushed me aside, called me a rude name, and stormed out of my house."

"Did he hurt you?"

"Oh, I was a little black-and-blue where he grabbed my arm, but you know, it's my own fault for agreeing to go to dinner with him. Bad enough to go through what I did, but then to find out he's a married man? Well, I was mortified."

"He's married?"

"Apparently. I'd never heard anyone mention him having a wife. I asked him if he'd ever been married and he told me he was divorced. Said his ex-wife lives in Florida. It turns out the Florida part is true, but they never got a divorce."

"Did you tell anyone what happened?" I asked. "Did you call the police?"

"Oh, heavens no. It wasn't that big of a deal. And besides, do you think they would've believed me? Potter's a hotshot at the biggest bank in town. And look at me. I'm not exactly some glamorous femme fatale. The police would've had a good laugh and told me to move along on my merry way."

"I don't believe Chief Jensen would've done that," I said. "First of all, you're beautiful. And second, nobody in town likes the man, so the cops would probably be more than willing to take your word against his."

"That would be nice, but it's too late to make a fuss now. I'd appreciate it if you'd simply forget I ever said anything."

Daisy had made up her mind, so it would do me no good to continue arguing with her. "If it makes you feel better, I'll drop the subject."

"Thank you, Shannon. Oh, here comes Marigold."

A minute later, she was buckling her seat belt and I waved good-bye to both of them. But I had every intention of talking to Marigold later about Daisy's close encounter with Peter Potter. All she had to do was say the word and I would be happy to contact Chief Jensen on Daisy's behalf. I wanted the chief to know that while Peter Potter might be a very important person around town, he was also a bug-eyed bully, capable of pushing a perfectly nice woman around and hurting her. I didn't suppose that was enough to arrest him, but I would give anything to see that old-goat mug of his behind bars.

Chapter Six

I was inside Forester House and starting for the stairs when I heard the front door open behind me. I turned and saw the ponytailed woman who had slapped Santa Claus step inside the foyer.

"I thought you'd left for the day," I said.

"I did," she said, glancing around uneasily. "But I had to come back because I, uh, forgot something. And then I saw you out on the lawn with that lady, so I followed you inside."

"Oh." Why was I creeped out that she had followed me? Probably because I hadn't seen her first. And why hadn't I seen her? Was she hiding? Deliberately trying to avoid me?

Was I looking for a freaky weirdo where only a suspicious stranger existed? I had to get a grip. But still, I paused to wonder if she'd seen Daisy trying to smack Mr. Potter. I hoped not. Daisy was one of the sweetest people in town and I wouldn't want a stranger getting the wrong impression of her.

I shook off the nerves. "Listen, I tried to track you

down earlier but I was told you were working in the attic and I didn't find you there."

"I was there. You didn't look hard enough."

She was really getting on my nerves. I didn't bother mentioning that the contractor in the attic told me she never showed up. I wasn't sure why, except that I didn't want to make her more defensive than she already was. Mostly I just wanted her to go away and not come back. But I took a deep breath and said, "Would you like to talk about what happened this morning?"

"Not really."

"Well, I think we should, especially if you plan on working here after today."

"I do."

"I'm not sure that's a good idea, but we'll deal with that later. Right now I'd like you to tell me exactly what happened."

"I already did."

"I'd like to hear it again, from start to finish." I motioned toward a fancy old settee arranged along the wall of the foyer, so we both moved toward it but neither of us sat down. She still didn't say a word, so I said, "I haven't talked to everyone but the people I've talked to say that the man you slapped was not actually the person who pinched you."

She didn't look surprised. "Did any of them see who did it?"

I gritted my teeth. "No."

She crossed her arms and gave me an imperious glare. "So you're calling me a liar?"

Her anger was palpable and frankly contagious. I wanted to snap back at her, but I resisted. I tried to remind myself that she'd been the one to get pinched and had just reacted. A little violently, but who was I to judge? On the other hand, I hadn't found anyone who'd actually seen the pinch occur, which could mean that the pinchee was lying. It would probably be rude to suggest it, but I was tempted. It was hard for me to be nonjudgmental when she insisted on being so defensive.

"No, of course not," I said patiently. "It's just that no one saw it happen and Santa swears he didn't do it. Granted, I haven't questioned everyone yet, but I will. It just might take a while."

"I think you're covering up for that man. I'm not surprised, though. Everyone in town would rather bury their heads in the sand than face the music. I'm so sick of it."

Everyone in town? Had she been living in Lighthouse Cove for long? Why had I never seen her before? And what was with her back-to-back nonsensical clichés? Nobody was burying their heads. And what music was she talking about? Something else was going on with this woman and I wanted to know what it was. First off, I loved my little town and didn't appreciate strangers trying to make trouble. Second, I just didn't like her much and I sure didn't trust her. What was she trying to pull?

And so much for me not being judgmental.

"I think you're being unfair," I said after a brief pause in which I tried to tamp down my own irritation. "I understand you're angry."

"Darn right I'm angry."

"I don't blame you. I would be, too."

"So what are you going to do about it?" Her hands curled into fists and I wondered if she was tempted to take a swing at me.

"I plan to talk to everyone who was in the area at the time you claim you were assaulted."

"Claim?" she cried. "I'm not 'claiming' anything. I'm telling you it happened. Deal with it."

"That's what I plan to do." I gazed steadily at her. "What's your name?"

"Why does that matter?"

"It matters because I'm in charge of this construction site and I like to know the names of the people I work with. My name's Shannon Hammer."

"I know your name," she said curtly, still fuming. She stared at the ceiling for a moment, possibly determining her next move. "My name is April."

"Okay, April. How about if we—"

"Look, maybe I'll just handle this on my own."

"What exactly is there to handle?" I asked. "You already slapped the man you think pinched you."

"I'll just talk to him. Make sure he understands that he's not to touch me again."

"No."

"But you're not—"

"No."

"But—"

I held up my hand. "I said no, April. I'm in charge and I don't want you going around causing problems."

Her nostrils flared. "I'm not the one causing problems."

That wasn't what it looked like from where I was standing. Yes, she was the victim here. At least, she claimed to be the victim and until I could investigate further, I would treat her as such. But she was so annoying! Why was she here? She hadn't shown up to work in the attic as she'd promised and now she was vowing revenge. On my work site. Was I being unfair to her? Maybe, but she was coming across as someone who enjoyed stirring up the pot no matter what.

"You're obviously ready to lash out at certain people in this house," I said. "And that's not going to happen." I took a breath myself, trying to get a firm grip on my dissolving patience. "I understand you're angry and upset and you probably think you're the only one capable of finding out anything. But you're wrong. My crew and I will handle this. We'll figure out what happened, one way or another."

"What if I don't believe you?"

Okay, threshold reached. "Then you should leave and not come back."

She flopped back against the wall, deflated. "That's harsh."

She looked completely flattened and frankly, that made me feel better. If I could keep her calm, maybe she'd let go of her angry revenge act. "Look, I told you I would deal with it and I will. We basically have eleven days to finish this massive job and I won't allow my people to be distracted. Either follow my rules or leave."

"Fine. Whatever." And with that, she pushed herself away from the wall, stomped past me, and ran up the stairs, leaving me feeling impotent and furious and determined not to help her at all. Ever.

Not a very mature reaction on my part, but April rubbed me the wrong way. Honestly, she could swing from Godzilla to a bratty child and back again in seconds. Neither of the two were appealing. I took some deep, calming breaths and wondered if it would be wrong to follow her upstairs and demand that she leave the property. But then she would raise an even bigger fuss. She might even talk to the newspapers, which would just bring Potter back to rail against me and every other volunteer.

With that possibility hanging over my head, I decided I would discuss the situation with Wade as soon as I could. He would have a cooler perspective. It would be smart of me to explain the situation and have him ask around for any eyewitnesses to April's assault. Together we would maybe get some answers more quickly.

Heading down the hall toward the ballroom, I thought more about April. Lighthouse Cove was a small town and I knew almost everyone living here. April was completely unfamiliar to me. Who was she? Where did she come from? Had she made up the entire Santa Claus pinching incident? And why was she here supposedly volunteering but not actually working? I was leaning heavily toward believing she had made up the whole thing. But why? It was too weird. Who would do such an odd, mean-spirited thing?

I hadn't believed her from the very start that morning. I couldn't say why. She had seemed sincere at first, but then I'd heard Slim's plaintive protests and I began to suspect that April might be lying. Again, I had to ask why.

It didn't give me much pleasure to realize I'd been right when I sensed earlier that she would be nothing but trouble.

I hoped she wouldn't try to hunt down Slim Daley and deal with him on her own. The thought sent an odd shiver across my shoulders. And it reminded me that I hadn't seen anyone from the Santa Brigade in a while. Maybe they had all left at lunchtime as most of the early volunteers had. But just in case, I decided I had better check all the rooms. And I would do that just as soon as I looked in on my father and his posse.

And speaking of trouble, I wondered where Mr. Potter had disappeared to. I rubbed my forehead as I traipsed down the hall. Officially this was my first day on the job, now that I had all my contractors and volunteers working at full capacity. But already I had to wonder, was the Forester project going to be wrought with this much trauma all the way through until Christmas? If that was the case, I would never get into the spirit of the holiday.

I had to laugh, because all of this minute-to-minute drama was working to keep my mind off my own angsty problems. I had that to be thankful for, at least, because my pitiful roller coaster emotions had been driving me crazy lately. Here on the job, there were so many more important issues to tackle. And it was refreshing to know that nobody working here gave a hoot about the fact that it had been six long weeks since MacKintyre Sullivan had talked to me.

It wasn't the sort of news I was inclined to share with anyone, including my dearest friends.

But it was true. Mac hadn't picked up a phone to contact me in exactly forty-two days. And apparently he'd never heard of e-mail either. Or texting. Or faxing. I hadn't received a letter, a telegram, or even a tweet. Not one word from him.

Disgusted, I shook my head. Fine. Even though we'd been pretty close for a few months, that didn't mean he had to check in with me all the time. He was a busy man, living his life, traveling around the country on his very important nationwide book tour and hobnobbing with his publishers in New York City. Apparently one of his agents had a farm in the Hudson River Valley and often invited Mac to visit and unwind. How super groovy for him.

For two months before that, he'd been jetting around Europe filming his latest Jake Slater movie. I mean, I was thrilled for his success and I wished him joy and happiness, really. I knew how much his work meant to him, so of course I was pleased to know he was enjoying the fruits of his labor. Why would I expect him to take time out to call me when he was so busy? You know, it took a lot of energy to deal with all those beautiful actresses and supermodels surrounding him all the time.

"You're an idiot," I muttered, and viciously pushed those feelings right out of my mind. Why was I dwelling on any of it anyway? It was so humiliating. Let's face it, I'd been a fool to fall for him in the first place—if only because of my previously dismal track record with men.

Don't go down that road, I thought to myself. I had always been happy with my life. I enjoyed my town, my job, my wonderful friends and family. I was fulfilled, darn it. Granted, until Mac moved to town, I hadn't really dated since college—well, except for that one awful blind date last year that went tragically wrong. But that was another reason why it would be smart to be more careful with my choices.

And besides, what business did I have being attracted to someone like Mac? The man was a superstar thriller writer and his circle of friends included movie stars and high-powered business moguls, along with the aforementioned supermodels, lest I forget.

And me? Let's face it, I was essentially a small-town girl.

The fact that I'd had a crush on Mac before I ever met

him was something for which I could forgive myself. His stories were riveting, after all, and his protagonist, Jake Slater, was the most awesome dark hero ever. And Mac's author photograph on the back covers of his books was simply mind-blowing. The guy had a face that stopped women's hearts.

And then there was the way we'd met, when he rescued me from a bad fall from my bicycle. He'd driven me home and carried me up the stairs and into my house, igniting all sorts of juicy rumors and gossip around town. And then, instead of moving into the fanciest hotel in town, he had chosen to rent one of my garage apartments, so we had been neighbors for months. We met for dinner on a regular basis. Sometimes he would grill steaks and I would make a salad, other times we would walk up to the pier. He helped me with my gardening. I brought him snacks when he was on deadline. He was thoughtful and funny and sexy and smart. He made it clear how much he liked me and how impressed he was by my professional abilities when he hired me to renovate the famous lighthouse mansion, the home he'd bought when he first moved to town.

And over time, my feelings for him had grown. I thought those feelings were mutual, but I'd been wrong about such things before. I thought it meant something that he had never really moved out of the garage apartment, but had instead stayed close to me. Now that the renovation on the mansion was completed, though, it was only a matter of time. And, oh God, I was really going to miss him.

Like I did now.

"Ugh, stop," I said, louder this time. Where had all this emotional residue come from? Had the unpleasant run-in with April brought it all to the surface? Whatever the cause, I didn't have time for it, so I shoved it all back into my subconscious and walked into apartment three wearing a determined smile on my face.

It was good to find my father and his cronies hard at work. My two crew guys, Sean and Douglas, were both up on ladders, opening up the dozens of cracks in the ceiling in preparation for spackling and painting. Seeing everyone working hard was all I needed to effectively cut off the self-pitying blather that had been spiraling around in my head.

"Hey, kiddo," Dad said cheerfully. "How's it going?"

"I was just going to ask you the same thing. You guys look busy."

Phil Chambers finished tightening a screw on an outlet and slipped the screwdriver into his tool belt before walking over to give me a hug. "Good to see you, Shannon."

"You, too, Phil. Have you had a chance to see Wade today?"

"He stopped by earlier to tell me to be careful." He glanced around at his buddies. "My boy thinks I'm ready for assisted living."

"Why do you think my girl is checking up on us?" Dad said, winking at me.

"I'm checking up on everyone," I said mildly. "That's my job. And Wade's, too."

"Well, come on over here and check out what we've done." I followed him to the doorway leading into the butler's pantry.

"Wow. You've already got the wall framed. That's great."

"Yup. Pete's always been the best framer in town.

Anyway, we'll be hanging drywall later this afternoon and start taping the seams. Tomorrow we'll add the first coat of mud and keep on going from there. I'm guessing the wall should be ready for priming by Friday."

Four days from now; that was probably about right. I estimated that I'd personally hung a thousand miles' worth of drywall—give or take a few hundred—in my young life. I considered the job particularly hellish, mainly because of the amount of time it took to get it just right. Dealing with the unwieldy boards and attaching them correctly to the frame was only the start. Then came the real endurance test. It started with covering each seam with a wide strip of drywall joint tape made of a thin, fibrous paper that resisted tearing and stretching. They also made a fine mesh tape that worked well. This was followed by the first thin coat of drywall compound, commonly referred to as "mud," applied over the tape along the seams and joints, using a drywall knife. Once that first layer of mud was dry, usually overnight, it was sanded down to a smooth finish. Then came the second coat of mud, covering a wider swath than the first coat. You let that dry overnight, then sanded it in the morning. Then more mud and more drying and sanding, repeating until the surface was completely smooth and wiped clean. There were a lot more tips I could give, like coating the vertical seams before the horizontal ones, and using gradually larger drywall knives as you smooth the mud over the seams. But basically, once these first ten thousand steps were completed, your new wall was ready to be primed and painted.

You could grow old in the meantime.

"While we're waiting for the mud to dry," Dad continued, "we'll be working on closing up those cracks in the ceiling and then painting over them. After that we'll demo the bathroom floor."

"We're lucky we don't have to deal with wallpaper," I murmured.

"Yeah, our team lucked out with this space," Dad agreed.

"The crews working on the second floor weren't so fortunate," Phil said. "I took a look around up there and every bedroom is covered from baseboard to ceiling in wallpaper."

Dad just grunted at the thought and I couldn't blame him. Removing wallpaper was another truly time-sucking task. And when your life's work centered on the renovation of Victorian homes, wallpaper was your constant companion. The Victorians had been in love with wallpaper, the more mind-numbingly flowery the better. So in removing it, you invariably ran into layers and layers of old sheets on every single wall. And occasionally on the ceilings. And with each layer you removed, the history and culture of past decades revealed themselves to you. It was fascinating, if labor-intensive.

I glanced around the ballroom, where beaded wainscoting and delicate bas relief designs graced the walls. Most of the surfaces were still in beautiful condition and wouldn't need any work done to them. "You all might finish ahead of schedule because of that."

Dad nodded. "If we finish early in here, we'll give some of the other crews a hand."

"Absolutely," Phil said.

"Thanks, guys," I said. Looking down, I noticed that they had peeled away the ancient linoleum so the new wall frame stood directly on the wood subflooring.

Dad followed my gaze. "Once the drywall is painted,

we'll put in the new tile floor. If any of my guys are available this weekend, we can get it done before Monday."

I should've known he would be ahead of schedule. "All the floor tile is being stored in the garage. Sean and Douglas will bring it into the house whenever you're ready."

"Sounds good," he said. "Now, about the cloakroom."

I frowned. "Yeah, I've been having second thoughts about the cloakroom."

"You're not the only one." We crossed the length of the ballroom with Phil tagging along. "Arnie stopped by with his blueprints and I explained to him what we wanted to do."

We had both worked with Arnie the architect for years. "Did he have a problem with it?"

"He has a couple of problems."

"To be honest, I have some, too," I said, stepping inside the large, dark cloakroom. "I just don't think we can get enough light in here to make it cheery enough for a little girl. Any window we add will be under the veranda roof."

"Right, and it's always going to be shady on the veranda."

"Exactly."

"Plus, Molly is only six years old," I said. "According to Sophie, her little girl has had a pretty tough life up to now. Under those circumstances, I'm not sure she would want Molly sleeping in a dark, windowless room." I shrugged. "But maybe I'm projecting. Once I thought about it, I realized I would hate it."

"Arnie completely agreed," Dad said. "And not only because the window might compromise the integrity of that stretch of the porch."

He grinned as he said it and I smiled, too. "We wouldn't want that."

"No way. But Arnie's against the idea because he has his two little girls. He just couldn't picture either of them sleeping in that closed-off space."

"Okay," I said with a nod. "I guess it's settled. We'll cancel our bedroom plan and go back to turning it into the world's most fabulous closet."

I was a little disappointed, but I'd find some other way to give Molly her own space.

Dad held up his hand. "Now, on the off chance that Molly and her mom love the idea of turning that space into a bedroom, I want you to know that Phil and the guys agreed that we'd all be happy to do the work anytime after they move in."

"That's so nice." I smiled at both of them. "Thank you."

"You bet."

"So we go with the original plan?" Phil said.

"Yes."

"Makes it easy." Phil glanced at Dad. "Ready to go back to work?"

"Yeah."

They left me staring at the walls of the cloakroom.

The original plan for the space had been to line the walls with light cedar planks in order to freshen up the space. We would build a modern closet using modular pieces that fit together. Open shelves for shoes and purses, pull-out shelves and drawers for shirts, sweaters, and scarves, and multiple areas for hanging clothes. We would add canned lighting above each shelving column and hang a couple of wall sconces to brighten and warm up the space. Of course, adding wall sconces would mean rewiring the space, but Dad was an expert at that.

The plaster walls would slow them down a touch so it was a good thing they were running ahead of schedule. So far, anyway.

I pictured a colorful stuffed ottoman in the center of the space where Sophie could sit down while deciding what to wear. I would ask the designers to add a smaller, poofy ottoman for Molly. This would be a closet fit for a queen and her little princess.

I returned to the ballroom where Dad and his guys had gone back to work in various parts of the room. Sean and Douglas were starting to spread spackle across the ceiling cracks. The only sounds were the putty knives scraping against the ceiling and the occasional pounding of a hammer and the hum of Phil's power drill as he finished the framing in the hall by the butler's pantry. The men were working quietly and industriously, which made me instantly wary.

Dad must have been feeling the vibe because he glanced over at me and grinned like a loon. "Everything's hunky-dory in here, honey. You can go check on your other apartments."

Why did I get the feeling that the minute I left, they would break out the pretzels, beer, and poker chips and start the party? But he was right: I had to go check on other things. "Okay, Dad. I've got my phone with me, so please call or text me if you need anything."

He winked. "You bet I will."

But I knew he would rather chew glass than call me for help. And for some reason, that thought sent a chill right down to my bones.

Chapter Seven

I managed to choke down a granola bar for lunch. In between talking to Angry April—aka Ponytail Girl, aka the Santa Slapper—and checking out my dad's work in the ballroom, I had lost track of Mr. Potter. The good news was that I hadn't heard any shouting for the last hour. The bad news was that his car was still parked out on the street, so I knew he was around here somewhere. And I didn't like not knowing where.

A glance out the window on the stairway landing told me that the local news reporters had long since finished interviewing Santa Steve and a few other volunteers. Everyone was gone from the spot I'd seen them earlier and I wondered if Steve and the rest of the Brigade had left for the day with the other morning volunteers. I sort of hoped so. Things seemed to be quieter now, but maybe that was my imagination.

It was one o'clock when the afternoon volunteers began to gather at the usual place near the veranda by the back ballroom door. Standing a few steps above the group, I plunged right into my prepared speech.

"Hi, everyone. I'm Shannon."

"Hi, Shannon," everyone shouted.

I grinned. Right off, this group seemed a lot happier than the morning group. To be fair, though, these folks hadn't had to wake up at the crack of dawn to get here.

I glanced around at all the familiar faces and was thrilled to see two of my closest friends, Lizzie Logan and Jane Hennessey, in the crowd. I gave them an extra special wave and was about to start talking when I noticed two younger girls, Kailee and Alyssa, standing on the other side of the crowd. They giggled and waved at me and made me smile. I waved back.

Those two were part of a group of homeless teenagers who had been attending a construction and carpentry class I'd been teaching for the past eight months at the Cove Community Center. It was DIY stuff, mostly, and how to do minor repairs like unclogging sinks and fixing cracks and caulking sinks and tubs. I taught power tool safety and even the best way to climb a ladder and paint a room. Pretty basic information. Kailee and Alyssa and their girlfriend Lauren were my three best students and I was happy to see two of them here to get some on-the-job training.

I worked with both boys and girls in the group, but I had to admit I was a big proponent of bringing more women into the construction field—if only so I wasn't always the sole representative of my gender in Lighthouse Cove.

I took a quick head count and then launched into my usual spiel about what to expect this afternoon. When I was finished, I divided the group into smaller teams and sent them off to their assigned crews.

Kailee and Alyssa rushed over and hugged me.

"I'm so glad you're here," I said.

"We got a special pass to work here this afternoon," Kailee said.

"On-the-job training," Alyssa said. "Isn't that cool?"

"It's fantastic," I said. "How's Lauren doing?"

They exchanged a quick, wide-eyed glance, and Alyssa said, "She's sick."

"Oh, I'm sorry. Maybe she'll make it next week."

"Um, yeah. We'll tell her you said hi."

"Good. Now I've got to go make sure everything's running smoothly, but I promise I'll stop by and see how you're doing later. And we can talk some more after you're finished for the day, okay?"

"Yay!" Alyssa said, and they went running for the back door. I laughed as I watched them go. Their enthusiasm was infectious.

Lizzie and Jane waited until the younger girls were gone before grabbing me in another big hug.

"I'm so glad to see you guys," I said.

My desperation must have been obvious because they exchanged glances, and Jane said, "You sound a little freaked out. Are you buried in work?"

"Something happened," Lizzie said after scrutinizing me a little more carefully.

They had always been able to read me like a book. That wasn't necessarily a good thing. "Guess you could say I've had a day. It started with Robbie escaping first thing this morning."

"And I heard Frank and Maureen are moving," Jane said, "so I guess you're down one contractor."

"You already knew that?" I shook my head. "I'm always the last to know."

"Is that what's bugging you?"

"Not really. There's more." I listed all the horrors that had made up my bad, bad, very bad day, including the Santa Clauses and the ponytailed woman, and Mr. Potter of course.

"Potter's always been a jackass," Lizzie said. "But let's talk about these Santa Clauses. Really? Ten of them?"

"Yes, each in full costume," I said, "right down to the white beards and the *ho ho ho*s. Oh, and then my father showed up wanting to work. So I gave him my assignment."

Lizzie's eyes widened. "Will he be okay?"

The fact that she was concerned enough about his health to ask the question made me want to hug her again. "I'm keeping an eye on him."

"Good. Don't let him overdo it."

"I won't. But enough about me," I said, laughing. "What's new with you two?"

"Well, you already know my big news," Lizzie said, now visibly excited.

I frowned. "I do?"

"But I haven't told Jane yet."

"Told me what?" Jane said. "You're holding out on me?"

"No, no," Lizzie insisted. "We just finalized the plans last night." She wiggled her eyebrows at me.

I had no idea what she was referring to, but I smiled and played along. "Spill the beans, Lizzie."

She paused for dramatic effect, then blurted, "Mac Sullivan is going to do a major book signing at the store this weekend in time for the big Christmas rush."

I gasped. Not to be overly dramatic, but it felt kind of like taking a punch to my stomach. I tried to mask my reaction, but it wasn't easy. Lizzie thought I knew of course, because she assumed that Mac had been keeping in touch with me. I hadn't even told my closest friends that the man I was nuts about had clearly forgotten my existence over the last forty-two days. It was just too humiliating.

Lizzie and her husband, Hal, owned Paper Moon, the book and gift shop on the town square. Mac had been in to sign books for her before, but Lizzie had never been able to schedule an official event with him and his fans. Until now, apparently.

"What's wrong?" Lizzie demanded. "Are you sick?"

Jane was staring too intently at me. "You didn't know, did you?"

"You didn't?" Lizzie looked puzzled. "But you and Mac talk on the phone all the time, right? I figured he would've mentioned it."

You know, I owed Mac for this, too. Now I was put in the position of having my friends feel sorry for me. If he wanted to dump me, why didn't he just write me a Dear Shannon letter and get it over with? "No, he didn't, but—"

She suddenly clapped her hand over her mouth. "I'll bet he wanted to surprise you. He said he was coming home tonight. I'm sorry I ruined the surprise."

She had no idea, but I breezily waved her words away. "Don't be silly." Inside, though, I was thinking, *Tonight? He's coming home tonight and didn't even tell me that much?*

Jane sighed. "He is so romantic."

Despite my inner turmoil, I had to smile. Jane was unwavering in her belief that there was such a thing as happily ever after. I couldn't bear to tell either of them the truth. And oh, when I finally did see Mac, I would have plenty to say before I turned my back on him forever. Not that he would care. "Look, I have to get back to work, but I'll come find you both later and we can chitchat."

I jogged off toward the front of the house. I didn't dare turn around in case they got another look at my pale, shocked expression. I didn't need the world to know what a mess I was. Because I wasn't a mess, darn it. I was as fine as could be. And that was my story and I was sticking to it. Besides, I was tired of being sad. I'd rather have been furious. That emotion didn't make my stomach hurt as much.

Before I could get ten feet into the house, a woman stopped me in the foyer. "Hello there. Can you tell me where I can find Mr. Potter? He's in charge of this project."

No, he isn't, I wanted to say, but restrained myself. I recognized the woman I'd seen earlier that day at the door to the ballroom. Dad had identified her as Potter's secretary, Patrice, so I was instantly on guard.

"No," I admitted, "I haven't seen him in a while. Actually, I was about to go upstairs and look for him myself."

"Do you mind if I tag along? I need to give him his messages." She patted her very large shoulder bag, which could have contained half of her office along with the messages. She had one of those soft southern accents and was petite and beautifully dressed in a taupe wool knit suit. Her shoes were sensible but expensive Etienne Aigner heels. (I recognized the brand because Lizzie had a pair in high school that she prized above all else.) Her blonde hair was coiffed to perfection. I guessed she was in her late thirties or early forties but her style and wardrobe belonged to a woman a decade older. It truly wasn't a criticism, simply an observation. She was very pretty.

"You're Patrice, right? You work for Mr. Potter."

"Yes," she said. "And you must be Jack Hammer's daughter, Shannon. I saw you with him this morning. It's nice to meet you."

"Nice to meet you, too." I led her toward the curving grand staircase and began the climb to the second floor.

"Your father is a lovely man," she said.

"I agree," I said, smiling. "Thank you."

But I noticed her frowning as she said it. "He doesn't care much for Mr. Potter. They've had run-ins before."

"Yes, they have," I said. And it still bothered me not to know if there was a specific thing Dad hated about Potter or if it was just on general principle. But I didn't ask the question out loud.

Patrice sighed. "I know people think Mr. Potter is short tempered, and I suppose he can be. But I've always been able to get along with him. Do you want to know my secret?"

"Definitely."

She smiled. "I let him think he's in charge of everything and then I go ahead and handle things. You know how it is. All a man really needs is for someone to assure him that everything is fine and that it's all being handled properly."

I tried not to choke. She sounded like she was describing a spoiled child, not the senior vice president of a bank. Her attitude matched her expensive clothing; both were just old-fashioned enough to be charming to some. Maybe that's what she'd been raised to believe. It wasn't generational. My friend Emily was about the same age as Patrice and she would have bitten off her tongue before she would ever say something like that.

I stopped at the top of the stairs and looked down at her. "It would be great if you could assure him that this project is running smoothly."

"I wish I could, Shannon, but he wouldn't believe me. He has to get a firsthand look at things and he gets truly nervous when there are so many variables. So many things can go wrong, you see. It drives him crazy when there are too many chefs in the kitchen, so to speak. It makes him jittery and that's when he goes off on a tear."

I smiled tightly. "There's only one chef in this kitchen, and that's me."

"And you're a woman," she said apologetically.

"Why, yes, I am."

Her smile was sympathetic. "He's funny about that."

I groaned inwardly. Potter was *funny* about a lot of things and, frankly, I didn't find any part of it *funny*. He was just a cranky old toad, as Daisy had said. None of that mattered, though. I was in charge and the work would get done on time and this place would look fantastic. I wouldn't let Potter's attitude—or that of his secretary—get me down.

Patrice was wildly myopic when it came to defending her boss, but she was also nice and friendly and she thought my father was lovely, so I decided not to argue with her. But she was ridiculously wrong about Potter. He enjoyed causing trouble. I would bet he even thrived on it. And I didn't know what particular character flaw allowed him to hold such low opinions of people, but he had no problem letting them know it, always belittling and sneering while at the same time demanding the impossible and ordering them around. And that made him an arrogant bully and a dangerous man.

And in my book, the fact that he didn't respect women was the last nail in the coffin. Having grown up working in a man's world, I'd often had to work twice as hard as any man to gain the respect of clients and peers and others in the field. I was used to the Potter mentality and there was no way I would let him make decisions or interrupt work on my job site.

I glanced up and down the hall. "He could be anywhere in the house, so I say we start checking all the rooms up here until we find him."

"That's as good a plan as any, since he does enjoy getting involved in every aspect of the work."

I almost laughed at her pleasant way of calling him an interfering menace. Again, it wouldn't do any good to call out her inability to see the man for what he really was. Instead, I just shook my head and started toward the first door. And that's when someone downstairs began screaming at the top of her lungs.

"What in the world?" Patrice cried.

"That's Lizzie!" I shouted and raced down the stairs.

I found my friend in the front tower room, a large circular space now known as apartment one. The door was wide open and I ran inside. Lizzie stood alone near a doorway that led out to the side yard and driveway.

"Lizzie," I shouted, running across the room. "What happened? What's wrong?"

She was visibly shaking and I had to grip both her arms and ask her again, "What is it? Talk to me."

"I'm sorry I screamed, but it's just so frustrating talking to that horrible man."

"Who?"

She gazed at me, but I wasn't sure she was really seeing me. "He—he threatened to close down our store."

"Who?"

She pointed toward the side yard. "Mr. Potter. That man is a monster. I swear, if Hal doesn't kill him, I will."

Chapter Eight

I ran outside to confront Potter and kick him off the property once and for all. I didn't care if he was a big muck-a-muck at the bank. How dare he threaten Lizzie! Or anyone else. I was tempted to call the bank right there and then to let them know that until this job was finished, Potter was not welcome on the work site.

But glancing around, I didn't see him anywhere and some of my rage was replaced by bewilderment. How did he vanish so quickly? The garage was only a hundred yards away. Was he a fast runner? Was he hiding in there? It was a ridiculous thought, but where else could he be?

I glanced down the driveway and saw that his car was still out front. So where was he?

I walked along the side of the house and had a "Duh!" moment when I realized he could have walked back inside using any one of six entrances. I'd been too freaked out by Lizzie's screams to think about it rationally. Potter was probably upstairs by now, harassing someone else for some other absurd reason.

As an executive with the biggest bank in town, where so many local people had bank accounts and confidential loan applications and all sorts of other sensitive information on file, Potter would be privy to information about hundreds of people. Knowing he was capable of using such private information against one of my dearest friends made my skin crawl.

Patrice came running outside after me and turned in four directions, looking for her boss. "I don't understand. He's not out here. Where did he go?"

"He probably walked around to the front door and right back into the house."

"I should go look for him." But instead of leaving, she leaned in close and said, "Did you hear your friend just now, threatening to murder Mr. Potter? Don't you think we should call the police?"

I gaped at her. "That's ridiculous. Lizzie didn't mean anything by it. Your boss threatened her livelihood for no good reason, so she has every right to be upset. But that's all it is. If you want to do something helpful for everyone here, I would suggest that you track down Mr. Potter and make him go home."

She shot a quick glance at Lizzie. "But she could be dangerous. Is she on medication?"

I was beginning to wonder if *she* was on medication. Did she honestly not know that everyone in town hated Potter? That hundreds of people probably muttered, *I'm going to kill that man* over and over again every day? How could she be so clueless?

I took another deep breath before speaking again. "I understand that you have to defend your boss, but you're wrong about Lizzie. She's the most solid citizen in Lighthouse Cove and Potter deliberately harassed her. If anyone deserves police scrutiny, it's him."

I walked away before I said something even more offensive and hurried back inside to give Lizzie a hug. She was sniffling back tears.

"He's full of it," I said. "You know that, right? He can't close down your store. It's one of the most popular shops on the square and it's doing great business."

Her hands were still trembling. "But his bank owns the deed, so he can do whatever he wants."

"No he can't," I insisted.

"Shannon, get serious. The bank owns every store on the square. If they wanted to tear us all down and put up a new bank building, they could do it."

"Not without the entire town protesting and boycotting them." I grabbed her arms and gave her a gentle shake. "Look at me. Nothing's going to happen to your store. He's just a big bully and he'll say whatever he can to get a rise out of you."

I heard a footstep and turned to see Patrice standing a few feet away. I could tell by the look on her face that she'd been listening in on our entire conversation. Now she was staring at Lizzie and frowning.

Lizzie stared right back at her. "You. I know you. You're his girlfriend."

Patrice blinked. "Who?"

"Potter's girlfriend."

Her mouth rounded in shock. "What?" She blinked. "No, I'm not. I'm his secretary."

"But you . . ." She frowned in confusion. "Weren't you having dinner with him at the Lobster Pot last weekend?"

"Of course not. He's a married man."

"But . . ." Lizzie's shoulders sagged. "Sorry. My mistake."

I watched Patrice roll her eyes and circle her finger around the side of her head, indicating that Lizzie must be crazy. She whispered, "I think she's having a mental breakdown."

I pointedly ignored the woman and concentrated on Lizzie. Since my friend was several inches shorter than me, I hunched down to make direct eye contact with her. "I'm calling Hal."

At the mention of her darling husband, Lizzie's eyes widened and she snapped back to reality. "No, Shannon. Please don't. He's busy at work. I don't want to bother him with this."

"Then I'll drive you home."

"No, no. Come on, forget it. I'm fine." She swiped her hair back from her forehead, looking drained but a little less frenzied and generally better than she had appeared a few minutes ago. "I was just shocked, that's all. You're right. Potter was trying to torment me because he can. He sneaks up and attacks when you're least prepared. But I'm okay now. I want to keep working."

"If you're sure."

"I am."

"Okay, I'm glad." But I had every intention of telling Hal exactly what that old bugger had done to Lizzie.

She sat down at the utility table that was set up along the wall of apartment one. "I was having so much fun until Potter walked in here." Holding up a plaster mold, she explained what she was working on. "Spencer showed me how to make a new plaster corbel from this mold."

Sections of the beautiful old corbels were disintegrating but we had managed to salvage parts of two of them to create the new mold that Lizzie was working with. I looked around for my contractor. "Where is Spencer?"

"He had to run out for a little while. We were going to clean the wooden doors next and he said he knows of a super-deluxe-formula wood cleaner he wanted to pick up somewhere."

"Probably the auto supply," I murmured.

"No, it's for wood."

I smiled. "If it's the super deluxe wood cleaner I'm thinking of, he's actually going to pick up a bottle of car engine degreaser."

"That's crazy."

I shrugged. "It works."

"You would know best, I guess."

She stared at the corbel without speaking and now I was afraid to leave her alone. "Do you need help with anything?"

She scowled. "If that old blowhard Potter hadn't interrupted me, I might've had the corbels done by now."

And that was another strike against him, I thought. Just because he was the money man on this project didn't give him the right to hover over the people actually doing the work. What was wrong with him?

Lizzie was working in what used to be the elegant front salon, now known as apartment one. It was as large as the ballroom, with just as many interesting features, especially the circular outer wall. I had asked Spencer to work in this room because he was a genius at recreating these wonderful old touches of Victoriana, like the elaborate ceiling frieze and the ornate corbels that Lizzie was working on. The decorative brackets would be used to accent the graceful archway that separated the main part of the room from the circular tower space. This was where the Foresters had once housed a fancy bar for their parties. But soon that portion of this space would become the bedroom for apartment one.

Floor-to-ceiling windows lined the circular wall, allowing a dramatic view of both the wide front lawn and the rows of graceful eucalyptus and sturdy pine trees that formed a natural border along the eastern side of the property.

I looked around, but Patrice seemed to have taken the hint and disappeared, just like her boss had. Maybe she had even managed to track down Potter and convinced him to leave. I could only hope so. I couldn't take much more of this crazy negativity today.

I supposed Patrice was essentially a nice person and I even understood why she'd said those things about Lizzie. It was her way of standing up for her boss. Unfortunately, Potter's behavior was indefensible.

Never mind her, I thought. If she showed up again, I would try to use her as a buffer between Potter and my crew. If she could do that much for me, I would forgive the other stuff. And honestly, until she began insulting Lizzie, I had thought she had her heart in the right place, unlike her awful boss. I hoped I wasn't wrong.

After a quick debate with myself, I ran upstairs to find Jane and tell her what had happened to Lizzie. She was working in apartment five, another large round tower apartment on the second floor at the front of the house, directly above Lizzie's room. I found Jane in the bathroom on her hands and knees, prying up old tile squares with a gooseneck pry bar. Half the floor was done and Jane didn't look ready to quit anytime soon.

"Anytime you want a job on my crew, you've got it," I said, impressed by her commitment to ripping up that floor.

She chuckled, sat back on her feet, and wiped a trickle of perspiration from her temple. "Thanks. I'll keep that in mind in case my hotel ever closes."

"Not much chance of that."

Jane owned the elegant Hennessey House, a beautiful Victorian inn that was always at full capacity. I had helped her renovate it over the years until she opened the doors to the public just last winter. Ever since then, the place had been receiving rave reviews from travelers around the world.

"Are you here to help me?" she asked hopefully.

"I suppose I could." Looking down into my friend's eyes, I really hated that I would upset her as much as I was about to, but she had to know. "But unfortunately, I just came up to tell you that Mr. Potter cornered Lizzie a few minutes ago and threatened to close her shop."

She froze at the words and then clutched the pry bar like a weapon. "Where is he? Let me at him."

"Down, girl." I patted her shoulder. "That's exactly how I feel. Which is why I'm telling you. Friends get to be ticked off together, right? Anyway, I've decided to ban him from the site. He's ruining the work vibe, messing with the volunteers. I have no choice."

She gave me a look. "Good luck with that."

"I know." I had to stretch my neck around to get rid of the tension that had been building up inside me all day long. It didn't work. I couldn't wait to get home and soak myself in an Epsom salt bath tonight.

"Poor Lizzie." Jane checked her wristwatch, then glanced with regret at the chunks of tile on the floor. "Does she want me to take her home?"

"No, she wants to finish the project she's working on."

"Good girl. I'm glad." Jane looked as furious as I felt. Somehow that made me feel better about everything.

"I just wanted you to be aware of what happened. You know, in case she says something on the drive home."

"I'll try to get her to talk about it." She gazed up at me. "So what can we do about Potter?"

I felt my jaw clench and Jane shook her head. "I know what that look means. I'd better hide this pry bar before I leave for the night."

I didn't find Potter, so instead of focusing on him, I concentrated on doing some actual work. I spent the rest of the afternoon helping the attic crew with the framing. I figured they had the most to do, and I also thought there was a chance that maybe I would run into Angry April, the bizarre volunteer, up there. But according to Blake, the contractor in charge of the attic space, April hadn't shown up until after lunch and then disappeared a little while ago, right after he asked her to help with the cleanup.

"Was she any help at all?" I asked.

He glanced around the room and shrugged. "Not really, but it doesn't matter. It's like we talked about at the meeting. The work up here is pretty intense, since we're building the rooms from scratch. We'll be framing for another few days, then hanging a lot of drywall and installing electrical outlets, running wires and plumbing up the walls."

"Not much a volunteer should be helping with."

"Right. So I didn't want to give her anything too complicated because I thought she might get hurt." He quickly held up his hand. "And I don't mean, you know, because she's a woman. It's because she was the one who insisted she didn't know anything about construction or tools or, well, anything. So there was also the worry that she'd do more damage than good."

"I know what you meant," I said, smiling.

"Okay, good." He chuckled ruefully. "Don't want to get myself in trouble. But anyway, you know how some of the volunteers are so eager to help out?"

"I know. It's so great to see that, isn't it?"

He made a face. "She isn't one of those. So basically, I just had her passing tools to the guys while they did the heavy lifting and nailing. In between, she mostly walked around, exploring the attic. Oh, and she stopped to talk to that guy from the bank."

It was so random, it took me a few seconds to figure out who he was talking about. "You mean Mr. Potter?" But why was I surprised? It seemed only logical that two horribly difficult people would find each other in a place like this. And knowing Potter, he would want to talk to anyone interested in sharing negative opinions of me. "What was he doing up here?"

"He walked around criticizing everyone's work," Blake said. "Told me I was hanging the drywall wrong."

"What's that supposed to mean?"

"I hang the sheets horizontally."

"As you should."

"He thought they should go vertically."

It was official: I wanted to wring Potter's neck, not only for being annoying, but for being stupid. "Did you tell him to buzz off?"

"Nah. I just ignored him."

"You're a lot nicer than me," I said, feeling another rush of irritation. Being a banker didn't make him a construction expert. Seriously, something had to be done to keep him from interfering. "I swear, someone's going to punch his lights out one of these days."

Blake chuckled. "It might be Willy."

"Oh no. What'd he do to Willy?"

"He told him not to wear those jeans anymore. You know, the ones with the hole in the knee?"

This was a new high in lows. "You must be joking."

"Nope. Said they were obscene."

I couldn't speak without muttering expletives, so I just shook my head.

Blake was grinning now. "Willy just laughed, told him the ladies love to see his knees. Potter's face got all red and he stormed off."

"Good." I took a deep breath to rid myself of the now-familiar frustration I was feeling. "So what did he say to April?"

"I only heard a few words of their conversation. They were whispering over by the banister and we were all pretty busy over here."

"Oh, darn," I said with an easy smile. "I really wanted to know what they talked about."

Still grinning, he said, "Next time I'll listen better."

"No worries. I just hope he didn't tell her to do something we haven't authorized."

Blake shrugged. "I doubt it. All I heard was him asking her if she got it. She said no. I couldn't hear the rest of it."

"Got it?" I repeated, confused. "Got what?"

"Sorry, Shannon. That's all I heard."

"It's no big deal," I said, and patted his arm. "But you said she was exploring the attic. Could she be looking for something up here?"

He glanced around. "Until we started framing, there were four walls and nothing else. What does she think she'll find?"

"I don't know," I murmured. "They used to have a lot of vintage stuff stored up here but we moved everything to the garage."

"She must not know that."

"No, I guess not."

Blake folded his arms across his chest, pondering. "Maybe Potter lost something."

"Yeah, maybe." I shrugged. "If she comes back up here tomorrow or anytime this week, will you text me?"

"You'll probably see her before I do, but sure."

"Thanks, Blake."

He reached into a pocket on his tool belt and pulled out the biggest, fattest tape measure I'd seen in a long while. Moving to a doorway, he caught the end hook on the top edge of the doorjamb and measured the distance down to the floor. Then he scribbled the measurement on the exposed drywall.

"Nice tape measure," I said.

"Yeah, thanks." He held it out for me to take. "Try it. It's like a weapon. Weighs about a pound."

I hefted the thing in my hand, feeling its weight. "Too heavy for me. You're lucky you've got big hands."

He grinned. "It's a curse."

I chuckled, shaking my head as I handed it back to him. "I'd sprain my wrist if I had to use that thing all the time. But it's pretty cool."

"I think so." He slid it back into his tool belt.

"I'd better get going," I said, heading for the stairs. "See you tomorrow, Blake."

"Okay," Blake said, then remembered something. "Hey, if April does come back up here, you want me to tell her that everything got moved to the garage?"

I thought about it and smiled. "Sure, why not? But if that happens, will you let me know?"

"You bet."

If I got the high sign from Blake that April was back here looking for something, maybe I could catch her in the act. There were probably some interesting things to be found in the Foresters' old trunks and dressers. We had also moved an old-fashioned rolltop desk, a baby carriage, two old sofas, and a fainting couch. But other than some interesting antiques, I couldn't imagine there was anything particularly intriguing or important hiding in there.

But then, maybe I would find out for myself one of these days.

It was close to five o'clock, official quitting time for the afternoon volunteers, so I stopped by each room on the second floor and said good night to each of the teams. I found Alyssa and Kailee cleaning up in apartment ten and stopped to talk for a few minutes. I asked about the other kids in the program and how everyone was doing.

"Alyssa has news," Kailee said.

Alyssa was practically bouncing with excitement. "My dad got a job."

"Oh, honey." I gave her a big hug. "I'm so thrilled for you."

"Me, too." She wiped her cheek, where a happy tear had escaped. "My mom is starting to look for a place for us. She wanted to try and move in here, but none of the apartments are big enough. Of course, after living in a minivan for six months, these rooms kind of look like palaces to me. But anyway . . ."

Her voice faded and Kailee grabbed her hand. "You'll find a place," she said lightly.

Alyssa nodded somberly. "And just think, when we do find a place, I'll be able to caulk the tub and unclog the toilets."

They both laughed and I joined in. I couldn't begin to imagine how these girls and their families had survived without a home for so long—and still maintained a sense of humor about things. They were so much braver than I could have ever hoped to be.

I gave them each hugs and told them I'd see them Thursday afternoon for our regular empowerment meeting at the community center, then said good-bye and headed for the stairs.

"Oh, hey, Shannon."

I turned and saw Zach Penn, the contractor working on apartment nine. He waved me over and I stepped into the room.

"We have a little problem in here," he said.

"What's up, Zach?"

"We were just cleaning up and about to clear out for the day when this happened." He pointed to the corner where Heather Maxwell was sitting on one of the five-gallon paint tubs, crying her eyes out.

"Heather, what's wrong?"

"Oh, Shannon," she moaned. Jumping up, she ran over and wrapped her arms around me, dissolving into more tears and heartbreaking sobs.

"Tell me what's wrong, sweetie." I patted her back while giving Zach and two of his crew a baffled look. They all shrugged in confusion. The combination of women and tears could mystify almost any man.

"I've lost my diamond charm bracelet," she wailed.

"What?" I pulled away and stared at her. "No, you didn't."

"I did. Look." She pulled the arm of her sweater up and her wrist was empty. "It's gone. I took it off while I was working and put it in my purse." She held up her purse, a big, baggy thing that was very chic, I supposed, but it had no way to secure the contents, no zipper or clasp. "And now it's gone." She burst into a fresh round of tears.

"It's got to be around here somewhere," I said, and turned to Zach. "Was she working in here all day? Have you looked for it?"

"I watched her empty out her entire purse," he said. "Nothing."

"Was she working in here all day? Have you looked for it?"

"Yeah. It's nowhere, Shannon."

I thought for a minute. "Did you all take a lunch break?"

"Heather stayed and worked," Zach said. "I brought her back a sandwich."

I looked at Heather. "You've been here all day? But you only signed up to work the morning session."

"I was having so much fun, I didn't want to leave. Zach let me stay." She batted her damp eyelashes in his direction and he had the good grace to appear embarrassed. I hid my amusement. It wasn't easy being a studly contractor wearing a tool belt. "I only left the room to use the bathroom a few times."

"Don't worry," I said, squeezing her arms with more

confidence than I felt. "We'll find it. Tomorrow I'll ask every single person to be on the lookout for your bracelet."

Her lips quivered. "I must've shown it to a few dozen people today. Do you think someone stole it?"

"If they did, they'll never be able to wear it around town. Everyone knows it belongs to you."

"I guess you're right about that."

"Of course I'm right." I grabbed a tissue from my tool belt—yes, I kept a packet of tissues on hand at all times—and passed it to her.

"So once you started working in here, did you take the bracelet out of your purse to show it to anyone?"

"Yes. A bunch of times."

"Do you remember who saw it?"

She named a few people and vaguely described a few others whose names she couldn't remember. I didn't recognize anyone from her descriptions.

"Anyone else?"

"I can't think of anyone."

"Okay, but if you remember someone else, you'll let me know. Are you coming back tomorrow?"

She sniffled a few more times. "Can I?"

"Of course." I rubbed her arms, trying to comfort her. "And please don't cry anymore. I know we'll find it tomorrow."

She wrapped me in another tight hug, then let go and grabbed her backpack. "Thank you, Shannon. Bye, Zach." She practically skipped out of the room.

"Thanks, Shannon," Zach murmured. He walked me to the door.

"Good luck with her," I murmured.

"She's no problem. I can handle a few tears."

I smiled in understanding. I'd gone to school with his wife. "So how's Julie doing?"

His smile faded. "Not so well. You know we've been trying to have kids, right?"

"She told me."

"Yeah, well, looks like that's not going to happen."

"Oh no. I'm so sorry." Julie had been one of those girls who'd always wanted children. She loved babies, the more the merrier. But over the past few years, she'd had a series of miscarriages. "Are you doing okay?"

"Me? Yeah, I guess so, but it's tough. They told us that Julie had some kind of internal problem when she was like ten years old and now . . ." He shrugged helplessly and I gave him a hug.

"I'm so sorry, Zach. I wish there was something I could do."

"I know. I appreciate it."

"Please give Julie my love." What else could I say?

"I will," he said. "Don't spread the news around, okay? But I wanted you to know."

"You know I won't say a word."

He nodded, as he zipped up his backpack. "Yeah, I know."

"See you tomorrow."

I watched Zach jog down the stairs and then checked the rest of the rooms to make sure everyone had left for the day. Only then did I head for the stairs, taking each step deliberately. My mind was filled with thoughts of Zach and Julie. I felt so bad for them. Especially Julie, who had always been a little mother to all of us. I hoped that once the initial pain wore off, they might think about adopting.

As I rounded the stairway's inner landing, my mind

drifted back to Heather. Had someone stolen her brace-let? Or had it slipped out of her purse one of the times she was showing it off? Would we find it tomorrow? I hoped so. Otherwise, we would have a hysterical teen-ager on our hands.

My thoughts moved on to Alyssa and Kailee, the two homeless teenagers whose young lives had been so dif-ficult up until now. They were so different from Heather, who had been pampered and doted on from the time she was born. Heather was a sweet girl, but I doubted she'd ever had to deal with the kinds of real-life problems the other two had faced.

What would a fifty-thousand-dollar diamond-studded charm bracelet mean to Alyssa and Kailee? Three years' worth of rent on an apartment for their family? Grocer-ies for a couple of years? Clothing? A car? A college ed-ucation? Maybe. And yet, I knew without a doubt that those two girls would never be tempted to take some-thing that wasn't theirs.

But someone else around here might not be that im-pervious to temptation.

And if nobody had taken it, then where was the bracelet?

My mind still wandering, I stopped on the outer land-ing to take in the partially tree-shrouded view out of the gorgeous leaded glass window—and almost tripped the rest of the way down the stairs.

"No," I whispered. It couldn't be.

I wanted to cry out at the injustice of it all. With my hands splayed against the window, I stared down, pray-ing this was some kind of bad mirage that would fade into the ether and disappear.

But it didn't disappear. It just came closer.

Could this day get any worse? Obviously it could. Because walking up the driveway, wearing a typically inappropriate outfit of stiletto heels, black spandex pants, and a sparkly top, was my high school archrival and still worst enemy, Whitney Reid Gallagher.

Chapter Nine

I felt like I'd been standing on the landing for hours watching Whitney's progression toward the house, but it had only been a few seconds. I felt frozen, unsure which way to turn. I was bone tired and in no shape to deal with that woman. There were plenty of days when I didn't mind sparring with her, but today was not one of them.

She had almost made it to the front door when I considered my options and quickly, maybe-not-so-bravely chose to retreat. I scurried all the way downstairs and hid in the open space under the stairway. I glanced around, but I didn't think anyone was still in the house. Thank goodness I had no witnesses to my shame.

But could you blame me for hiding? Whitney had been the queen of the mean girls in high school and she'd never outgrown it. For some reason she still considered it her mission in life to make me as miserable as she could.

I shook my head in disgust. After admiring the courage of Alyssa and Kailee only minutes ago, it was humiliating to find myself crouching behind the stairs.

What was wrong with me? I could face down a six-foot-tall ripped-to-the-max carpenter with a nail gun and an attitude, but I couldn't deal with a skinny woman in spandex? Whitney Gallagher was the last person in the world I should be afraid to face. I chalked it up to the totally weird day I'd just had. Between Potter and April, I'd had enough of crappy attitudes for the day. And then Heather's tears. And Lizzie's freak-out. And Dad's confrontation with Potter. Okay, there were plenty of reasons to make a strategic retreat. This was not a case of tucking tail and running away. And still . . .

"Enough of this," I muttered, and stood up, squared my shoulders, and prepared to walk out into the open hallway to face the evil queen. I was emboldened to repeat my new mantra to myself: *I am in charge here. This is my turf.*

And yet, when it came to Whitney, I sometimes reverted to my sixteen-year-old self.

Strangely enough, Whitney was the one who'd been jealous of me since her first day in high school, mainly because my boyfriend was Tommy Gallagher, football team quarterback and all-around high school Adonis. She had funneled that jealousy into a relentless attack campaign, criticizing everything I did and said and wore. Her circle of mean girlfriends jumped on the bandwagon and I only survived because I had so many good friends of my own. When we were seniors, Whitney shocked the world and me, winning Tommy by getting pregnant. So that was a bummer, to say the least. But I got over it.

These days, she and Tommy were married with three kids and if I had ever thought her lifestyle would make her so happy that she would back off, I was wrong. She still took every opportunity to rub my nose in the fact that she had Tommy and I didn't. If only she knew how little I cared. The funny part was, I had managed to stay friends with Tommy, and that drove her crazy. So, that helped.

I heard the front door open and shut and without thinking, I took a giant step back under the stairs. So much for my personal mantra. I heard her heels tapping against the marble floor of the foyer and then I heard a door click shut, followed by a whirring sound.

Instead of taking the stairs like a normal human, Whitney was taking the fancy antique elevator. In her defense, those stilettos she wore probably made it impossible to climb stairs like regular people.

I took a tentative step out into the hall, listening for the loud clunk that signaled that the elevator had made it to the second floor. Seconds later, the whirring stopped and the elevator door clicked open.

"There you are," Whitney said in an accusing tone. For a second I froze, thinking she was talking to me. But then someone else spoke.

"I'm right where I said I would be. What do you want?"

Oh my God, I knew that voice. It was Mr. Potter. Where had he been all this time? And what had he been doing? And more important, Whitney and Mr. Potter were having a meeting? Could this day get any more bizarre?

Whitney's high heels tip-tapped across the hardwood floor. I moved over to the newel post at the bottom of the staircase and leaned over the banister to see if I could catch sight of them. And that's when I saw Whitney with her finger pointed right at Mr. Potter—and it wasn't a friendly gesture.

"I want the money you stole from my father."

He laughed, sending a shiver down my arms. "I'll give you credit, girly. You've got more gall than your father ever had, but you're just as foolish if you think I'm going to change my mind."

"You're the foolish one if you think I'll walk away without getting what I want from you."

He patted her cheek. "That was a very brave statement. Now go home to your little family and mind your own business."

She slapped his hand away and her chin jutted defiantly. "This *is* my business. My father still owns the home I live in and you've stolen it and everything else out from under him. He might not be willing to face you, but I am. I'm not afraid of you."

"You should be," Potter said in a voice so malicious, it made me shudder again. He was no longer amused and I really didn't want to see what happened next. "I can make your life miserable. Don't tempt me."

"Do you deny that you stole money from my father?"

"Is that the story he gave you?" Potter laughed. "The fact that your father's broke is not my problem."

I was tempted to run, not walk, right out of the house and call it a day. I knew if I kept watching them, they might see me. But I couldn't do it, couldn't walk out the door. Call me crazy, but I couldn't leave Whitney alone with him.

A small voice inside my head said *You're nuts. Those two deserve each other.* But while that might have been true, I stayed where I was, just out of sight below the stairway.

I had a hard time hearing the rest of their discussion until Whitney finally raised her voice angrily. "I said, give me back our money."

"Or what?"

"Or you'll wish you were dead."

"I don't respond to threats, little girl. When you get old enough to play with the big boys, give me a call."

Heavy footsteps moved across the floor to the stairs. I dashed back under them and waited. I could feel each footstep hitting the stairs directly above me. Seconds later, Potter reached the foyer floor and walked out the door, leaving it ajar.

Whitney shrieked in frustration, "You crook! How dare you walk away from me? If you think this is over, you're dead wrong."

He didn't respond, just kept walking.

She went running after him, her stilettos tapping loudly on the hardwood and marble surfaces as she made her way down the stairs and out the door, slamming it behind her as she left.

I tiptoed over to the front door and peeked through the decorative glazed glass to watch them squabble for another minute on the front veranda. It was a tribute to the builder of Forester House that I couldn't actually hear their conversation through the double-plated glass and heavy oak doors. But I caught the gist, with Whitney screaming and threatening and Potter simply mocking. Then he jabbed his finger inches from her face as though he might be threatening her back.

And then he turned and walked away. She stood there, not moving, and I could feel the waves of impotent fury emanating from her. And I couldn't blame her one bit. Because I knew Potter, knew his tactics, and knew something was terribly wrong with this picture.

I hadn't realized that she and Tommy didn't own their home, but maybe I should have. They were married right out of high school and moved directly into one of the expensive modern Victorian houses perched along the beautiful Alisal Cliffs. Ironically, my father had built their home and given Tommy a very good deal on the property. I always figured that Whitney's father paid for the house in full, but now I guessed I was wrong.

Had Mr. Potter's bank reneged on the loan? Was Whitney's father really broke? He had once been an extremely wealthy man. Had Potter invested money for her dad and lost it? Despite Whitney's threats, it seemed clear that Mr. Potter held all the cards.

I was dying to find out the story, but I had a feeling that if I asked Whitney, she wouldn't exactly be forthcoming.

But I knew someone else I could ask. My father.

It took another long moment, but Whitney, standing tall with her shoulders back, finally walked back to her car. No way would she have allowed them to droop in defeat, even if that was how she felt. Strangely enough, I had nothing but sympathy for her. As soon as she got into her shiny black Jaguar and drove away, I grabbed my stuff and left the house.

Once I got home, I took an exuberant Robbie for a walk around the block. He seemed to be interested in every last bush and tree and patch of grass we passed, while all I wanted to do was climb into a bathtub and soak my weary limbs.

It wasn't until we made the turn back onto our street that I remembered what Lizzie had said earlier: Mac Sullivan was coming home tonight.

"That'll be nice," I said to Robbie. "Don't worry. I

can handle it. We're friends. I'll offer him a glass of wine to prove it."

Robbie tilted his head at me, as if to say, *Exactly when did you become delusional?*

I glanced down the block and didn't see Mac's SUV parked anywhere, so I assumed he hadn't made it back to town yet. Good. I began to jog the rest of the way and Robbie was happy to join me. Once we got home, I greeted Tiger, my marmalade cat, picking her up to bury my face in her soft fur. Her deep-throated purring was a comfort to me, but after a moment I felt her getting ready to squirm, so I set her down. Once I'd freshened the water in both of their bowls, I gave them each their dinner.

Duties completed, I walked upstairs, found the Epsom salts under the sink, poured half a box into the tub and turned on the hot water. I added some yummy homemade bath salts and breathed in the fragrant scent of lilies and lavender, then scooped my tangle of red hair up off my neck and clipped it securely.

And finally, finally, I slipped into the bath and moaned in relief. My achy bones were in hot-water heaven.

And that was when I remembered that the Festival Committee was meeting tonight. In a half hour. At my house!

"Oh noooooooooooo!" I couldn't help it; I uttered a little shriek. I shut my eyes and slipped under the water to avoid reality for a second or two. I might have sobbed once or twice, maybe even slapped the water around a little, because a good-sized wave slopped up and over the rim of the tub. So now I would have to mop that up. Oh, the unfairness of it all!

"Rats," I grumbled, unplugging the tub and listening to the water draining out while I grabbed a towel and dried off.

Twenty minutes later my hair was dried and I was dressed in a sweatshirt and yoga pants, fixing up a few savory snacks of chips and salsa and cheese and crackers. Wine and glasses were set out and I even had fancy cocktail napkins placed on the table. So there. None of my friends would ever have to know that I'd completely spaced out on the most important committee meeting of the year.

Lighthouse Cove was famous for its annual parades and festivals. There were five each year, celebrating various events and holidays. The first one was our Valentine's Day Festival in mid-February, then the Spring Festival—which was more about Saint Patrick's Day and green beer than anything else—followed by the Fourth of July Parade, the Harvest Festival in October, and finally, the Christmas Festival.

My friend Jane was the head of the Festival Committee and I was her second in command. Our friends Ellie, Pat, and Sylvia completed the committee, and we had almost two hundred volunteers working with us. The five of us always had a good time, and by all accounts the festivals kept getting better and better each year. Every hotel in town was booked solid whenever we had an event, and even the local campgrounds were booked months in advance. All of that added up to extra revenue for the town and its businesses, which meant that the festivals were essential to the financial vitality of everyone in town.

So how in the world could I have forgotten something as important as this meeting? Let's face it—I was *this* close to comatose when I got home from work. And I blamed it all on Mr. Potter.

"And that's the last time I'll say his name tonight," I vowed aloud.

Thank goodness the doorbell rang just then, happily distracting me from any thoughts about the man who would not be named again.

"Come on in," I said, holding the door open for Jane and the others. "Did you all come in one car?"

"No, we just happened to arrive at the same time." Sylvia walked inside carrying an interesting pink box.

"Good," I said, leading the way to the dining room table. "We can get started right away."

Jane sat and reached for a chip. "I think we've got everything under control, right?"

"All systems go," Pat said, giving her a thumbs-up.

"That's right," I said with more confidence than I felt at the moment.

"I'll admit I've been nervous about this one," Jane said.

"Well, it's our biggest festival of the year," Pat said. "But we're a well-oiled machine at this point, so don't worry."

"Okay," Jane said, letting go of a breath she must have been holding. "I'm hoping we can just go down each of our lists and check everything off."

"We're getting good at this," Ellie said, grinning. "And we're still having fun, so that's a bonus."

I gave Jane a look. She was still worried, not having any fun at all, but maybe that would change with tonight's meeting.

"So what's in the box, Sylvia?" I asked.

Sylvia batted her lashes. "I thought you'd never notice."

"I noticed right away," I said. "But I was being polite."

Jane snickered and the others laughed, including me.

"Guess I'd better open it." Sylvia pulled the string off the box and lifted the pink lid. "These are from the Buttercup Bakery. They wanted us to sample the cupcakes they plan to sell at the festival."

Jane's eyes widened. "What a good idea."

The box contained eight mini-cupcakes piled high with glossy green frosting covered in red and white sparkles with a candy gold star on top. They looked like glittery little Christmas trees.

"Oh, they're adorable," Pat whispered.

Jane sighed. "So cute."

Sylvia reached for a cupcake. "I'm wondering why every other bakery in town doesn't do this for us."

I laughed. "Just what we need—a few hundred cupcakes to sample."

Ellie winced. "That sounds really dangerous."

"It does," Sylvia said with a grin. "I would just hate it."

"Oh, this is delicious," Jane murmured.

I had to agree. The cake was moist and chocolatey and the frosting was the perfect combination of sweet and fluffy. And they were small enough to be consumed in two bites.

After oohing and ahhing over the cupcakes and then quickly devouring them, we got down to business.

"Let's go down each of our lists one by one so I can make sure everything's been taken care of." Jane picked up her pen. "Sylvia, why don't you start with the vendors?"

"Okay." She quickly licked frosting off her thumb and stared at her list. "I've checked in with every one of the vendors, and they've all got their permits updated. I've received each of their risk assessments and insurance details, and wherever applicable I've got their temporary sale of alcohol notices. They've each assured me that they'll post the notices in their booths the night of the event. And they're all publicizing it like crazy."

Pat nodded. "Those flyers Marigold designed are so gorgeous, everyone wants one in their store window. They've been handing them out to customers and posting them on every telephone pole in town."

"I've heard them talking about it on the radio stations, too," Sylvia added. "Not just playing the advertisement, but actually talking it up."

"That's free advertising," Jane said. "I love it."

"Nothing better than free," Sylvia agreed, then continued with her vendor lists. "I've got assurances from every single vendor that they've signed up at least two volunteers to help them set up their booths and break them down once we're done."

Over the last few Christmases, that big breakdown at the end of the night had become its own party. It was always the diehard volunteers and hardest workers who stuck around despite the late hours and the cold, and we liked to reward them with free food and goodie bags of gift items to take home to their families. It seemed only right to give them something for their trouble, and they all really appreciated the goodies.

As event organizers, our main duty was to plan, manage, and monitor the festival to make sure that the public was not exposed to any health and safety risks and that everyone had a good time. And beyond that, we liked to go the extra mile for our hardworking volunteers.

"Anything new and interesting this year, Sylvia?" Ellie asked, skimming the list.

"It's mostly the same regulars returning, and we love them, of course."

"Of course," Pat said with a grin.

"But we do have a few newbies I'm excited about," Sylvia continued. "I'm sure you've all seen the new fudge shop on the pier, right? Well, they'll be selling fudge to eat at the festival, plus lots of boxed gifts for last-minute presents."

"Fudge makes me happy," Pat said, and everyone smiled.

"The Hog Roaster is back, too."

"Hallelujah," Ellie said. "I love their stuff."

"Me, too," I said. "Pulled pork, yum."

"This year they've packaged up their syrup-soaked bacon chunks in gift bags."

"Oh my God, I'm salivating," Jane said.

Sylvia grinned. "They promised to cook lots of extra food, since the parade will break up around dinnertime and it's going to be chilly outside."

Jane smiled as she made a note. "I'm sure they'll sell out, no matter how much they cook."

"It's supposed to get a lot colder between now and Christmas." Pat glanced around at each of us. "Do you think it might snow?"

"No," Jane said, grabbing another chip. "I just hope it doesn't rain."

"If it does, we can always hand out umbrellas. Or better yet, those disposable plastic ponchos," Ellie suggested.

"That's a good idea," Jane said, making another note to check the cost.

I frowned. "I really hope it doesn't rain."

"It would be nice to have snow, though," Pat said.

I pictured the town square dusted in white. "It would be a miracle. It hasn't snowed in Lighthouse Cove for over eighty years."

Jane scanned her lists. "Anything else, Sylvia?"

"Just one more thing," Sylvia said. "Do you remember the Twigsters?"

"I do," I said. "I bought a beautiful willow bowl from them a few years ago. They're really talented."

The Twigsters were two sisters who lived east of town on a large plot of land where weeping willow trees cheerfully proliferated along a narrow creek that ran through their property. The sisters used the thin branches and twigs of the trees to create their artistic gifts.

They also produced stunning studio art that could be found in galleries all over the world. The sisters would fashion hundreds of the thinnest switches into large, wildly whimsical sculptures of men or women or animals, through a complicated twisting and turning of each individual branch. With a few bends of a twig, they could make a creature look as if it were happy or angry or about to blow away in the wind. It was amazing.

"They've promised lots of smaller Christmas gift items this year," Sylvia said. "And they wanted us to know that they've added gourd lamps to their repertoire."

Pat frowned. "I love their willow stuff but I'm not convinced I could live with gourds around my house."

"They're not for everyone," Sylvia said diplomatically.

Once she was finished with the list of vendors and booths, Jane turned to Pat and me. "Okay, parade people. What have you got to report?"

Pat went first, since she was in charge of the nuts and bolts of permits and parking areas for the floats. She had volunteers lined up to walk next to each float for safety purposes. We would have a record number of floats this year, and that didn't even include the marching bands, baton twirlers, fire trucks, and the skateboarding Christmas elves. (Ellie's son had suggested that a bunch of his friends skateboard as a troupe in the St. Patrick's Day parade and they had been a crowd favorite ever since.)

When Pat was finished, it was my turn. I listed the latest additions to the parade line, then added, "And my big thrill this week is that I get to interview Santa Claus." As I said it, I wondered how many of the Santa Brigade members would be applying for the one-night gig at the festival. Our Santa would ride the last float, tossing out candies to the parade watchers and then visit with children in our North Pole Village after the parade was over.

Once I was finished with my report, Ellie took over. She was in charge of vendors and events that didn't fall under the parade or booth categories. For instance, at the last Spring Festival, she hired a company that brought a rock climbing wall. We made a boatload of money at one dollar per climb. For the Christmas Festival, she'd hired a local farmer to set up a reindeer petting zoo. The kids were going to go nuts over the baby reindeer. Ellie had also scheduled various school choirs to perform on the festival stage throughout the evening.

"Those poor kids are going to freeze," Jane muttered.

"Oh, that reminds me," Sylvia said. "I ordered six more gas heaters for the food court."

Jane nodded, made a note. "We'll need them."

Ellie jumped in. "And we've ordered one thousand Santa hats to hand out during the parade."

"I'm glad we came up with that idea," Pat said. "They're cute and they'll keep people warm."

One big problem with the Christmas Festival was that it was held at Christmas. Duh! But it was the middle of winter, so it was a given that the weather would be cold. The parade started in the late afternoon and the Festival ran into the evening, so we were always trying to come up with ideas to keep people warm. The heaters would help and the hats were a stroke of genius.

Last year we'd handed out candy canes for our give-away. Fun and tasty, but not much in the way of heat producing. Hats were a lot smarter and not too horribly expensive when you bought a thousand of them. And people were going to love them.

Once we'd finished with business, the girls stayed another half hour to chitchat and gossip and munch on the chips and crackers. At that point I was having a hard time keeping my eyes open, and when Jane finally noticed she hustled everyone out.

"Alone at last," I said to Robbie, who had been sleeping under the dining room table all evening. He let out one happy bark and then followed me around as I tidied things up. Then he and Tiger raced me up the stairs to bed.

Ten Shopping Days Until Christmas

No big surprise that, despite feeling exhausted, I didn't sleep well that night. At four a.m., I gave up on sleeping, got out of bed, got dressed, and went downstairs to pour myself a cup of coffee. While I fixed a piece of toast for breakfast, I took care of watering and feeding and playing with Robbie and Tiger. Once they were happy and resting in their respective beds, I ate some yogurt and granola and looked up at Mac's apartment over the garage. There were no lights on, which made sense. Most normal people were still sleeping at this hour.

After cleaning up the kitchen, I jogged out to my truck and drove over to Forester House to get an early start on the day. Call me a coward, but leaving before the crack of dawn had the added advantage of avoiding Mac. I just wasn't sure how I would handle the first time I saw him after so many weeks without any contact, and I didn't want to find out just then. At the very least, I knew it would be awkward after the sleepless night I'd had. I wanted to feel strong when I finally ran into him, and all I felt right now was vulnerable.

It was just past five a.m. when I parked my truck along the side of the Foresters' massive six-car garage. I was obviously the first one to arrive. Most of the neighborhood was still asleep.

This area of Lighthouse Cove was known as Hillview because it was on a hill in the eastern part of town that overlooked the coast for miles in either direction. Here were some of the town's oldest homes, glorious Victorians set back from the road, each on an acre or two of land, surrounded by rolling lawns, splendid English gardens, and the occasional croquet field or tennis court.

Twice a day, the local tour bus drivers rolled into the area to enthrall their passengers with intriguing tales of our town's history. This was where they pointed out the homes of the founding fathers, the wealthy dairy magnates, real estate tycoons, and lumber barons who had first settled in Lighthouse Cove and built the stunning homes that our town was famous for. Homes that had stood the test of time. Homes like Forester House.

I grabbed my backpack and headed down the driveway, under the porte cochere and around to the front door. I enjoyed wandering around my job sites alone in the quiet morning, enjoyed studying the old bones of a house when no one else was around to distract me. I took a lot of pride in seeing the progress my crew had made the day before. At this time of the morning I would be able to peek inside each apartment before anyone else arrived, especially the volunteers. Once they showed up, organized chaos would reign again.

I crossed the foyer and headed down the hall toward the ballroom, anxious to see how much Dad and his crew had accomplished yesterday, especially the progress made on the butler's pantry wall.

I opened the ballroom door and walked inside—and was shocked by the first thing I saw. Dad's heavy red tool chest sat on the floor next to the marble fireplace, its cover wide open and the top drawer pulled out. A collection of screwdrivers were scattered on the floor.

So much for locking up your tools at night, I thought, rolling my eyes. Dad must have been awfully distracted before he left last night. It was unlike him, but maybe he and the guys had been busy planning their trip to the pub for drinks and dinner.

I walked over and grabbed the screwdrivers that had rolled away, along with a wrench and a plastic box of miscellaneous screws. Tossed onto a folded paint tarp sitting next to the tool chest was the black cloth sheath that had covered Dad's new ax.

"That's not like you," I murmured. My father was

scrupulously neat with his tools, especially a treasured new one like the demo ax he'd shown me yesterday. Had he taken the ax home with him? I wondered. Without the sheath? And why were the other tools on the floor? What were the guys doing last night?

Still wearing a frown, I walked over to check on the butler's-pantry framing, hoping the guys had gotten a good start on the drywall.

The door wouldn't budge. I pushed harder and got nowhere. There was something propped against the other side of the door, obviously, but what was it? If one of the guys had left their tool chest blocking the door, how had they gotten out of there? With the new wall built, there was no outlet. It didn't make sense. Maybe something had fallen against the door. A ladder, maybe?

I pushed again and finally managed to budge the door a few inches. That gave me enough leverage to clutch the door's edge and push harder. My arm muscles were straining, but I finally managed to open it enough to poke my head around and see what the impediment was.

"Oh!" I scrambled backward as far as I could get from the door, but it wasn't far enough. I couldn't catch my breath. "No. No way. Not again."

Leaning against the farthest wall of the ballroom, I wrapped both arms around my stomach and bent over, willing myself not to be sick. It wasn't easy. The impediment behind the door wasn't a toolbox or a ladder. It was a human. A big, heavy one.

It was Mr. Potter. And without a doubt, the man was dead.

Chapter Ten

I knew the drill. Sadly, I had experienced the aftermath of violent death before, so I knew the first thing I had to do. I called Eric Jensen and the police chief answered on the second ring. He actually sounded happy to hear from me, even though it was barely five o'clock in the morning. I knew that happy vibe wouldn't last long.

"Hi, Eric," I said, not even trying to sound cheery as I paced back and forth across the ballroom. "I'm working over at Forester House and wanted to get an early start this morning, so I apologize if I woke you."

"You didn't. I like to get an early start most mornings myself."

"Good. That's good. Real good. Okay." I was stalling and there was no reason for it. After all, it wasn't like I had killed Potter myself. As a shiver crossed my shoulders, I tried to banish that thought from my mind. Because, let's face it, even though I hadn't killed the man, I had certainly threatened him with bodily harm once or twice. At the time it hadn't bothered me because, frankly, he deserved my wrath. But now I just hoped no one had overheard those conversations. In my defense, though, I'd heard a half dozen or more people say much the same things to him. Now one of those people had gone one step beyond just saying the words.

I took a deep breath and blurted, "I found Mr. Potter dead in the butler's pantry. I think someone killed him."

There was a long pause in the conversation and I played back my words. *You think someone killed him?* Yeah, duh.

Finally, Eric said, "Potter. Are you talking about Peter Potter? The bigwig over at Lighthouse Cove Bank and Trust?"

"That's the guy."

"And you think he's dead."

I recalled that quick glimpse I got of the man. "Actually, I *know* he's dead."

"Are you anywhere near the body right now?"

"Uh, no, not exactly. Well, I mean, I'm closer than you are, but, yeah, he's in the room right next to this one and the door between us is closed, so . . ." I was yammering nonsense. It happened once in a while when I was under stress. You'd think I would have, oh, I don't know, gotten used to finding dead bodies? But how did anyone ever get accustomed to stumbling across death?

"He's in the butler's pantry," Eric reiterated, as though he might be writing down notes.

"Yeah, he's in there and I'm in the ballroom and there's a door . . . never mind." He didn't care where I was, I thought, rolling my eyes. "Can you come soon?"

"Give me ten minutes." And he hung up.

All the breath in my lungs deflated and I had to grab a folding chair and sit. Talking to the chief of police about a dead body could do that to you. Still, at least Eric knew me well enough now to be reasonably sure I hadn't killed Potter myself. At least, I hoped he did.

I couldn't sit still for long. I grabbed my phone and called my father, pacing the floor as I listened to his phone ringing.

"Yeah?" Dad whispered.

I could tell I woke him up. "It's me, Dad. Sorry to call so early."

"What's wrong, honey?"

"Mr. Potter's dead."

There was a long silence, then, "How?"

"He was murdered." I closed my eyes and brought the image back. "Stabbed to death, I think."

"Whoa." He exhaled. "Wow. Well, I'm shocked, but I can't say I'm sorry. And probably not all that shocked, either, when you come to think of it. If there was anyone in town asking to be killed, it had to be Potter. So who did it?"

"I don't know. I just called Eric Jensen and he's on his way."

"You called the cops?" He paused as the subtext of my words sank in. "Honey, where are you?"

"At Forester House. Dad? Here's the thing."

But I couldn't say it. I was still shaking inside. This was what I hadn't wanted to say out loud. To Eric. To anyone. But there was just no getting around it.

"What is it, sweetheart? Are you in danger?"

"No, but . . . Dad, Potter was killed with your ax."

He whispered an expletive. "I'll be right there."

It took Eric eight minutes. I was waiting inside the front doorway, shivering despite my down vest and a heavy turtleneck, when his black, police-issued SUV turned

into the driveway and stopped at the spot where the veranda began. I stepped onto the front porch as he
climbed out of the car. He saw me and lifted his hand in
a brief greeting.

He looked good—really good, as usual—in his faded
brown leather bomber jacket, worn blue jeans, and
boots. In his rush to hurry over here, he hadn't bothered
to dress in his chief's uniform and I appreciated it.

"Thank you for getting here so fast," I said, hating to
hear my voice crack. But honestly, how many dead bodies did one person have to come across before they went
completely bonkers?

"There was no traffic. Hey, are you all right?" he
asked, and wrapped me in a warm, secure hug. He was
big and muscular and handsome and blond, and since
the first day I met him at a much different crime scene, I
had thought of him as Thor. You know the guy. Super-
hero. Nordic god. Carried a big hammer. Yeah, that guy.

"I'll survive," I said, adding, "That's more than I can
say for Potter."

"Indeed."

We both turned at the sound of another vehicle turning into the driveway. I recognized Tommy Gallagher's
brown SUV and both of us waited for the assistant chief
of police to park and jog over to join us at the front door.

"Hey, beautiful," he said, giving me a hug and a kiss
on the cheek. "You okay?"

"I'm fine," I said, sighing as I hugged him back. "It's
good to see you."

Not only was Tom Gallagher the assistant police
chief; he was also my former high school boyfriend *and*
Whitney's husband. I wondered if Tommy knew about
Whitney's private meeting with Potter the afternoon be-

fore. I was willing to bet she hadn't mentioned a word of it to her darling husband. And did Tommy know their home was in jeopardy because of Mr. Potter's connection with Whitney's father? If he did know about the threat to their home, was that enough to make Tommy a suspect, too?

Tommy was still just as tall and adorable as he'd been in high school, with surfer blond hair and a charming smile. He was warm and sweet and funny, and why he had ever chosen Whitney over me remained one of the great mysteries. But he loved her madly and he was a terrific dad to his three kids, so that only made him sweeter in my book.

I stared at the two cops and sighed. If one was inclined to compare humans to animals, then Tommy was like a big cuddly bear while Thor was a powerful stallion. A tall, golden-haired, brawny, take-charge stallion. Tommy was a warm, wonderful cutie-pie, while Thor—Eric—was tough, compelling, and resolute. He was blue twisted steel come to life. He didn't smile a lot, because when he did, women tended to melt into puddles at his feet.

It wasn't easy being around two such manly dudes, but I managed to make it work for me.

"Why don't you show us where you found the body?" Eric said, bringing me back down to earth with a thud.

"Right," I said, shaking my head at my errant thoughts. "It's this way."

I led them into the house and down the hall to the ballroom, crossing the wide, hardwood floor to the door of the butler's pantry. That's where I stopped and pointed. "He's right inside there. You'll have to push hard to get the door open because his body is pressed up against it."

"Is there another way into that room?" Eric asked.

I had been wondering that same thing earlier when I'd tried to push the door open, and while waiting for the cops I'd realized there was a simple answer. "There are two windows in there that lead to the side of the house by the driveway."

"Then let's take a look through the windows first," Eric said, "rather than disturbing the scene right off."

Oops. I had already disturbed the scene by pushing on Potter's body, but I decided not to mention that right now. Besides, since I'd told them that Potter's body was blocking the door, they'd probably already guessed that I'd done some pushing. I had them follow me outside using one of the French doors that led to the veranda and around to the side of the house.

One of the windows was wide open.

"Screen's been removed," Tommy said, pointing at the large, thin screen leaning against the stone foundation. "Looks a little rusty."

Eric frowned. "I can see that. Not sure if we can get prints off an aluminum frame. But don't touch it, just in case."

The chief moved over to the windowsill and studied the surface from several angles, then turned to Tommy. "Give Charlie a call and tell him to get his guys over here. We'll need to lift these fingerprints."

Tommy walked away to make the call to Charlie Samuels, their crime-scene investigator, while Eric stood as close as he could get to the window's ledge without touching anything. He leaned over the sill and stared down into the hallway space for a long minute. Taking out his cell phone, he snapped several pictures.

"There's a lot of dust in there," he muttered to himself. "Might catch a break and find some footprints."

"They were hanging drywall yesterday afternoon," I said. "That's where the dust came from."

"That's lucky for us."

I frowned a little. "You realize everyone working here has been through this room and probably handled the windowsills and God knows what else."

"We'll get prints from your workers if we need to."

I coughed to clear my suddenly dry, guilt-ridden throat. "I should mention that I did try to push the door open, so Mr. Potter might be in a slightly different position than he was originally."

"Was he lying on his stomach when you saw him?"

"Yeah."

"How did you know it was Potter?"

"I, um, had some run-ins with him yesterday. I recognized his blue pinstripe suit and his bald head." *Oh God,* I thought. *Why did I mention run-ins?* That didn't sound good. Would it make me a suspect? I almost whimpered. Not again.

"So you saw the ax sticking out of his back?" Eric asked, his voice flat. It wasn't really a question.

I gulped, then took a deep breath, then another, and tried not to hyperventilate. The ax had been closer to his neck, I thought, and there was a lot of blood pooled under his head. I imagined the weapon must have severed one of the vertebral arteries. I knew something about arteries because of the tool-safety classes I used to teach at the local junior college. Yes, believe it or not, part of my curriculum included teaching students how to avoid cutting an artery with one tool or another. Kids enjoyed all those sorts of blood-and-guts details. But I digress.

"Yeah, I saw the ax," I said. "It looked to me like it was sticking out of his neck."

"I stand corrected," he said dryly, then gave me a hard look. "Did you recognize the ax?"

I couldn't speak, just nodded slowly.

"Shannon, whose ax is it?"

It was like I was standing in quicksand. Time slowed down to a crawl and stars began to burst in my eyes. Was I having a stroke? Was I going to faint?

"Shannon?"

I couldn't say the words.

"What's wrong?" he demanded. "Are you going to pass out?"

I shook my head rapidly. "No." But the word echoed around in my head, and I must have stumbled because he grabbed me and held on until I was steadier. He put his arm across my shoulders and walked me away from the window. We took a brief stroll down the driveway while he murmured words of encouragement. "It's okay, Red. You're going to be all right. Come on. You're stronger than this."

I was, usually. But this time was different.

He stopped walking and turned to look at me. "Tell me who the ax belongs to."

I swallowed around the lump in my throat. "It belongs to my father."

Dad arrived ten minutes later, parking his truck on the street and running up the driveway to the front porch. "Shannon?"

"Dad." I jumped up from the veranda patio chair and dashed over to meet him. The crime-scene guys had arrived moments before and I was trying to stay out of their way while still sticking close by the action.

My father grabbed me in a tight hug, then held me at arm's length, squeezing my shoulders as he stared at my face. "Are you all right?"

I was still shaky but there was no point in telling my

dad that. He already looked worried enough, for good reason. "I'm better than I was earlier. And I'm just glad you're here."

We walked back up the steps to the veranda and sat on the cushioned outdoor sofa. He turned and met my gaze. "Honey, I have to ask you this."

"Anything, Dad."

"Did you see the ax? I mean, did you see it in Potter? Are you sure it's mine?"

"I saw it, Dad. It's yours. It's got the hard foam black handle with the leather cord. There's no mistake."

He shook his head in disgust. "So someone stole my brand-new demo ax and used it to kill Potter."

"Yeah." But as I heard him say the words out loud, I suddenly wondered, did the killer deliberately plan to set up my father? But why? Who would do that? Everyone loved my dad. And I wasn't just saying that because he was my father. He had been born and raised here and knew everyone in town. He'd built dozens of homes and designed a number of beautiful neighborhoods in Lighthouse Cove. Anyone who knew him admired him. I couldn't imagine who would try to frame him for murder. It didn't make sense.

No, I preferred to think that the murder had occurred in the heat of the moment, which made it a crime of passion. Potter had to have been arguing with someone—the killer—and then he'd walked away, leaving the killer feeling helpless. Frankly, it was a scenario I'd seen several times yesterday. But in this case, Potter had used up his allotment of mockery and scorn, and the killer, in a fit of rage, searched around desperately for a weapon. Dad's tool chest was sitting right there and the killer had rushed to open it to find a weapon.

Maybe Potter had been looking for a way out of the house and used the door to the butler's pantry, not realizing it was a dead end, so to speak. The murderer came running after him with the ax and thrust it into his neck. Stunned by the act of violence he—or she—had just committed, and realizing that he—or she—couldn't budge the pantry door open with the victim wedged next to it, the killer opened the window, removed the screen, and jumped to freedom.

It made as much sense as any other scenario. More, in fact, if you knew Potter. I did, and I'd experienced that same feeling of impotent rage. I wouldn't have reacted the same way, of course, but I definitely could understand how it might have happened.

So until I learned the truth, I would call Potter's murder a crime of passion—or even temporary insanity. It sounded a lot better than going with a premeditated theory in which the killer had purposely tried to set up my father as the main suspect.

But would Eric believe it? He might, if he'd ever had to deal with Mr. Potter. Either way, I was going to have to try my darnedest to convince him. Because the pure truth was that my father had nothing to do with it.

The only questions that continued to bug me were these: Why was Potter in the ballroom last night? What were he and the killer doing in there after everyone else had left for the day?

Dad bent forward and rested his elbows on his knees as he considered the situation. "This is all my fault. You warned me to lock up the tools but I didn't have the key with me. It was stupid, but instead of taking my tools with me, I just closed up the box and laid one of the tarps on top of it."

"It's not your fault, Dad. Some killer went searching for a weapon and happened to rummage through your tools. When I got here this morning, the chest was wide open and some of your screwdrivers and other things were on the floor. And your ax sheath was empty. My first thought was that you and the guys had been joking around before you left for the night and you just got distracted and left everything open."

He frowned at me. "You know I don't work like that."

I held up both hands. "I know. It was my brain trying to justify what I knew couldn't have happened. And I realized it as soon as I had the thought."

"The guys and I worked until about five thirty," he said, staring off into space as if seeing it all again. "Then we cleaned up and went to the pub for some beers and fish and chips."

"Who went with you to the pub? How late were you there? Do you have an alibi for afterward? Did anyone see you after you left?"

My barrage of questions caused him to grimace. "Jeez, honey, slow down." He thought for a moment. "Okay, we stayed until nine and then I walked home. I doubt if anyone saw me."

"Are you sure? Someone must have seen you." Yes, I was grasping at straws.

"Not that I know of. I walked back to the RV and slept like a baby all night."

Dad had bought himself one of those great big recreational vehicles about five years ago, after he had recuperated from his heart attack. He and my mom had once dreamed of touring around the country in an RV. Mom died when I was eight, but instead of letting that dream die with her, Dad was determined to follow through in hopes of keeping her memory alive. Once he hit the open road, though, he realized it wasn't much fun driving the humongous thing without a loving partner beside him.

So he drove the RV back home, parked it in our driveway, and turned it into his man cave. Eventually, he moved into the RV full-time, and why not? It had a huge flat-screen TV and a comfy living room, a nice-sized bedroom, a galley kitchen, and a full bathroom. These days, the only time he came into the house was to use the laundry room. And two weeks out of four, he was off fishing with Uncle Pete.

As I said, the RV was usually parked in my driveway, but it wasn't last night.

"Where did you park the RV?" I asked.

"I've got it parked over by the marina."

That was odd. "How come?"

He gave me a crooked smile. "Lately I've been thinking of buying a boat. I wanted to check out the scene for a few days."

His boyish enthusiasm made me want to laugh, but his answers to my questions were too critical to his own fate to allow me the luxury. I especially couldn't laugh because I had experienced the fear and dismay of being a murder suspect and it wasn't fun. I didn't want the same thing to happen to my dad. I hated the image of him sitting in a squalid room for hours while the police chief interrogated him, wondering all the while whether they were going to lock him up in a cell or not.

To be fair, the Lighthouse Cove Police Headquarters was actually quite pleasant and nowhere near squalid, but it suited my mood to think so. And Eric wasn't stupid. He'd been in town long enough to know my father and his reputation, so that all worked in Dad's favor, too.

The marina was only a few blocks beyond my house, so Dad's walk home from the pub last night wouldn't have taken him more than fifteen minutes. But since we didn't yet know what time Potter was killed, it was foolish to try to pin down his whereabouts to a particular time. I would just have to let the police do their job.

This feeling of helplessness was starting to make me crazy, and it was barely past sunrise. I figured I'd be a basket case by noon.

"There you are, Shannon. Hello, Jack."

I almost jolted off the couch at the sound of Eric's voice. I guess I was a little edgy, but who could blame me?

Dad stood immediately and went over to shake his hand. "Hey, Eric. Looks like you've got yourself some trouble here."

"You could say that."

"I'll do everything I can to help out."

"I'd appreciate that." He glanced at me, then back at Dad. "You will have already heard about the ax."

"Yeah, Shannon told me. I'm confounded as to why anyone would open up my tool chest looking for a murder weapon." He scratched his head in frustration. "All I can say is, I'm sorry. I wish I could go back in time and put a lock on the darn thing."

"I wish you could, too," Eric said, and gave me another look before continuing. "I'm sympathetic to both of you needing to share information with each other, but I would appreciate it if you'd keep everything between the two of you. I don't want any details leaking out to the general public."

I winced at the admonition. Maybe it had been stupid to tell my dad how Potter had been killed, but what else was I going to do? He deserved to know the truth. And besides, he was my *dad*.

"We won't tell a soul," Dad said, touching his heart. "You can count on us."

"That's right," I said. "Nobody will hear another word from me."

"I'm grateful for your discretion. And I'll want to talk at length to both of you at some point later this morning." He looked at me with sympathy in his eyes. "For now, though, I need to shut down your construction site."

"What? No!" I hadn't even considered the reality that Forester House was now a crime scene. "But we only have nine days to complete the work. The families are moving in on Christmas Eve. This is our biggest charity event of the year. You can't just shut down the whole house."

He said nothing, just gazed at me with infinite patience.

I waved my hands in the air. "I mean, of course you can shut it down because you're the police. But if you could just allow us to work in some of the rooms, it would be a huge help."

He thought for a moment. "In the spirit of the holiday, I'll have my people search through as many of the rooms as we can get to this morning and then we'll try to open up a section or two by lunchtime."

I released a big sigh of relief. "Thank you."

He held up his hand. "Except for the butler's pantry and ballroom. That space is off-limits for now."

"That's okay. Thank you, Eric." I jumped up and

hugged him, much to his surprise. I mean, we'd hugged before, but not when there was a freshly dead body in the vicinity.

"I really appreciate it," I said, letting him go and stepping back. "You have no idea how critical every hour is to the success of this project."

"I have an inkling," he said kindly. "And I'll try to get things back on track as quickly as possible. We just need to get some answers."

"I understand."

He checked his wristwatch. "It's six twenty-five. My crime-scene guys are already working. Hopefully we're only dealing with the one crime scene, but that's what we've got to determine before we let you go back to work."

"I know." I rubbed my stomach where it was twisted up in knots at the possibility that there were other bodies strewn throughout the house. My mind instantly went to any number of horror movies, laying out bloody, awful scenes that couldn't possibly be true.

"What time do the volunteers arrive?" he asked.

I blinked away the imaginary carnage. "They'll be here at eight."

"Are they the same group as yesterday morning?"

For a moment my mind went blank. I couldn't recall my numerous lists of volunteer names, even though I'd practically memorized everything about this project. I blamed it on my anxiety over finding a dead body. I took a few calming breaths and was soon able to focus on the information he needed. "About half of yesterday's group should be back today. That's ten people, give or take a few. The rest of them are new."

"Good. I'll interview the returnees. I can do it right out here on the porch."

"Are you sure you don't want to move inside to the foyer, at least? It's awfully cold out here." And there I went, inserting my own opinion once again. I pointed toward the front door, glancing through the decorative wrought iron glassworks. There was the red settee and plenty of wide stairway steps in case people wanted to sit down.

"That should be fine," Eric said. "I'll ask Mindy—I mean Officer Payton—to do a complete search of that area first."

I'd gone to school with Mindy Payton, so I knew who he was talking about. "Do you want me to explain to the new volunteers that the house is closed for today?"

He frowned in thought. "I'd better talk to them."

"Okay. But don't, you know, scare them off with your death stare."

Eric grinned. "But that's what I'm good at."

Trying not to smile, I shook my head.

With the question of volunteers settled, Eric asked my father to please wait out here on the veranda.

In other words, I thought ominously, *don't leave town*.

Gazing back at me, the chief said, "And I'd like you to come with me to the ballroom. I want to go over every single step you took when you first arrived this morning. And maybe, while we're at it, you can come up with a good theory as to why you're the one person in Lighthouse Cove who's always encountering dead bodies."

I shook my head, completely baffled. "It's a mystery."

Chapter Eleven

Eric and I went over and over what happened that morning and I showed him every step I took, starting with parking my car by the garage and walking him down the central hall and into the ballroom. He wanted to know why I was driven to open the butler's-pantry door first thing and I told him I wanted to see how far my dad and his crew had gone with the drywall.

That was the easiest question to answer. They got harder after that.

"What did you think when you saw his tools scattered on the floor?"

"Honestly? At first, it didn't make sense to me at all. I thought something must've happened to distract him, because ordinarily my father would never leave tools out like that."

"Never?"

"Never," I insisted. "My sister and I used to hang out on his construction sites when we were little kids and even back then, Dad was adamant about discipline. Tidying up at the end of the day. Taking care of your tools.

He even insisted that his crew wear clean clothes every day. He was convinced that it not only instilled *self*-respect in his guys, but it also showed their clients that they had respect for the job. And all of that went a long way toward building his guys' self-confidence. And it led to more jobs for everyone. It was all connected. This was a big deal to him."

"So you figured he was distracted last night?"

"Yes."

He considered for a moment. "After all those years of building up discipline and self-respect, why would you think he was distracted last night?"

My shoulders sagged. "Oh, boy. You can't tell him I said this."

Eric folded his strong arms across his chest. "Just go ahead and tell me what you're thinking."

"All right." Oh God. Did this make me a traitorous daughter? It felt weird talking about my father behind his back. Even to Eric. Still, it wasn't like I had a choice. "See, Dad hasn't worked a steady construction job in almost five years. I mean, he helped Uncle Pete add a new room onto his winery, but that was mostly supervising. So I'll admit I was nervous about him working here with me. And then Wade's dad showed up to help and that doubled my worries."

"Phil Chambers? Why would you worry about him?"

"Phil used to be my father's foreman. A couple of their former crew members showed up to help, too, so the old gang was back together again. They were having a great time, reliving their glory days, I guess. I thought Dad might overdo it, trying to look tough in front of his buddies. I was concerned that they would egg each other on and try to outdo each other, and someone would end up spraining their back or worse."

"Because they're a bunch of old guys."

"I never said *old*, but yeah. That's why I asked you not to tell him."

"I won't say a word. But your father seems too smart and businesslike to mess around like that."

"I agree. I was wrong, okay?" It was lowering to admit that I had been acting like a jackass about the man who had taught me everything I knew. "I don't know what came over me. I was like the paranoid parent and he was my unruly child."

Eric bit back a smile. "Sounds like it."

Great. Even *he* was amused. I quickly got back on track. "Anyway, when I saw all the tools lying around, I thought my nightmare scenario had come true. That Dad and the guys had been screwing around on the job and forgot to tidy up." I gazed up at him. "Little did I know, the real nightmare was waiting for me behind the pantry door."

Eric paused at that, then pointed to the ax sheath lying on the tarp. "What did you think when you saw that?"

"Oh God." It physically hurt to look at it and I rubbed my eyes. "I thought Dad had been showing off his new toy to his buddies."

"So you still had no inkling that something might be wrong."

"None at all." I threw my hands up. "Why would I? My only thought was that I would have to try to curtail my father's shenanigans."

Eric nodded thoughtfully, then gazed at me with a

troubled expression. "And when you saw the ax sticking out of Potter's neck? What did you think then?"

I shivered. He was being brutally straightforward for my own good, I supposed, to get me to talk. But ugh. "It made me sick. My mind went blank for a few seconds and I screamed. I raced to get out of there as fast as I could. And as soon as I could think clearly, like maybe a minute or two later, I called you."

"And when did you call your father?"

"As soon as I hung up from talking to you."

Ten minutes later, Eric and I walked out of the ballroom through the French doors and circled around to the front of the house where we found Wade sitting and talking to Dad.

"I'm glad you're here," I said to my foreman. I had called him right before I went with Eric to tell him what had happened and to ask him to call the other contractors. I wanted them to show up after lunch instead of first thing this morning.

Wade stood. "Are you all right?"

"I'll be fine."

"I still can't believe it, Shannon." He waved one hand at Dad. "I'm sitting here talking to your father about this and we're both in shock. Do you know how it happened? Who did it?"

"I have no idea. I'm leaving it to the police to figure it out." I glanced at Eric, who gave me a twisted smile. He knew my penchant for tracking down murderers. It was a bad habit of mine. I had no idea how it had *become* a habit, but there we were.

Eric's gaze was fixed on me. "We'll be talking some more."

I nodded, taking his words as a promise, not a threat. Even though it was sometimes hard to tell with Eric.

Wade and I walked away so the police chief could talk to my father privately, but once we were out of sight on the side of the house, Wade stopped and glanced down at me, his expression troubled. "This is really bad. What in the world happened here last night?"

"You said you talked to Dad about it."

"Yeah. So Potter's dead, killed by Jack's ax. He said you found the body and saw the ax sticking out of his neck."

I swallowed uneasily. "That pretty much sums it up. And please don't mention the ax or anything else to anyone. It's evidence."

"Jeez, Shannon, tell me the truth. Are you okay?"

"Right now I'm fine, but I'll probably fall apart at some point this afternoon when nobody's watching." I smiled. "And there will be some bad dreams tonight. Seriously, though, my biggest fear is that they'll arrest my father. But they shouldn't, because he didn't do it."

"Of course not."

"And luckily there are plenty of suspects to go around."

"How do you know? I mean, yeah, Potter was a jackass, but how many people would actually be inclined to kill him?"

"Better to ask how many *wouldn't*. Heck, I'm not a violent person and even I wanted to take a shot at him once or twice yesterday. I saw at least six different people fighting with him. He seemed to enjoy enraging everyone he talked to. Including me, by the way. So if Dad goes to jail, I may feel compelled to start naming the others I saw fighting with the old goat."

"He was an egotistical tyrant," Wade said darkly. "The man made everyone's life a misery and he was ruining this job site. I don't think it's out of line to say that anyone who's ever had to deal with him should be considered a suspect."

"Probably true." We began walking with no particular end point in mind. It was a cold, crisp morning, close to freezing with the temperature hovering in the mid-thirties. The pine trees lining the property looked stunning against the clear blue sky. I knew it would warm up as the sun rose higher, but right now I shivered and zipped my vest up for warmth.

"So who are all these suspects you're talking about?"

I grimaced. "Well, there's my father, for one."

"Yeah, I overheard their argument myself."

"You and everyone on the property heard it." I sighed. "Santa Claus Steve heard it, and Potter's secretary. And probably most of the volunteers who were standing right outside the glass doors."

"The crew in apartment two heard everything, too," Wade told me. "That's where I was working before I came into the ballroom."

"Oh, great. More witnesses against him." And that reminded me that I would have to deal with the venting issues. It would be a real problem if the new tenants could overhear conversations in other apartments.

"Don't worry, your dad will be fine." Wade gave me a hearty pat on the back. "Everyone in town loves him and hated Potter. It's gonna be okay."

"From your lips," I muttered.

"So who else did you see Potter fighting with?"

"I'm not sure that they were fighting, but Blake said

he saw that woman April, the Santa Slapper, talking to Potter up in the attic."

"Potter was up in the attic?"

"Yeah. Don't ask me why. I have no idea. He sure got around, though, didn't he?"

"Sure did."

Now that I'd brought it up, I was recalling more of my conversation with Blake yesterday. "Blake thinks Potter and April were looking for something up there."

"In the attic?"

"Yeah. I guess they didn't know we already moved everything over to the garage last week."

Wade scowled. "If Potter was looking for something up in the attic, I'm doubly glad we moved the stuff."

"But what were they looking for?" I asked, thinking about it for a long moment. "And why? Maybe we should go look and find it before April does."

"But what are we looking for?"

I laughed. "I have no idea. And another thing, what's the connection between those two? I've never seen April before yesterday, but she acts like she's been around here for a while and she obviously knew Potter. And how did they know there was something in the attic worth finding in the first place? Is there some connection between April and Potter and the Foresters? Is that why she volunteered? And what about her accusing Santa Slim of assaulting her? Nobody else saw it happen. I'm not saying it didn't happen, but I can't help wondering if she's trying to pull something over on someone. I mean, who in heck is she?"

Wade was watching me carefully and finally nodded. "You're good at this, you know?"

"You mean I'm good at asking questions. Too bad I don't have any answers."

"Still, maybe Eric should hire you as a detective."

"Oh, he would love to hear that," I said, smiling. "I'm nothing but a pain in the neck to him."

Wade's eyebrows lifted. "I wouldn't say so."

"Trust me."

We turned and strolled the opposite way down the driveway toward the street, watching for any morning volunteers to arrive. We met several and shepherded them around to the back of the house. I asked them to wait there until everyone else had arrived. There were other pieces of elegant wrought iron patio furniture all along the back veranda, so I knew they would be comfortable enough.

Wade and I continued our stroll. My mind was working, considering several possible theories regarding April, when Wade said, "Are you sure you're all right?"

"I told you, I'm fine."

"Yeah, you did, and I know the circumstances today are grim, but you've seemed down for two days now. I didn't pursue the conversation yesterday, but now I really want to know what's going on with you."

I stopped walking and stared at him, but he was gazing so intently at me, I had to look away. "I have no idea what you're talking about."

He laughed. "You're a terrible liar. Come on, Shannon. We've known each other too long. Yesterday you seemed sort of bummed. You were trying to hide it, but I can usually read you pretty well. And today, well, you're still unhappy."

"Because someone's dead on my job site!" I crossed

my arms tightly and gazed at the trees. "Other than that, I haven't got a clue what you mean."

"I mean I can tell when you're off your game, Shannon. It has nothing to do with Potter's death, because I saw it yesterday. You're not often out of sorts, but yesterday was one of those rare days. There was the Robbie escape and the whole *Bah, humbug* thing, and you were late for work. And then today, I don't know, but . . ." He frowned. "I'm getting a vibe from you."

"No vibes here," I insisted, walking faster in the fervent hope that he wouldn't root out any more of my vibes. Wade was right. I was a terrible liar. "Stop trying to psychoanalyze me."

He stayed where he was and I finally turned to see him staring at me as if I were a particularly fascinating smear on a microscope. "What?"

"Heard anything from Mac lately?"

My gaze narrowed in on him. "No. Why would I?"

"Ah." Wade's lips pursed in thought. "Hmm."

I glared at him. "What's that supposed to mean?"

He laughed. "It means I have my answer as to why you've been in such a crabby mood. You miss him."

"I am never in a crabby mood."

With a grin, he said, "True, until recently."

Staring up at the sky, I wondered when, exactly, had I turned into such a transparent doofus? I really had to lighten up about this whole Mac situation. If my own foreman could read my moods so easily, I probably needed to get myself an attitude adjustment.

I flipped my hair back, squared my shoulders, and looked him in the eye. "I'm sorry I've let my personal life affect my work environment. It won't happen again."

"Hold on a minute. I'm not asking for an apology, Shannon." He draped his arm across my shoulders and squeezed. "This isn't affecting your work, pal. I was just asking as your friend. You're not happy, so I'm concerned."

It was so **unexpected**, I almost burst into tears. Wade had been my friend for over twenty-five years. Our fathers had worked together, so we'd often helped out on the same job sites. I had been a bridesmaid in his wedding. We were partners at work. We should have been discussing the problems brought about by Potter's death and the temporary halting of the Homebuilders project. My feelings for Mac should have been the last thing on our agenda. But since he was a trusted friend and he'd expressed concern, what else could I do but spill my guts?

"You're right," I said. "I do miss him. He hasn't called once since he left for New York and his book tour. And before that, he was in Europe with the Jake Slater film. And in between everything else, he was visiting his family for the Thanksgiving holidays."

"Sounds like he's been busy."

Just what I'd been telling myself. Making excuses for him. But seriously? How long did it take to text "I miss you"? "Yeah, he's been busy, but apparently he came back to town last night. And you know how I found out? From Lizzie. He's doing a big book signing at her shop this weekend. And I had no idea."

He winced on my behalf. "Ouch."

I appreciated the gesture, since that was exactly how I felt. But enough already. "Look, it's dumb to even talk about it. He's got a whole life out there that has nothing to do with me. We had a little flirtation for a while, but it's over. That's okay. I figure he was out on the road and had time to rethink this whole thing, and what the heck? He decided to cut me loose. That's fine. We'll still be friends."

"If you want, I'll go beat him up for you," he offered, giving me a worried smile.

"Thanks, but you're the one who taught me how to fight, so I can take care of it myself if I have to."

"True, but I'd be willing to hit him for you anyway."

"That's so sweet, Wade. Thank you."

"I don't like to see you unhappy," he murmured, and wrapped one arm around my shoulders again, this time pulling me in for a friendly hug. "It's just unnatural."

I smiled up at him. "I'll be fine. Promise."

"Good," he said firmly, and let me go.

I shoved my hands into the pockets of my vest. "Now if the police would just solve Potter's murder and let us get back to work, I'd be even happier."

"If only," he said.

"Let's go check on Eric and my dad."

We headed that way, but before we could make it all the way to the front, where we'd left Dad and Eric, I saw a black Jaguar drive up and park. "Oh, great. The icing on the cake."

Eric strained to see who it was. "Is that Whitney?"

"Yeah."

"Wonder what she's doing here."

"Probably wants to make sure Potter's really dead," I muttered, and managed to shock him into silence. "Sorry if that sounded harsh."

"A little. Where'd that come from?"

I glanced around to make sure we were completely alone. "Before I left here last night, I went around checking all the rooms. I was coming down the hall when Whitney drove up, so I watched from under the stairs to see what she was doing here."

He smirked. "Under the stairs?"

I shrugged. "I wasn't ready for a confrontation."

"I don't blame you. I know you two don't get along."

That was putting it mildly. "She took the elevator up to the second floor, where guess who was waiting? Potter. The two of them proceeded to have a rip-roaring fight, yelling and screaming and threatening each other. It was creepy. And a little scary. She was furious when she left."

"Holy moly."

"Yeah. So I'm not accusing her of murder or anything, but if Dad is on Eric's suspect list, she definitely belongs there, too."

"Wow," he said, his voice a whisper as we watched Whitney check her makeup in the car mirror. "Do you think Tommy knows she was here?"

"What do you think?"

He thought for a moment. "I doubt it."

I had to smile. "Interesting, isn't it? I hate to think of Tommy being upset, but I have to say, it was nice to see Whitney giving someone besides *me* a hard time."

"I feel bad about what this might do to Tommy. But he's married to her. He's got to know what she's like."

"I'm not sure he does," I murmured, and left it there. Since Wade had grown up in Lighthouse Cove and we'd known each other since kindergarten, he was well aware of my feelings for Whitney. But I still didn't feel right mentioning the bitter details of the fight or the fact that Whitney had accused Potter of stealing money from her father. That would be taking friendly gossip to a dangerous new level and I wasn't ready to go there.

I checked my watch. "I'd better get back to Eric. He

wanted to talk to the volunteers and they're probably all here by now."

"Okay. Look, since we can't get any work done until this afternoon, I'm going home to have breakfast with Sandy."

I smiled. "Give her my love."

"You bet. I'll be gone about an hour and a half, but call if you need me sooner."

"Thanks, Wade."

He ambled over to the driveway while I took off in the opposite direction. I had left my dad and Eric talking for the past half hour and I was worried. I had a sudden image of Dad being handcuffed and taken off to jail. That spurred me to move faster and I rushed around the corner—and almost rammed right into Whitney.

"You!" She made it sound like an expletive. "What are you doing here?"

She was so full of bluster, I almost laughed. "That would be *my* question to *you* since this is *my* job site."

She tossed back her perfect fringe of dark hair and eyed me as if I were scum floating on a pond. "I'm looking for Tommy."

For once she wasn't wearing stilettos and it occurred to me, not for the first time, that she wore them as part of her basic armor. Evidently she didn't need them this morning because there was no battle to be waged. Potter was dead. And also, her big, strong husband Tommy was lurking around here somewhere, always ready to protect her. She was safe here, or so she thought.

"Really?" I said, perplexed. "Because I was thinking you came here to make sure old man Potter's really dead."

"That's a horrible thing to say."

"He was a horrible man."

"That's for sure," she muttered. Lifting her shoulders, she held her head high and tried to tower over me. It wasn't easy, since I was four inches taller than her. No wonder she wore stilettos. "So once again they've found another dead body on one of *your* job sites. They should lock you up for the good of the town."

I laughed. The woman simply never changed. Heck, I'd even saved her life twice and she still acted like Queen Bitch of the Universe. "That's really funny, coming from you. But I wouldn't be so quick to send someone else off to jail if I were you."

She was instantly on guard. "What's that supposed to mean?"

I folded my arms across my chest and looked down at her. "Let's cut to the chase, shall we?"

"Okay." But she frowned and her voice was tentative. She hated looking up at me and she had no idea what I was talking about. I enjoyed having the upper hand, at least for the moment.

I leaned in close and said softly, "I saw you here last night, Whitney. I heard you arguing with Potter."

The color literally drained from her face and she looked like she might faint. "You eavesdropped."

"It was hard not to. You were screaming at him."

She sucked in a huge breath of air. "You can't tell Tommy."

"Oh, really?" I cocked my head to one side and looked down at her. Boy, I enjoyed being taller than her.

"He can't ever know."

"Huh." She looked worried and I didn't blame her. "Wonder what you'll owe me if I keep my mouth shut."

"Anything. Whatever you say."

I didn't hesitate. "You have to be nice to me."

"Oh, for God's sake." Her mouth screwed up, her eyes narrowed, and that lofty nose went up in the air as if she'd caught a bad scent.

I started to walk away. "Tommy's around here somewhere. Good luck explaining why you're here."

"Wait!"

I turned and gazed at her, waiting for her to agree to be nice. But she couldn't say it. It was enlightening and humorous and painful all at the same time. "You have a real problem, you know that?"

"No, I don't. And I don't hate you." She sighed and shrugged. "I mean, not exactly."

"Yeah? Well, you do a really good impression of it then." I laughed. "You're pathetic."

Her lips pressed together in frustration and finally she stomped her foot and blurted, "You had what I wanted!"

I snorted softly. "Really? We're still back in high school? Okay, fine, I had what you wanted. But you fixed that, didn't you? You took Tommy, married him, and had three kids with him. Now you have everything. So get over it."

"It wasn't just Tommy. It's just . . . you were so . . . *friendly.*" She waved her hand vaguely, searching for the right words. "So . . . *nice.* You always wanted to . . . *help* everyone. It was a little sickening."

"I can see why that would be unpleasant for you. So you had to try and destroy me?"

"Oh, please. You're stronger than I ever was."

She said it so offhandedly, I almost missed it. She thought I was *strong?* Was that why she'd pounded me down for years?

She was still talking, so I had to pay attention.

"Watching you being so darn nice to everyone made me feel awful. I felt better when I picked on you."

"That's ridiculous."

"It's true."

"Well, gee, no wonder Tommy fell for you."

"I *love* Tommy," she said defensively.

"I know, Whitney. He loves you, too. But he's my friend—*just* my friend—so how about you stop acting like I'm the bad guy here?"

"I'll . . . try." She paused, then blinked dramatically. "I'm about to get kicked out of my house, you know. I'll have to sell my clothes and my Jaguar." She sniffled and her eyes began to water. "It's not fair."

"Don't tell me you're going to cry."

She sniffed again. "I wouldn't shed one tear in front of you."

"So, this is you trying to be nice?"

"It's not that easy," she snapped.

I rolled my eyes. "You know you're insane, right?"

She took another big breath of air and pulled herself together. "Look, I'll work out my money problems. Just don't tell Tommy what you heard."

"Tell Tommy what?"

She let out a little shriek and Tommy laughed, grabbed her around the waist, and kissed her. "Hi, baby. What a nice surprise. What were you two talking about?"

He turned to me and grinned boyishly. "What is it you heard that you're not going to tell me?"

Behind his back Whitney stared at me wild-eyed and vigorously shook her head as if to shout, *No!*

It was a test, and I knew it. If I betrayed Whitney, she would treat me like dirt for the rest of my life. And if I *didn't* betray Whitney? Heck, she would *still* treat me like dirt for the rest of my life. So, what to do? What to do?

I sighed and batted my eyes at Tommy. "I heard one of my friends saying how cute you were, and Whitney didn't want me to tell you because you already know how cute you are."

His eyes narrowed as he tried to gauge my honesty. I continued smiling innocently until he finally chuckled and gave Whitney another kiss. "You girls are the cute ones."

"Love you, babe," she said, patting his cheek.

"Love you more." He gave her one last squeeze and walked away. And Whitney almost collapsed with relief.

"Oh my God, oh my God," she said in a breathless whisper.

"You're welcome," I said, knowing she wouldn't thank me out loud unless forced.

"Okay, yes, thank you. I'm going to take care of this," she swore. "I need to talk to the board of directors at the bank and . . . and I'll talk to Tommy."

"Please do," I said. "Because if Eric puts my dad in jail, all bets are off. I'll hand him a long list of people who wanted Potter dead just as badly as my father. And trust me, your name will be on it."

She shook her hair defiantly. "From what I hear, you're on it, too."

I scowled. "Let's face it, everyone in town is on that list."

"For good reason," she grumbled. "Potter was a monster."

I realized that while I'd been talking to Wade and arguing with Whitney, Eric had finished speaking to the volunteers. He had disappeared into the house, but I counted twelve volunteers who had stuck around. They stood in small groups on the backyard lawn or sat on the edge of the veranda, dangling their feet, chatting with each other and waiting for the police to finish searching the house.

I felt compelled to say a few words, so I thanked them for staying but also let them know they were free to leave. Everyone insisted they were perfectly happy to hang out and visit with each other until we were ready to get back to work. I appreciated their devotion, even though I would bet most of them just wanted to catch up on the murder gossip. I couldn't blame them. You wouldn't find much bigger news around here than murder.

I circled to the front of the house and was happy to find Dad still sitting in the same chair on the veranda. The good news was that he hadn't been dragged off to police headquarters. Not yet, anyway. Instead, he was deep in conversation with Phil Chambers, who waved at me but kept talking in low tones to Dad.

I didn't want to interrupt them, even though I was dying to know what Eric had said to my father. But I resisted, heading instead to my truck, where I climbed inside to work quietly on my tablet.

I recalculated the list of job priorities and moved around the tasks I had hoped to have finished this morning. I shifted a few crew members around, too, to make things work out time-wise.

I checked the list of volunteers from yesterday who had told me they would show up again this afternoon. Gazing at the list, I was struck once again by the number of people who'd carried a grudge against Peter Potter. Counting myself and my father, there were almost too many suspects to deal with. Not that all of us could seriously be considered murder suspects, but these were just the ones who'd clashed with Potter yesterday. Who knew how many other people had locked horns with him before that?

So far, Eric hadn't made any moves to bring my father in for questioning. Our police chief was nothing if not fair, but I also knew that he played by the rules. The ax was the primary clue in the death of Potter and it belonged to my father. But Eric wouldn't simply arrest him and stop looking for more evidence. That wasn't his style. He knew my father, so he had to believe he was innocent, right? Okay, yes, everyone in the known universe had heard Dad and Potter yelling at each other yesterday. And of course, a bunch of people had seen Dad brandishing his shiny new ax over Potter's head while threatening to kill him.

Still, Dad wasn't the only one who had a bone to pick with Potter yesterday.

I continued to stare at the list of names on my tablet until they began to blur. Was there a murderer on the list? Were my crew and I working side by side with a killer? Had my father been set up deliberately to take the fall? Would the police see it that way? I seriously doubted it. It was becoming more and more obvious that if I wanted to keep my father out of jail, I was going to have to track down Potter's killer myself.

Chapter Twelve

Sitting in my truck, I forced myself to go through all the lists of volunteers, contractors, crew members, plumbers, electricians, painters, and decorators. I even checked the names of the families and single people who were moving in on Christmas Eve, since each adult family member was required to put in some work as a volunteer.

I would bet money that someone on one of my lists knew exactly what happened in the ballroom and the butler's pantry last night.

Naturally, I recognized many of the names because they were townspeople I'd known most of my life. Either that, or they were fellow contractors or crew members I'd worked with on other jobs over the years. The thought that one of them could be a killer was chilling.

Then, all of a sudden, one name bounced out at me.

"Lizzie!" I blurted, then immediately covered my mouth and glanced around to make sure no one had heard me. And didn't I feel stupid? I mean, I was alone in my truck, parked back by the garage with the windows rolled up. Still, it was after eight o'clock in the morning, so a few more people were ambling about the property. Most notably, there were more police officers and crime-scene techs. Everyone looked busy with their own work, thank goodness, but I would have to be more careful with my outbursts.

How could I have forgotten to call Lizzie? What kind of a best friend was I? She needed to know that Potter was dead!

Of course, Lizzie was another one who had an excellent reason to want Potter dead. Not that I believed she was guilty, of course, because she wouldn't hurt a fly and neither would her husband, Hal. Unfortunately, though, Potter's secretary had heard Lizzie screaming out her threats. And if the police interviewed Patrice—and they would, of course—she would point the finger at Lizzie in a heartbeat. That's what I was most concerned about.

I pulled my phone from my pocket, slipped on my Bluetooth, and punched in her number.

"Shannon!" she cried when she answered the phone. "Did you hear about Potter?"

"Of course I did," I said, a little annoyed that I wasn't the first to tell her the news. "He died on my construction site. I found the body." Now I was just bragging, which was ludicrous. But it was that kind of a day.

"Oh no, Shannon, you didn't! Not again. Are you all right? Where are you? Do you need me to come by with a latte and a scone?"

I smiled. That was my friend Lizzie. "I love you and, yes, I'm fine. A latte sounds fabulous, but it's not necessary."

"That's good, because I'm still in my pajamas. Hal's got the first shift at the store."

"Lucky you," I said with a laugh but I quickly sobered. "How did you hear the news about Potter so soon?"

"Don't you remember Hal's police scanner?"

I buried my head in my hands. I'd forgotten all about Hal's fixation on listening to police calls. Not that we got a lot of excitement from the Lighthouse Cove cops, aside from the occasional drunk-and-disorderly call. Well, and except for those times when I happened to find a dead body.

"I thought he was going to throw that thing away."

"Are you kidding?" she said. "He's just as obsessed as ever. Still has it going every morning. So we heard the dispatcher call Tommy with the news."

"Great. I was calling to warn you, but I guess it's not necessary."

"Warn me about what?"

"About the fact that Potter's dead. I mean, in light of what you said to him yesterday."

There was a pause, then she said slowly, "Shannon, I have no idea what you're talking about."

"Lizzie, Mr. Potter's secretary heard you threaten him."

Another beat, and Lizzie asked, "But I didn't say anything bad, did I?"

Was she kidding? Had she been in so much of a rage that she couldn't even remember threatening the dead man? I suppose it could happen. "Are you feeling all right?"

"I'm fine. I just can't honestly recall saying anything that would get me into trouble."

"You remember Potter coming into the room and threatening to close down your bookstore, right? And how you shouted something about killing him, right?"

Again, she paused before groaning loudly. "Oh no!

But that's just an expression. You know I didn't mean anything by it."

"Of course I do. But his secretary, Patrice, was right there and she will never forget what she heard. In fact, when she heard you say that, she thought we should've called the police right then and there."

"That's crazy," she said. "It—it's just an expression. You know I would never kill anyone."

"I know that. But she doesn't know you and I suppose she was being protective of her boss."

"But he was so awful," Lizzie said. "I've never been so furious and so frustrated all at the same time before, Shannon. Potter kept nagging and mocking me. He called me names, said Hal and I were incapable of running a successful business. He wouldn't stop. I guess I snapped."

"I think you did snap, Lizzie. Just for a minute, anyway." I tapped my fingers against the steering wheel and stared off at the house, watching the police and a few of the remaining volunteers wander around the property.

"Yeah, I did," Lizzie admitted quietly. "I don't even know what started it. He just saw me and took off ranting. He was so condescending and mean. It was weird."

Poor Lizzie sounded miserable and there wasn't a thing I could do to help her. "It sounds like you were traumatized. And you're not the only one."

"What do you mean?"

"Potter was on a rampage yesterday. He had violent arguments with at least five other people."

"Please don't tell anyone I said this," Lizzie whispered, "but I'm glad he's dead."

"You're not the only one." I glanced at the clock on the dashboard. "Look, I should get going. I just thought

I'd better warn you that, as soon as the police talk to Patrice, you'll probably get a visit from Eric Jensen."

"Oh, Shannon," she moaned. "Hal is going to kill me."

"You need to stop using that particular phrase."

"Oh God."

"Don't worry, honey. You've got an alibi with Hal."

"I'm not so sure about that. He might be so angry with me, he'll stand there giggling as they cart me off to the pokey."

I chuckled. "I've never heard Hal giggle in my life."

"No, you're right, he doesn't. But what a mess." She covered up the phone to say something to whoever walked into the room just then. "I've got to get going. Marisa's got a dentist appointment. Will you keep me posted?"

"You bet, and you keep me posted, too. And by the way, I was one of those people who tangled with Potter yesterday, so we might end up sharing a room in the pokey."

"You're the best friend ever."

Even though it was no laughing matter, I was smiling as I disconnected the call.

I walked back to the front of the house and found Dad's entire crew commiserating with him. Uncle Pete and Bud were sprawled on the couch with Dad sitting on the chair facing them. Phil Chambers chose to pace the perimeter of the group, banging his fist against his palm. "What I want to know is this: what the heck were Potter and the killer doing in our ballroom?"

"Good question." Dad took off his baseball cap and scratched his head in frustration. "And why in blazes did they go for my tool chest? I mean, I'm not saying I wanted them to use any of yours, but still, it's a mystery."

"I stashed mine in the cloakroom," Uncle Pete said, wearing a concerned frown.

"I took mine home," said Bud. "Promised the wife I'd hang some pictures on the wall."

"Lucky you," Dad grumbled, then grinned. "I mean that. You're a lucky man."

"Don't I know it?" He wiggled his eyebrows up and down. "Babs made chicken fried steak for my trouble."

"My cholesterol is shrieking," Phil muttered.

Uncle Pete rubbed his stomach. "But, oh, man, that sounds great."

"Sure does," Dad said.

In that moment, my heart wanted to break for my father. He and my mom had fallen in love and dreamed of a long life together, but Mom died from complications from diabetes. Dad rarely spoke about it, but I knew he had to be lonely sometimes.

Don't get me wrong—Dad enjoyed the ladies. He and Uncle Pete often dated and flirted with the tourists who came to town every year for their two-week vacations. And the ladies loved them both. But Dad had never been serious about another woman since Mom died.

Maybe I would cook up some chicken fried steak this weekend, just for fun. And for Dad.

It was ten o'clock and I was starting to get nervous. The cops had two hours to finish searching the house, according to Eric's self-imposed deadline. So we had two hours to wait. I hated sitting around with nothing to do. I had other job sites I could be checking on, but I wasn't about to leave Forester House while we still had volunteers here, along with my Dad and his crew. The rest of the crews had received a call from Wade, letting them know we wouldn't be starting until one o'clock. If we were lucky.

Would Eric and his crime-scene people be able to finish by one o'clock? I hoped so. I'd already rescheduled and reconfigured my calendar to accommodate the lost hours. Would it be wrong to check in with Eric to see if he was any closer to making a decision? He was right inside the house somewhere, completely off-limits to me. If I sent him a text, would he consider it pushy?

"That never stopped you before," I muttered, and pulled out my phone to text a message.

"Is one o'clock still workable?" I texted to Eric.

I got his reply in less than a minute. "This place is gigantic."

"Is that a no?" I asked.

"No."

I smiled. "No, it's NOT a no?"

"U R not helping."

I laughed. I didn't know why, but sometimes Eric's gruffness was charming. Despite the momentary lightness, I had a feeling he would end up sending us all home. After all, he was right about one thing: the house was enormous. How could they possibly search thirteen thousand square feet of nooks and crannies and corners and cubbies in four hours or less?

I felt bad about the volunteers sitting around doing nothing. Would it be silly to suggest they start pulling weeds or something?

"Good grief, yes." I almost laughed out loud and figured it was stress related. I really wanted to get back to work.

On the off chance that Eric did allow us to go back to work, we still wouldn't have access to the butler's pantry for a few days, and probably the ballroom as well. In that case, I would have to ask Dad and the guys to split up and work in other rooms in the house. They wouldn't mind, but I knew it wouldn't be the same for them. They'd been having a great time with the old gang being back together again for one more construction job.

Thinking about the butler's pantry being cordoned off made me think about Mr. Potter. Why had he always been so horrible to everybody? What had his problem been?

Without warning, the image of his dead body appeared full-blown in my mind's eye. Sprawled across the pantry floor. ax buried in his fat neck. Blood pooling under his head.

"Oh, yuck," I muttered, and rubbed my stomach. Yeah, I could still see him lying there like a beached whale in a five-hundred-dollar suit, his starched white shirt collar stained with blood. And for the fiftieth time today I wondered what in the world had brought him into the ballroom and then the pantry last night. Had he just been wandering around? Had he scheduled another meeting to harangue some other poor sap? What if he'd been looking for my father? He knew Dad had been working in the ballroom.

Another chill skittered across my shoulders and I took a few deep breaths to try and calm down the internal turmoil.

Had Potter been after my father? If so, who had he run into instead? Was it someone who'd been working here yesterday? Or had someone new entered the house in pursuit of Potter?

With another deep breath, I stepped off the veranda

in search of a distraction. I strolled around to the driveway, crossed under the porte cochere, and headed for the back lawn. Pulling out my phone, I punched in my friend Jane's number, hoping she would be willing to cheer me up. It occurred to me that she had been working here yesterday afternoon and I suddenly wondered if she had seen anything unusual. But there was no answer, so I had to leave a message.

I was going stir-crazy and it didn't help that the body remained in the butler's pantry. I suddenly realized it might be hours before the coroner finally showed up to take Potter's body away. Our town didn't have an official medical examiner, so that meant that the Mendocino County sheriff would have to drive over from Ukiah, the county seat, and declare Potter deceased.

I was pretty sure they wouldn't have to investigate any further into the cause of death. It was pretty clear from the ax in his neck and all that blood that an artery had been severed. So once the sheriff made it official and signed his formal declaration of death, the cops would probably take Potter's body over to Bitterman's Funeral Home, where it would be prepared for burial.

And how gruesome was it that I knew so much about the procedures following a violent death? It just proved that Eric was right. I really was the only person in town who kept encountering dead bodies. But it wasn't on purpose, believe me.

I continued to stroll mindlessly until I happened to pass the window leading into the butler's pantry. It was still wide open, so I ventured closer.

I could see our local crime-scene team doing their thing, swirling fingerprint powder everywhere and obviously tiptoeing around the body, which was still lying on the pantry floor. The tech was wearing latex gloves and I knew he had Tyvek nonskid booties over his shoes. I'd seen those booties a few times before on the feet of the cops going through the houses of friends who had died. They wore them so they wouldn't destroy evidence or leave additional footprints.

I didn't want Eric to catch me snooping, so I continued around to the back veranda and up to the French doors leading to the ballroom. I tried to peek inside but the curtains made it difficult. I did manage to find a sliver of an opening, though, and was delighted to be able to watch the two cops inside as they searched the room.

Talk about snooping.

I recognized my old friend Mindy Payton, now *Officer* Payton, kneeling next to my father's tool chest. They would have already fingerprinted the shiny red metal cover and possibly some of the tools I'd found on the floor. Now Mindy was carefully sifting through the tools still left in the box. I prayed she would find some clear evidence of the killer's identity. Not inside my father's tool chest of course, but somewhere in that room. There had to be some proof, somewhere, that would tell us who had opened up the box and stolen my father's ax to kill Potter.

Suddenly Mindy grinned and called her cohort over. Even from this far away, her excitement was contagious and I held my breath as she pulled out her phone to snap a few photos from different angles. Then she turned the phone over and used it to make a quick call. She looked excited as she spoke.

Once she ended the call, her latex-covered fingers reached into the tool chest and extracted something from among the tools and supplies. She held it up so the other cop could see the object glistening and sparkling in the ambient light. And I felt my stomach go spinning out of control.

It was Heather Maxwell's diamond-encrusted charm bracelet.

I must have stared at that bracelet for a full minute before tripping away from the French doors. I managed to make it to one of the patio chairs, where I slumped down like a wet noodle.

"It doesn't mean anything," I whispered. But I was kidding myself. Finding that bracelet in my dad's toolbox would mean everything to the police.

But what was it doing there? There was certainly no connection between the missing bauble and Potter's murder. Was there?

Eric and his men might consider the possibility that the bracelet had slipped off while Heather helped herself to my Dad's ax. But Heather, a killer? There was no way. Heather had made such a huge deal about showing off the bracelet, *anyone* working in the house might have been tempted to steal it from her purse. But who would plant it in my father's toolbox?

Pondering the possibilities, I came up with an idea that made more sense. Namely, that the bracelet had fallen out of Heather's purse while she was working yesterday. One of Dad's crew found it and thought it belonged to me. And he put it in Dad's tool chest for safekeeping.

I shook my head. That was possibly the dumbest theory I'd ever come up with. But how else could I explain it? Dad hadn't stolen Heather's bracelet. And Heather wasn't a killer. So how in the world had it gotten into his toolbox?

I rubbed my temple where a headache was forming.

I had no choice but to face the possibility that this was a premeditated act. A crafty killer had set up my father to take the fall for Potter's murder. That meant that the same person had taken Heather's bracelet and left it in Dad's toolbox. Had the killer stolen the bracelet in the first place or just been lucky enough to find it somewhere? I guessed it was the latter.

As a theory, I suppose it made a lot of sense. Although to be perfectly honest, *none of it made any sense at all!*

But it might make sense to the police if they didn't know the whole story. Did they know that Heather had been showing off her bracelet to the entire group of volunteers yesterday? Would the subject come up when Eric interviewed the volunteers? And of course, Dad didn't know anything about that, either. He was already getting started in the ballroom when Heather decided to display her jewelry.

I needed to find Eric and let him know that this was a setup. That my dad knew nothing about the bracelet. I wondered if Heather had already told Eric about her missing bracelet or if this was a fluke. I wanted to tell him all my theories before he accused my father of murder and theft.

God, this was exhausting. Besides my father, I had no idea who Eric had interviewed this morning. I assumed he'd been searching inside the house, but maybe he'd gone off to talk to some of yesterday's volunteers. Had he already talked to Daisy? Or Lizzie? Or Santa Steve? And then there was *me*. I had given Eric my explanation of how I'd found Potter's body, but I'd said nothing about the argument I'd had with him yesterday.

I had to wonder again if there was a witness to our confrontation.

I took one more look through the curtains and saw Mindy and her partner turn toward the ballroom door. That's when I noticed that Eric Jensen had just walked into the room.

I needed to talk to him! This was so frustrating. I knew I wasn't allowed inside the house, but right now I didn't care. I began pounding on the door. They all turned and looked my way. I could see Eric scowling and Mindy looking puzzled. The third cop jogged over and pushed the door open.

"Hello," I said, smiling at the cop holding the door. Then I glanced beyond him to the chief. "Eric, hi. Can I talk to you for one minute?"

He looked irritated, then resigned, and walked toward me. I took a chance and stepped inside the ballroom to meet him halfway.

"This better be good," he said.

"It's about that bracelet," I said, speed talking so I could get everything said before he kicked me out. "It belongs to Heather Maxwell and she was showing it off to the volunteers yesterday, but here's the thing: My father wasn't around when that was going on. He would have no reason to steal it because he didn't even know about it. And besides, what does a bracelet have to do with Potter's murder? So here's what I think. I think my father is being set up."

Eric smiled thinly and I knew I was pushing up against every last nerve in his system.

That didn't stop me, though, because my father's honor—and freedom—was at stake. "Ask yourself, why would the bracelet be inside his tool chest? And why would his ax be used to kill Potter? There's only one reason. It's because he's being framed." I frowned. "I just don't know why. Who would do that?"

I ignored his scowl and forged ahead with my other brilliant theory. "One possibility is that maybe one of his crew saw the bracelet on the floor somewhere. They might've thought it was mine so they put it in Dad's tool chest for safekeeping. That sounds plausible, right?"

It sounded even dumber when I said it out loud.

"Never mind," I said, thoroughly disheartened. "Sorry to waste your time. I just . . ." My mouth was so dry. Where was a two-gallon bottle of water when you needed it? "Look, I don't know what's happening here, but my father is innocent."

"And that's what I'm trying to prove," he said, his voice deep and quiet.

I blinked in surprise, then stared up at him. "And I'm not helping?"

He shook his head. "Not really."

But I had one more point to drive home. "So you talked to Heather and the other volunteers about the bracelet? And you know there were at least thirty-five people out there who saw her showing it off and bragging about how valuable it was?"

"Yup."

"And you know my father wasn't one of those thirty-five people, right?"

"Go," he said through his teeth, apparently having reached the end of his patience.

"Oo-kay. Gone. Thanks for your time." I scurried across the shiny ballroom floor and escaped through the French doors. I was almost surprised when a barrage of bullets didn't follow me out.

I kept walking, not wanting to stop and talk to anyone. I was feeling chastened, and a little mortified, but definitely exhilarated at the same time. I would get over the mortification part because I'd succeeded in grabbing my moment with Eric. All I'd wanted was to try and convince him that my father was innocent. I think he got it and had been leaning that way already. Now he would have to prove it.

"Shannon! Wait up."

I turned and saw a tall, heavyset man running to catch up with me. I had no idea who he was, but I waited for him anyway. He looked pleasant enough and there were plenty of witnesses around, so I had no reason to be apprehensive.

And why was I thinking in those gloomy terms anyway? For heaven's sake, it wasn't like there was a marauding band of large psycho killers roaming the estate. My only excuse was that I'd been traumatized by Potter recently, another big, tall man who'd come after me.

Without warning, another image of Potter's body, now covered by a tarp in the pantry, sprang to mind.

"I'm glad I caught you," the man said, breathing heavily. "I can't believe what I just heard. Potter's really dead?"

"I'm sorry, do I know you?"

"Oh," he said, taken aback. "Oh! Yes, you do." He started to laugh. "Ho ho ho! Yes, you know me."

"Steve?" My eyes narrowed as I focused on his facial features. I still didn't recognize him without the white beard and red hat, but I knew that laugh. "Sorry. You look really different from your Santa Claus persona."

"I would've said something, but I was in a hurry and didn't realize you might not know who I was. Anyway, your father tells me you found the body. Are you all right?"

"Oh, well. Sure. As right as I can be, I suppose. Given the circumstances."

"Of course." He stroked his chin, which was completely beardless. It was probably an unconscious gesture on his part, something he did when he was dressed as Santa Claus. But it made me realize how flawless his costume was. "I can't say I'm sorry to hear the news," he said. "Potter was an awful man. But it's disturbing to know that you were the one who discovered him."

"Disturbing is a good word for it," I admitted. "So how are the rest of the Brigade taking the news?"

"Oh, most of them didn't know him very well. Just me and Slim. We knew him all too well."

I frowned. "Yes. Me, too."

"I noticed him out on the lawn yesterday," Steve continued, frowning. "I could tell he was hell-bent on shutting down our TV interview, so I want to thank you for intercepting him."

"That was my pleasure," I said firmly, feeling irritated all over again that Potter had been sticking his nose in everyone else's business. "He would've embarrassed you and the entire project on live television. It wasn't right."

"He was a raging blowhard," Steve said tightly. "He could've done some real damage to our cause. I appreciate your intervention."

"You're not the only one he inflicted damage on yesterday," I assured him. "I'm just glad I was able to stop him before he got to you."

He shook his head. "I truly believe he was crazy."

"I couldn't say, but he did seem to enjoy tormenting people and that's not normal." I scowled. Even dead, Potter was creating chaos. I tried to lighten the mood. "He definitely belonged on the Naughty List."

Steve threw back his head and laughed heartily. "Ho-ho-ho! Good one, Shannon."

Hearing his laughter, I couldn't help but smile, and finally I joined him. On a day like this one, it felt darn good to laugh.

It was one o'clock when the afternoon volunteers showed up. My contractors were here, too, and we met on the western lawn to discuss today's jobs. I was trying to be optimistic, even though Eric hadn't yet emerged from the house to give us the go-ahead to start working again.

I was going over my schedule of work that still needed to be done in each room when I received a text. "Be right out," it said.

"Is that a good thing or a bad thing?" Wade wondered.

"I have no idea," I said, but I didn't have a positive feeling about it.

"Guess we'll find out soon enough. Here he comes."

Eric walked across the lawn and splayed his hands in frustration. "I'm sorry," he said, clearly unhappy. "We're going to need the rest of the day."

There were groans of disappointment. I was bummed, too, but not surprised. There were just too many rooms and too much square footage for the cops to investigate in a few short hours.

I turned to Eric. "Do you need to talk to any of us today or can I send everyone home?"

"We've got everyone's contact information, so we'll be in touch."

Blake, my attic contractor, overheard him, and asked, "Are we going to have to come down to headquarters?"

"For the majority, the answer is no." Eric scanned the small crowd. "For some of you, we've just got a few logistical questions to ask."

"And we're good to go back inside tomorrow morning?" I asked.

"Yes. Except for the pantry and the ballroom. We'll be working in there for a few more days."

"Got it." I glanced at Dad, who nodded briefly. I was glad the work in the ballroom wasn't too involved and I was hopeful we could still finish it in a week or so. The pantry was a little more extensive with all of its woodwork, but with any luck, we'd have a full week to work in there once the police cleared the space.

I grabbed Sean and we walked with Eric around to the back porch, where the volunteers waited. The police chief told them the same thing and they took it well enough, sticking around to commiserate with others in the group.

I decided to say a few words and jumped up onto the veranda. "Thanks so much for coming today, and you heard Chief Jensen. You're free to go home, but if any of you would like to return tomorrow, we can definitely use your help. Give your names to Sean if you can make it either in the morning or afternoon." I watched Sean wave his hand at everyone and within seconds I was happy to see a crowd formed around him.

"We've got an eight o'clock call tomorrow morning," I continued. "Let's see if we can make up for lost time."

There was a smattering of cheers and I appreciated that. It had been a rough morning.

I was surprised when Marigold stood and waved at me. I had completely forgotten she was going to be here and I felt a weight lift from my shoulders. Marigold was like a ray of sunshine on a dreary day. I jogged over and gave her a hug.

"You poor thing," she said. "Another body?"

"It was awful," I admitted. I wanted to tell her about my father's possible connection to the crime, but Eric had warned us not to say anything. I trusted her completely and I usually confided in my friends about all sorts of things, but since this was about my dad being a suspect, I held off saying anything. It felt weird, though, not to share all that I was thinking with one of my best friends.

"Walk me to my car?" she said, weaving her arm through mine.

"Of course. I'm sorry you took time off work for nothing."

"I'm not," she said. "I got to see you."

I squeezed her arm. "I'm glad for that. So how's Daisy doing?"

"Fine. She's covering for me at the shop. She'll be happy to see me, what with all the Christmas shoppers we've been getting."

"Did she tell you what happened yesterday?"

She grinned. "She had the absolute best time. She thinks you've been holding out on us because there are so many good-looking men working in construction. We never knew."

"She got a big kick out of that," I said, laughing. "I think her crew really enjoyed her being here."

"Good, because she's coming back Thursday." She glanced over her shoulder at a few of my contractors as they headed for their trucks. "I may have to come with her. I see what she means about the eye candy around here."

"The guys will be happy to see you both." I hesitated, then said, "Did Daisy mention anything about Mr. Potter?"

"No," Marigold whispered, glancing around. "I just found out he was dead a little while ago. This may not sound very nice, but I can't say I'm sorry. He came into our shop a few times and he was very unpleasant. Just because his bank held the deed to our store, he thought he could boss us around, make demands, expect favors, you know? I explained that it doesn't work that way. We're not indentured servants, for goodness sake."

Honestly, the more I heard about Potter, the more amazed I was that he hadn't been murdered sooner. "I'm sorry you had to go through that. I know his temper could be nasty."

"I do sympathize with his family, of course."

"Yes, of course. Me, too." I wasn't sure how to broach the subject, so I just said it straight out: "But I wasn't talking about his death. I wanted to know if Daisy told you about their confrontation."

"Confrontation? Daisy?"

"Yes, and Mr. Potter."

"But they barely know each other."

That was what I was afraid of. "Actually, they seem to know each other better than you think."

She frowned. "What do you mean?"

"Did you know they went out on a date a while back?"

"No!" She stopped walking and gaped at me. "My aunt Daisy and Mr. Potter? On a date? There's no way."

"It's true." I glanced around. I didn't want anyone to hear us talking about Daisy's confrontation with Potter on the off chance that it would fuel speculation about Potter's murder. "And when they ran into each other yesterday, they had a big argument."

"I don't believe it," she said. "Aunt Daisy never argues. She's quite possibly the most pleasant person I've ever known."

"I agree. That's why I was so shocked when it happened."

Her eyes were wide with concern as she grabbed my hand. "Tell me everything, Shannon."

I related the conversation, including the remarkable name-calling. "She called him an old goat and a horny toad and a bug-eyed worm." I smiled in memory. "It was fantastic."

Marigold shook her head in disbelief. "I can't believe you're talking about my aunt Daisy. I've never seen her behave that way."

"That's the effect Potter had on people. She was really ticked off. He was mocking her and saying ugly things. He's just awful."

"And she hit him with her purse?"

"She tried. Unfortunately, it barely grazed his head. In fact, he just grabbed it and threw it across the lawn."

"What a toad."

I smiled at that. "But Marigold, there's more."

"Oh no. What else?"

I took a breath or two before divulging the rest. "She wouldn't go into any detail, but the night of their date, I believe he tried something and she wouldn't allow it."

She pressed her hand to her chest, breathless. "You think he tried to . . ."

"He tried to kiss her, but he didn't get anywhere."

"Good."

"It made him angry, though. He said some cruel things and I think she's still hurt by it."

"That brute." Marigold rarely showed anger, but now she was seething. "If he wasn't already dead, I'm not sure what I would do."

I gripped her hand. "I struggled with whether to tell you or not."

"I'm glad you did. And I'm going to find a way to talk to her. I'm just not sure how to approach her."

"Well, I have a suggestion."

"Anything, Shannon. You're always so smart and brave."

Smart? Brave? Nothing could have felt further from the truth. But it was nice to know my friend thought so. Still, I laughed. "And you're very kind. Crazy, but kind."

We both laughed, then Marigold sobered. "Tell me your suggestion."

"There was a witness to Daisy's confrontation with Potter, so I have a feeling that Eric Jensen may pay you a visit."

She gasped. "Are you saying Daisy is a suspect?"

"She won't be for long, believe me. But you might tell her that I warned you that Eric heard about her confrontation."

"Ah." She nodded slowly. "And that way I can ask her about her date with Mr. Potter."

"Yes. Do you think that would work?"

Her eyes narrowed in thought. "I'll let you know."

It was almost two o'clock in the afternoon when I trudged back to my truck, dragging my backpack alongside me.

The volunteers and crews had gone home for the day, but glancing down the driveway, I saw all the police cars parked on the edge of the lawn. Except for one. Eric's big black SUV was parked next to the veranda, and he and my father were getting into the car.

"What? No." I went running to the car and grabbed the passenger door handle. "Dad, what's going on?"

"I'm just going with Eric to answer some questions."

I glared at the police chief. "Are you kidding me?"

"Before I can clear him," he said with infinite patience, "I need some answers."

"I'll meet you there."

Dad squeezed my hand. "Shannon, honey, that's not necessary. You'll be waiting around the police station for hours when you could be home getting some work done."

I stared pointedly at Eric. "For hours?"

He shrugged. "As long as it takes."

His casual attitude annoyed the heck out of me and I pointed at him. "I'm following you."

"Suit yourself."

I turned and jogged back to my truck, then watched as the chief backed the SUV down the driveway and turned onto the street.

A mewing sound came from somewhere close by and I glanced around, trying to locate it. Then it stopped and I forgot all about it. Still irate, I started to toss my backpack into the back of the truck, but stopped when I noticed a large bundle of . . . something . . . in my truck bed.

Sudden chills rushed up my spine and I backed up slowly, not knowing what was inside the bundle or where it had come from.

In keeping with my foul mood, my first thought was that it was a bomb.

"You're ridiculous," I muttered. But what was it? It looked like a big pile of blankets inside a laundry hamper. Whatever it was, it didn't make sense.

I glanced around to see if anyone was nearby, preferably a cop. But all the cops were working inside the house. All of my contractors had taken off for the day. I was on my own out here.

Taking a deep, fortifying breath, I leaned over the side of the truck bed to get a better look at the bundle so I could figure out what it was. Maybe it was a Christmas present. Or a bale of cotton? Not that I'd ever seen an actual bale of cotton before, but I imagined it was thick and fluffy.

I moved to the cab door and opened it, tossing my backpack and tool belt inside. Shutting the door, I circled around to the back of the truck and reached for the tailgate—and stopped in my tracks.

The mewing returned and it sounded closer now. I wondered if the animal had crawled under my truck.

I stooped down to check but didn't see a creature hiding beneath the truck. Straightening, I lowered the tailgate and hoisted myself up into the bed, then hesitated. Was it smart to approach this thing when I had no idea what it was or where it had come from? Probably not. But it didn't look dangerous. It looked soft. Still, I was hesitant to get any closer. Who had left it here? Was it a friend or an enemy? One of my crew guys? Was it an April Fool's joke? In December? Would something jump out at me if I got within a few inches?

I returned to the idea of a Christmas present. But from whom? And why?

The mewing grew louder and more urgent. Some mama cat had her hands full, I thought with a frown. I glanced out at the tree line. Was there a new litter of kittens out there somewhere?

It didn't matter. I wasn't going to go exploring in the woods when there was something truly odd sitting right here in my truck.

I crept closer to the pile and stared, trying to figure out what it was. At least the blankets appeared clean. And pink.

The sound of kittens hushed abruptly and I felt nothing but relief. I took one more step toward the basket and the mewling suddenly erupted again. I jolted and almost fell backward.

The whimpering sounds were definitely coming from inside the basket.

Was this a joke? I pictured my friends hiding behind a tree, watching me and laughing their butts off.

"If somebody left me a bunch of kittens, it's not funny," I called out to no one in particular, then braced myself and reached for the top blanket. The soft crying turned into a pitiful wailing, growing even louder. It sounded as though there were some sort of phantom banshee living inside the pile. With a toothache, maybe.

But no, I knew what that sound meant, and it filled me with terror.

"This can't be happening," I muttered. Summoning my courage, I grabbed the blanket and pulled it open.

No way. If only it were kittens, I thought. They would be the least of my worries.

But there were no kittens. There was simply a baby.

Chapter Thirteen

A baby!

A screaming, mewling, newborn baby with a wet diaper and a bad attitude. It wore a pink, footie sleeper thingie and a pink cap, and it was wrapped in a pink blanket against the cold, so I assumed it was a girl. She had been buckled into a pint-sized car seat, also pink, and set inside the laundry basket. Her little face was red and turning even redder and I didn't know what to do. Hey, don't judge me. Just because I'm female doesn't mean I come with instinctive knowledge of tiny screaming humans. I searched the rest of the laundry basket, hoping for a bottle, some diapers maybe, or a note saying, "If found, please return me to [fill in mother's name here]."

I hadn't been around a baby this small since Lizzie's son Taz was born. I remember he was so tiny, he had to stay in the hospital for almost two months. Even though I visited with Lizzie almost every day, I couldn't remember hearing the kind of gut-wrenching wailing sounds that were coming out of this little one.

Which was my way of explaining why I had behaved so stupidly in the back of my truck. I mean, really, for a short while there, it had sounded just like a kitten. Maybe even a demon kitten. Never mind.

"Well, come here," I said, unbuckled the strap, and lifted the tiny creature into my arms. Immediately the crying stopped. I felt as if I'd accomplished something monumental as I bounced her gently on my shoulder.

"Who are you?" I asked, gazing down at her. "How long have you been sitting out here? You must be freezing. Probably hungry, too. That's not good. Do you have any food in that basket with you?"

She met my gaze with her own wide-eyed stare and I felt a punch of pure energy hit me. I held her a little tighter and marveled at the powerful bond that could be created within a heartbeat. Who would want to give that up?

"Where's your mommy?" I wondered aloud. "What's your name?"

Not only were her blankets pink, but she was wrapped from head to toe in a thick fleece pink pajama thing that covered her tiny hands and feet. It looked like a miniature sleeping bag and it even had a hood that was pulled up over the little cap she wore, completely protecting her fragile little baby head. I tugged on the zipper and saw that she was also wrapped in several thin cotton blankets, along with her diaper and a tiny undershirt. I assumed all of it was keeping her warm, but still, it wouldn't be smart to leave her out here too long.

Which begged the question: who in their right mind had left a close-to-newborn baby outside in my truck? Had anyone around here noticed someone placing a large pink bundle inside my truck bed?

I imagined whoever had done this had tried to do it

secretly, because no one had reported any strange activities happening around my truck. I figured none of the cops had seen anything, either. Nobody had come up to ask my permission.

Did the person—I assumed it was the mother—have any idea what kind of chance they were taking? There had been people all over the property today, coming and going all day long. And many of those people were cops. Someone must have seen whoever had done this.

And it was winter! I could have been working inside the house for hours. All night, maybe. This poor baby could have frozen during that time.

Which meant that whoever left the child probably knew my schedule and had counted on me showing up in time to find the baby and get her inside. So that meant it was someone I knew. Maybe. I turned and scanned the property. Was the person still here? And who was it? I didn't know anyone who had been pregnant lately.

I didn't see anyone, but the woods on both sides of the property were thick and there were plenty of places to hide. I asked myself again, who could have done it? Why would a stranger leave a baby in my truck? But then, maybe it wasn't a stranger. Except, again, I really couldn't think of anyone I knew who was pregnant.

This was a mystery.

And getting on to more practical matters, what was I supposed to do with a newborn baby? Raise it as my own child? Turn it over to the police? Was I supposed to protect it? Of course I would do that, but for how long?

Protection. Is that what the mother wanted from me? Safety, security, shelter for her newborn baby?

Was the baby in danger?

I almost laughed. A baby in danger! It sounded like

a plot straight out of a Jake Slater book. All that was missing were some ninjas and a courageous band of Navy SEALs jumping out of black ops helicopters.

The sun dipped behind a cloud and the wind picked up. The air grew chillier and I used one hand to lift my collar to keep my neck warm. I set the baby back in the car seat and buckled her securely, then slid the basket to the side of the truck. I hopped down to the ground and lifted the car seat out of the truck bed. I climbed into the backseat and struggled to secure the car seat. Finally, the seat belt cooperated and the baby looked well protected, but she still had a wet diaper so her happy cooing and gurgling would end any minute now.

I shut the passenger door and leaned against it, still thinking. Seriously, why would a mother want me to have her baby? I thought again about the possibility that the baby could be in danger. But why? A baby couldn't hurt anyone. It was so far-fetched, I had to shake my head.

But then another thought occurred. Maybe the *mother* was in danger. That made more sense than a baby being in danger. But still, why would she leave the child with me? If she was in danger, why didn't she go to the police?

I stared up at the imposing structure that was Forester House and thought of everything that had happened in the past two days. I tried to recall if I'd seen a pregnant woman anywhere on the premises. And then it hit me. Was it just a huge coincidence that this baby showed up the same day Potter was found murdered?

Had Potter been threatening the mother?

Wait a minute. Was the baby's mother the one who had *killed* Potter?

If that was the case, Potter was dead now and the

mother was out of danger. Okay, not exactly out of danger, because now the mother would be arrested for murder.

"Oh my God," I muttered as yet another thought occurred. What if Potter was the baby's father!

"Ugh, no way." I stared through the window at the baby in the basket. Nope, I refused to believe it. Just because the little darling sounded like a demon kitten when it cried, that was no reason to conclude that she was the child of the demon Mr. Potter. No child deserved that lineage.

And yet another thought suddenly occurred to me. Now that I had the baby, was *I* the one in danger?

Oh, great. More chills. Rubbing my arms, I took another quick scan of the property. It was the middle of the day, the sun was up there behind the clouds, and yet I was getting just as freaked out as if it were midnight and I was surrounded by darkness.

And besides, there were cops everywhere. Even though I couldn't see any of them right now, I knew there were at least eight or ten cops inside the house busily looking for clues to Potter's murder.

And since I was thinking about Mr. Potter again, I returned to the theory that my father was being set up to take the fall for his murder. I began to wonder, in an adjunct to that theory, if maybe I was being set up to take the fall for the crime of kidnapping the baby.

Could I get more paranoid?

But it made a certain kind of sick sense, didn't it? And if I was right, it meant that I could be in danger after all. I scanned the property one more time. So many places to hide. And so many windows. Was someone watching me?

I wasn't going to stick around and find out. Jogging

around to the driver's side, I jumped in and started the engine.

There were still police cars and a crime-scene van parked along the side of the driveway. What if they stopped me? What if they wanted to search my truck? How would I explain that someone had left me a baby without sounding like a crazy person?

I could just hear them. "Oh, reeeeally. Someone left a baby in your truck. A baby. Right. Joe, bring the strait-jacket."

Which wasn't fair. I mean, obviously I didn't make it up and I sure as heck didn't kidnap the little thing. Still, the police wouldn't be happy about this whole situation. And more important, they would take the baby away from me. That thought didn't sit right with me. Strangely enough, I already felt that she was my responsibility, so the idea that they would snatch her away was not a happy one. But of course they would, eventually.

But not right now. Which is why I had no intention of talking to the police. I put the truck in gear and drove away.

I checked my rearview mirror constantly, making sure the baby was still wrapped up in all those protective belts and buckles. After a minute or so, her eyes closed and she went to sleep.

So now I needed diapers. But I couldn't walk into a store with the baby. I'm not sure why, but until I figured out how she had come into my world, I didn't want anyone to see me with her. And besides, how did one go about buying diapers? They sold them at any supermarket, I figured, in size small. And she needed food, too. Or just milk?

I had to face the fact that I was clueless when it came to infant stuff.

The only person I knew who could help me with this important issue was Lizzie. She was a mom. And her house was a lot closer than the shopping centers out by the highway.

I was scared to death to drive much faster than ten miles an hour all the way to my friend's house. Twice someone honked at me and I wanted to yell at them, "Hey, quiet! Baby on board!"

Once I passed a police car and almost turned myself in.

As I drove through the town square, I realized it was just coming up on three o'clock in the afternoon. Lizzie would still be working at the bookshop and wouldn't be home until later this afternoon.

I wasn't about to bring the baby into her bookshop. But I didn't want to take her home until after I spoke to Lizzie and figured out how to take care of a baby. And I couldn't think of any alternative destination. Lizzie was clearly the only one of my friends who would be able to help me. So I pulled over onto a side street and called her.

"I know I'm asking a lot," I said, "but I need you to meet me at your place right now. Can you do it?"

She paused a moment, then said, "Hal can cover me for half an hour." There was another pause while she covered the phone with her hand, probably discussing the situation with Hal. Then she came back to me. "I'll meet you there in five minutes."

She hung up and I stared at the phone. Now *that* was a test of friendship. Lizzie had passed it with flying colors. I didn't even have to tell her the reason. She just said yes. I sniffled a little, feeling all *verklempt* to know I had such good friends.

I drove the rest of the way to Lizzie's and arrived a minute before her car came around the corner and pulled into the driveway. She jumped out and ran to my truck. "What's wrong? Are you all right?"

"I'm fine," I said, closing the truck door as quietly as I could. "But there's someone here who needs your help."

She glanced around, looking puzzled. "Who?"

I opened the back door and pointed to the bundle of pink joy asleep on the seat. "Her."

"You lead the most interesting life," Lizzie said as she strolled around the kitchen, patting the baby's back, trying to persuade her to burp. A while ago, when she realized what we needed, Lizzie had opened up her house for me and the baby and then jumped into her car and raced to the market. She came back with infant formula and disposable diapers. In her garage, Lizzie had found a box filled with bottles and a few dozen other baby accessories, along with her son's infant baby bouncer, which looked like a lightweight version of the car seat. The thing bounced and rocked and even vibrated, and Lizzie swore it worked miracles. She tossed the cloth bouncer cover into the washing machine while I started scrubbing the hard plastic casing on the back of the bouncer.

"I always thought my life was normal," I said, as Lizzie warmed a bottle of formula. "But I'm beginning to rethink things."

"And you truly have no idea who might've left this little angel in the back of your truck?"

I stared at the ceiling, trying to picture every female I'd met over the last year. "I got nothing. What about you? Can you think of anyone who was pregnant up until a few days ago?"

"No. And I probably see a lot more people around town on a daily basis than you do. Although you see a lot, too."

"Yeah, but I mostly work with men, so that doesn't help." I spread a couple of dish towels on the counter and placed the cleaned and disinfected car seat down to dry.

"Maybe it's one of their wives or girlfriends," she said.

"Seriously?" I thought about that for a minute. "If one of the guys had a girlfriend who was pregnant, would he really want me to raise it? Would he actually take the baby from its mother and put it in my truck? It defies comprehension."

"Boy, I'll say it does."

"You don't have to agree so quickly. I wouldn't be that bad a mother, would I?"

She grinned. "You would be a wonderful mother. I'm just teasing you."

Suddenly the baby burped and we both laughed.

"What a good girl you are," Lizzie said, rubbing her back. "Yes, you are. You're a very good girl."

I smiled. She sounded a little like me when I was talking to my dog, Robbie. "So now what do we do?"

She chuckled, shaking her head. "You really don't know much about babies, do you?"

"Only what I gleaned from watching you with Marisa and Taz. And it's been a few years since they were as tiny as this one."

"I know." She buried her face in the baby's blanket. "Oh God. She makes me nostalgic for those days."

"Oh no." I squeezed my eyes shut. "This is not good. Hal is not going to thank me for bringing up all those feelings."

"Don't worry about Hal." But then she sighed. "You know what you have to do, don't you?"

"What?" I stared at the baby, totally clueless. "Should we put her down for a nap?"

"I'm talking about calling Child Protective Services."

"Oh." I frowned. "But what if she's in danger?"

"There's no *what if*, Shannon."

"You're right." I sighed. "She's already in danger by virtue of the fact that someone left her out in my truck."

"Exactly."

I walked over to Lizzie and stood next to her, rubbing the baby's back. Now that we'd changed her diaper and fed her, she had been transformed into a sweet, happy, burbling baby.

I scowled. "I don't want her to be taken away and never see her again, you know?"

"I don't want that, either."

I gave her a hopeful look. "Maybe you could adopt her."

"Don't even think about it. Hal and I have already had that conversation. We're both counting the days until we're empty nesters."

"Oh, come on." I tossed a dish towel at her. "You love your kids. You guys have so much fun together as a family."

"We do, but you know . . . well, it would be nice to have some privacy sometime in the next ten years or so."

I smiled. "I get that."

"Still," she said, swaying slowly with the baby in her arms, "holding this little one makes me wonder if we made the right decision to stop at two."

*   *   *

While Lizzie held the baby, I made the phone call. I knew a girl from high school who worked in the Health and Human Services offices in Ukiah. They oversaw the Child Protective Services department so I thought I might talk to her first. I looked up her office number online and then placed the call. An office assistant answered the phone and I gave a vague explanation of the situation.

"I'll take your name and address," she said officiously. "We'll send someone over to pick up the child this evening."

"I'll call you back," I said, and quickly hung up the phone.

"What happened?" Lizzie asked.

I shook my head. "I'm not doing that."

"Doing what?"

I began to pace around the kitchen. "Having some anonymous civil servant pick up our baby and take her away."

"Shannon, she's not *our* baby."

"I know, I know." I tapped my fingers on the counter in nervous frustration. "I just need some time to think about this. Whoever left that baby in my truck was trusting *me* to make sure she's safe." I continued pacing, then stopped. "You must think I'm starting to go insane."

"No, I think you have already *reached* insane."

I covered my face with my hands. "You're probably right."

"Probably?"

I ignored the dig and glared at her. "Look, do you want some social worker picking her up and putting her into foster care? You've heard the horror stories."

"Shannon, she's a newborn baby. She won't go into

the foster care system. She'll be adopted by a loving couple who want a baby very badly."

"We should meet them first."

Lizzie's eyes widened and she started laughing. "Oh my God, you want to keep this baby."

"No! I don't. I mean, maybe. I mean, look at her—she's adorable. But no. No, no, absolutely not." Good God, I really was insane. I'd known this baby for less than two hours and suddenly I was lining up to be Mommy. What was wrong with me? "I can't. But look, she ended up in *my* truck, so I just want to have some input, you know? I want to know where she ends up after this. I want to know that she grows up happy. I mean, if you and Hal adopted her . . . ."

"Just get that idea out of your head."

"All right, all right." My shoulders drooped a little. "I thought it was a pretty good idea."

"Let's call Eric," Lizzie said. "He'll have some thoughts. And I don't think he would just take the baby away without discussing it with us first."

I gasped, then winced. "I'm not sure that's a good idea."

"Why?" She gave me a look. "What happened? What did you do?"

"I didn't do anything. That's the problem." I was cringing as I paced. How could I have forgotten? "I saw Eric a few hours ago and he was taking my father to police headquarters. I said I would follow and meet them there."

"Did he arrest your father?"

"I don't know."

"Well, is your dad okay?"

"I don't know!" I dropped my head down, ashamed.

"I spaced out. I was supposed to go there and wait for him. But then I found the baby and I forgot about everything else."

"Do you want to go see him now?"

"Yeah, I'd better." I reached for the baby. "I'll just take her with me."

"No way," Lizzie said, turning away. "I can take care of her for a few hours."

"Are you sure? I don't want you to get so attached that you refuse to give her up. Because Hal will blame me if that happens. And rightly so."

"He won't blame you because it's not going to happen." She walked around the kitchen island and into the living room, where she set the baby down on top of a blanket on the couch. "Because even though she's a sweet thing and I'm having lots of fun with her, I'll be able to give her up because I recognize that she doesn't belong to me."

I watched her doing all the right things. "You're so smart."

"And you're usually a lot smarter," she said, smirking. "I think you've got a sudden case of baby fever."

"Yeah, maybe," I said, frowning. "I've got to do something about that."

Lizzie sat down next to the baby and wiggled her fingers, causing the baby to gaze up at her with delight. "All I ask is that we make sure she goes to a loving couple who want her more than anything else in life. Deal?"

"Deal."

She looked up at me and squeezed my hand. "Don't worry, okay?"

"Okay." I bent over and touched the baby's soft cheek, then gave Lizzie a hug. "I'll call you."

*   *   *

"He already left?" I scanned the front-desk area, but I didn't see my father anywhere. "He went home?"

"Yes," Eric said. "He waited around for a while thinking you'd show up, but when you didn't, he called Pete. Where have you been?"

"It's a long story." Did I dare tell him? The real question was, did I dare *not* tell him? After quickly considering the ramifications of not telling Eric about the baby, I made an easy decision. "Do you have a few minutes to talk?"

"For you, always."

I laughed. "I'm not sure why."

"Always an adventure."

While leading the way down the hall to his office, he turned and asked, "Have you talked to Mac since he's been home?"

"No, I haven't seen him yet. I've been kind of busy."

He nodded. "Yeah, you've got your hands full."

"Why do you ask?"

"Just wondering." He shrugged. "Thought you might've talked to him."

"We'll talk one of these days," I said breezily.

We got to his office and he indicated the visitors' chair in front of his desk.

I paused before sitting. "Can you close the door, please?"

"Absolutely." He shut the door and moved around to sit in his big executive leather chair. "What's up?"

"Just listen to the whole story before you comment, okay?"

"That can't be a good sign," he muttered. "But I'll try."

That was all I could ask. "When I left you in the

driveway at Forester House, I had every intention of following you back here."

"You made that very clear."

"Right. So I walked back to my truck and that's when everything went kaflooey." I paused, wondering how I could explain this whole weird situation.

"I'm sitting on the edge of my seat," he said, interrupting my train of thought.

I gave him a look. "You promised you'd withhold your comments."

"I said I would try." He grinned. "Please go on."

"Okay. Well, I found something in my truck."

He looked appalled. "Not another body!"

"No! No, nothing like that." So I told him the story of how I'd found the baby in the basket and about Lizzie and about my phone call to social services.

"And there's no way we can just hand this poor baby over to some nameless Child Services person," I said, "without first trying to find the mother and find out why she would leave her newborn child in my truck. I mean, something must be really wrong. And I've got some theories."

He managed to keep from rolling his eyes. "I would be shocked if you didn't."

I was impressed that he hadn't immediately picked up the phone and called Child Protective Services himself. So I went ahead and listed all my theories, starting with the baby possibly being in danger and ending with *me* being in danger. "I admit that might be a stretch. But the mother could be in danger."

"Anything's possible," he murmured. "But why wouldn't she go to the police?"

"Maybe she's afraid."

"Of what?"

I thought about it. "Of the father?"

He gave an equivocating nod. "Maybe. But why would she choose your truck? Do you think you know her?"

"I have no idea. I don't know anyone who was pregnant recently."

"So again, why your truck?"

"That brings me to my personal favorite theory. See, what if the baby was kidnapped and then put into my truck to make it look like I was the one who kidnapped her?"

"I can see why that would be your favorite."

"Are you being snarky?"

"Absolutely." He grinned, but then sobered. "In all seriousness, you must know this woman, Shannon. Why else would she single you out?"

"I don't know, but if my theory is right and I'm being set up to take the fall for the crime of kidnapping, it goes right along with my other theory that my father was set up to make it look like he murdered Potter and stole Heather's bracelet."

"So someone's out to destroy your family."

"When you say it out loud like that, it does sound a little sketchy."

"Definitely sketchy."

I agreed with him, but still. "Okay, so you tell me: what was a baby doing in the back of my truck?"

"Good question, and I intend to find the answer."

"I appreciate that." I squirmed for a moment, then plunged ahead. "So you let my dad go home?"

"Yeah."

I waited, but he didn't give anything else away. I tried

a different tack. "You said earlier that you were trying to prove he was innocent."

"I am. We're still gathering evidence, but it might take some time."

"I understand. And I appreciate everything you're doing."

He looked steadily at me. "We'll find out who did this, Shannon. All of it."

"I hope so. But meanwhile, what should we do about the baby?"

"I'm going to have to call Child Protective Services, but they'll probably let me use my discretion for today. Not sure what'll happen tomorrow." His expression was solemn. "Tell the truth now. Would you like to keep her overnight?"

It was a difficult decision and I chewed on my lip until I settled on my answer. "If it's okay with everyone, I'd like to ask Lizzie to continue taking care of her. At least until we can find the mother or find a suitable couple to adopt her."

"Lizzie?" He sat back in his chair, surprised. "Is she okay with that?"

"I think so. And if she's not, then I'll keep her myself."

"And what about Hal?"

I frowned. "I'm not sure."

He pushed back from his desk. "Let's go find out, shall we?"

I followed Eric over to Lizzie and Hal's, where he sat with both of them and made sure they were willing to take care of the baby for a few days. Eric told us that on the drive over he'd contacted the head of Child Protective Services to explain the situation. The person in charge knew our police chief and trusted him to oversee things, but said they would send a case worker out to check on the child sometime tomorrow.

I glanced around the living room and noticed that Lizzie and Hal had already pulled some other baby things from the garage. There was a mobile attached to the bouncer and I spied the carved wooden cradle they'd used for both of their children. I admit it made me a bit sniffly to see how quickly they had made a temporary home for the little one.

"Does she have a name?" Eric asked.

"I'm calling her Angel," Lizzie said, and glanced at me. "Is that okay?"

I beamed a smile at all of them. "It's perfect."

Chapter Fourteen

I called my father on the drive home to make sure he was okay. He assured me that everything was hunky-dory, as he put it.

"Pete's here and I'm beating his butt at poker."

"Sounds like a perfect evening." I turned onto my street and grinned at the stunning array of Christmas lights on Mrs. Higgins's house. Dad's RV wasn't in my driveway, so I figured he was still parking it over by the marina. "I'm sorry I didn't make it to the station, Dad. Something came up and I was forced to take care of it."

"No problem, kiddo. Pete came and got me and treated me to a burger on the way home."

"Okay. I'm relieved that it worked out."

"You bet."

"Was Eric nice to you?"

He chuckled. "He's a good guy. He knows I didn't do this."

"Of course you didn't." I pulled into the driveway and came to a stop. "Will I see you tomorrow morning?"

"Bright and early and ready to work."

"That reminds me," I said, grimacing. "I hate to say it, but they probably won't let you use your tool chest for a few days."

"No worries, honey. I've got another one."

"I know you do." I was pleased by the easy way he was handling things. "I'll see you tomorrow."

Thanks to all the uplifting things that had happened with Angel and Lizzie and Hal and Eric and my dad, I was actually starting to feel a little Christmas spirit awakening inside me. I climbed the steps to the kitchen door, walked into the house, and was greeted enthusiastically by Robbie and Tiger.

"Hi, kids," I said, bending down to scratch and ruffle their fur. "I'm happy to see you, too."

My heart felt warm and cozy in my chest as I turned to lock the door, then I noticed there were lights on in Mac's apartment. He was definitely home and it hurt to realize I didn't have a clue how to handle our inevitably awkward first meeting. And that's when my fledgling Christmas spirit fizzled and fell to the earth.

Nine Shopping Days Until Christmas

I woke up the next morning surprised to find that I'd slept as soundly as I had. I'd been afraid of tossing and turning all night, thinking and worrying about Mac and the murder and the baby and the Forester House project and everything else going on in my world. But instead, I slept like, well, a baby.

"Cute," I murmured, smiling at the thought of baby Angel. I wondered if Hal and Lizzie had gotten any sleep at all—and was instantly guilt-ridden. Angel had probably kept them awake off and on all night long.

I tied my hair up and took a quick shower, then dressed in my usual uniform of jeans, Henley, down vest, and work boots. That was me, a real fashion statement. But hey, at least everything was clean.

I sat down at the kitchen table to drink my coffee and eat a piece of toast with peanut butter. Robbie sat at attention right next to me, waiting for any crumbs that might fall on the floor.

"I already fed you," I explained. "So you know you're not getting any of my food."

But he continued to stare up at me and finally, after I'd finished my toast—because he really wasn't getting any of it—I patted my lap and he jumped up.

"You're the best boy in the world, aren't you?"

He barked joyfully and leaned against my chest to lick my cheek. I was pretty sure he just did it so he could breathe in the sultry scent of peanut butter and maybe lap up a few errant toast crumbs, but I was okay with that.

"Yes you are. You're the best." I buried my face in his soft, clean fur and whispered, "I love you, Robbie Roy."

Tiger wound herself around my ankles and I laughed. "I love you too, Tiger Lily."

After cleaning up my dishes and adding more water to their bowls, I left the house and headed for the job site. The sky was dark gray and rain was threatening to pour down, but I felt happy anyway. On the drive over, I called Lizzie to make sure everyone had survived the night. "No worries. We all survived and we're all in love with Angel. Especially Marisa."

"I'm glad."

"But given all the mystery surrounding the way the baby was found in your truck, I'm afraid to leave the house with her. I'm going to call Eric to double-check, but I think I'm going to be housebound for the next few days."

"I never thought of that," I said. "I'm sorry."

"It's okay. Hal's happy to cover the store and we have extra Christmas help this week. And we love having Angel here. Marisa didn't want to leave for school this morning, but I'm a terrible mom and forced her to go."

"You're the best mom ever," I assured her. "I'll check in with you later and I'll stop by after work to see if you need anything."

"Thanks, honey."

Eric's SUV was parked at the side of the driveway when I arrived at Forester House and I experienced a long moment of apprehension. Had they found another body? Was he going to close down my site for a second day? With a heavy sigh, I grabbed my backpack and tool belt and walked to the large glass doors at the front of the house.

Eric was just coming through the foyer and he opened the door for me.

"Good morning, Chief," I said. "Are we cleared to work this morning?"

"Yes."

"Hooray! Thank you."

"I just wanted to check in with my crime-scene guys first and they reported that everything is good to go in the rest of the house."

"Great."

"But the ballroom and the pantry are still off-limits."

"I figured as much," I said. I had already worked out some contingencies, so I knew we'd be back on track within a day or so. "I'll keep everyone out of there until you give me the word."

"Good. I'll be in and out of there throughout the day, and I'll have at least one tech on the scene at all times."

"Okay. I feel safer knowing you're all within screaming distance."

"Always happy to be of service," he said, saluting me.

I smiled, then asked, "Any idea when we'll be able to get in there? I've got at least a week's worth of work to do with a full crew."

"Shouldn't be more than another day or two."

"Okay, thanks."

Wade showed up a few minutes later and we sat in the foyer, going over the lists of jobs and schedules. We had already chosen the apartments where my Dad and his crew could help out. I didn't want them having to climb the stairs all day, so they were all being assigned to the first floor rooms. I'd moved Sean and Douglas up to the attic to help Blake get caught up on the framing and drywall.

Wade checked his watch. "I wonder if any of the volunteers from yesterday will show up today."

"I hope so. I have a feeling we'll need their help after losing a day of work."

Wade's eyes widened. "Um . . ."

"What? You think we should cut them loose?" I glanced down at my tablet. "I was hoping we could get a few of them to . . . what's wrong with you?"

He shook his head. "Nothing. I've got to go check on . . . something." He ran across the foyer, dashed up the stairs, and disappeared on the second floor.

"What in the world is up with him?" I muttered.

"Hello, Shannon."

Oh. My. God. My heart pounded as I whipped around. "Mac."

I had to catch my breath. He was even more handsome than I remembered, if that was possible. He wore a denim shirt with black jeans and boots. His hair was a little longer and he looked a bit leaner, maybe from all the traveling he'd been doing. I wanted to throw my arms around him and just hold him, but those days were over.

"Long time, no see," he said.

"Yes." My throat was as dry as a desert. "Um, welcome back."

"Thanks."

And wasn't this the most sparkling conversation two people had ever had? Where was a wormhole I could crawl into?

"Hope you had a happy Thanksgiving," I said, grasping for topics.

"Yeah. You, too."

If this got any more inane, we would both fall asleep. I noticed a couple of my contractors walking up the long driveway and sighed. "I should get to work."

"Wait," he said.

"What?"

"Take a walk with me."

"I, um, shouldn't."

He took my hand in his. "Come on."

"Okay."

We walked out the front door and down the steps, then onto the lawn. I tried not to dwell on how good it felt to hold his hand. Even though I had pictured this moment in my mind for weeks now, I couldn't think of anything to say. I tried out a few lines in my head, but nothing seemed to feel right.

I've missed you.

Why did you stay away so long?

Why won't you stay here forever?

Nope. None of those would do. We would just have to stumble through our stilted conversation, say our good-byes, and wish each other well. And that was just heart-breaking to me.

He stopped walking and turned to face me. "I want to tell you a story."

"Oh. All right. But . . ." A story was a whole lot better than him saying he wanted to say good-bye forever. Although I suppose we were just postponing the inevitable. I glanced back at the house, wondering if Wade was staring out the library window. Probably. This was good juicy stuff here.

"This won't take long," he assured me, noticing my fleeting glance over his shoulder.

"It's fine," I said. "If anyone needs me, they know where I am."

He took a deep breath and began his story. "You might remember that, about two months ago, I left for New York to see my agents."

"Yes."

"I had been there less than a week when I ran into Whitney and her girlfriend."

"Whitney? Whitney Gallagher? She was in New York?"

"Yeah."

That couldn't be good, I thought. My shoulders were so tight, I was starting to shake. "Do you know who the girlfriend was?"

"Some blonde."

It was an easy guess. "Jennifer?"

"Yeah, that's her. She didn't say much, just snickered a lot."

"That's Jennifer." Great. If Whitney was the Evil Queen, then her best friend Jennifer was the troll who lived under the drawbridge and did the queen's dirty work. "So what happened?"

"I was walking out of my agent's office and there they were, standing on the sidewalk. It was a complete coincidence. They said they'd come to town for a long weekend to shop and visit another one of Whitney's old friends."

"How fun for them," I said, trying to keep the sarcasm out of my voice. "I had no idea."

"It's not something Whitney would've told you."

"Not likely." I pasted a smile on my face. "So, did you all go out for dinner or something?" *And why are you telling me this?* I wondered, but I sensed that if I asked, he would ask me to be patient. It wasn't easy.

"No," he said, "but we did duck into a coffee shop and spent an hour chatting. To tell the truth, I went a little overboard at the sight of a familiar face from Lighthouse Cove. I wanted to hear everything that was happening back home. I wanted to hear about you."

"But . . . you could've called." I wanted to swallow my tongue, I sounded so pathetic.

He held up his hand. "Let me finish the story."

"All right. Go ahead." Just as well we both ignored my woeful whimpering.

"Whitney seemed eager to tell me about a new relationship that had everyone in town talking." He scowled as he spoke. "She was delighted, couldn't say enough great things about the lovey-dovey couple. She went on and on about how these two people were clearly meant for each other. How happy they were. She wondered when they would set the date to get married. Her girl-friend jumped in, too. They were both giggly over the news."

I frowned, trying to think back a few months. "I wonder who she was talking about."

"Shannon," he said gently, "she was talking about you . . . and Eric."

"What?" I shrieked. "Are you kidding me?" I whipped around and paced away from him, angrily stomping on the ground, back and forth, back and forth. I couldn't speak. I couldn't think—except to wonder if I was killing the grass from all this frenetic pacing. If so, I was sorry about that. I only wished it was Whitney's head beneath my feet. Yes, that was a bloodthirsty thought, but could you blame me?

How dare she say such a thing to Mac? And poor Mac would believe her because she could be so convinc-ing, so sugary sweet, and so darned good at acting like the concerned friend.

I sincerely wanted to beat her with a stick. Besides avenging Mac, maybe a good smacking would prove to Whitney that I wasn't quite as sickeningly *nice* as she thought I was. And why was being *nice* such a bad thing, anyway? I felt myself shaking from all the anger I'd tamped down over so many years of having to deal with Whitney's lies. I was no longer sure I could keep all that rage from rising up and lashing out.

Mac was watching me carefully so I took some deep breaths and tried to speak rationally. "You do know she was lying, right?"

He grimaced. "I didn't at the time, but I do now."

I stared at his expression. "So you believed her." I knew it already, but it still took my breath away to think about it. "Wow."

Mac Sullivan, world-class tough guy, former Navy SEAL, and creator of the world's most dangerous hero, had fallen for Whitney's lies. I'd always known the woman was spiteful, but she was more than that. She was downright vicious.

"Yeah, I believed her." He shook his head in disgust. "She can really spin a tale, I'll give her that much."

"But none of it's true."

"I know that. A part of me probably knew it when I first heard it. But I was on foreign ground there, Irish. I couldn't get my bearings. I don't know how else to explain it."

I hadn't felt this much antipathy toward Whitney since she destroyed my relationship with Tommy. But that had been high school stuff and I was long over it. This latest trick she'd pulled on Mac, though, was the last straw as far as my tolerance went. I had the strongest urge to whip out my phone and call Tommy to fill him in on all of Whitney's secrets. I would gladly let him know that his father-in-law was broke and that his home was in jeopardy. But that would be stooping to Whitney's level and I refused to go there.

Besides, I wouldn't want to hurt Tommy that way.

"So that's why you never called?" I said. "You never wrote? You just believed the words of my worst enemy. Why, Mac?"

"Look, Irish." He grabbed my hand again and I tried to pull away, but he held on tight. "You're very important to me. I'll tell you the truth—I've never felt like this before."

I blinked at him, unable to speak.

He hurried on. "When I first left for New York, it was weird. All I wanted to do was jump back on a plane and come home to you. And that's not like me. I've always enjoyed traveling; I like adventures, meeting new people and seeing new places. And this was the first time I didn't feel that way. I was homesick and it was frankly baffling to me."

I wanted to hug him and tell him all was forgiven. But honestly, I wasn't sure all *was* forgiven. Not yet.

"I fought the feeling," Mac said. "Forced myself to go out and enjoy the city, see old friends and meet new ones. I mean, I'd only been gone a few days, but still, when I ran into Whitney and what's-her-name, I was so delighted to see someone from Lighthouse Cove, I wasn't thinking straight. I wanted to talk about you and have them tell me everything was okay back home. I guess that made me susceptible to her lies. I should've been paying better attention, but my head was all muddled up. When she told me about you and your new squeeze, it hit me like a shot to my kneecaps. It was awful. I was baffled and hurt and didn't know how to deal with it."

"I'm sorry, Mac."

"Don't be," he said tightly. "I was stupid to believe her. If it makes you feel any better, I was sick to my stomach for days afterward. Devastated."

"That's something, at least," I said, nodding. "I really do feel better."

He chuckled. "I deserve that. I'm a bonehead."

"Yeah, you are. First, for believing anything Whitney says. And second, for thinking I would do that to you. Because I wouldn't."

"There's more to the story."

I sighed. "I'm afraid to hear it."

"Oh, it gets better," he murmured. "When I finally got home the other night, the first person I tracked down was Eric. I congratulated him and he didn't know what I was talking about. When I told him what I'd heard, he was horrified. He adamantly denied the whole thing."

"He didn't have to be so adamant about it," I muttered.

Mac laughed. "Let's just say he was as baffled as I was."

Now I knew why Eric asked me last night if I'd seen Mac yet. Interesting.

"And earlier this morning," Mac continued, "I went to Whitney's house to talk to her."

"Really." I folded my arms across my chest and waited for it. "This ought to be good."

"She started to cry."

I rolled my eyes. "Naturally. What a drama queen."

"She insisted she was planning to confess everything to me."

"Oh, sure."

"She told me something I didn't quite understand. She said that when you didn't betray her to Tommy earlier that day, she knew she had to make things right with you."

I would have laughed if I weren't so upset. "Oh, please. She's just so full of it."

"Yeah, she is. But I finally got her to admit that she'd actually planned to track me down while they were in New York. Which wasn't too hard to do, frankly, since I'd been spending every morning since I got there in meetings at my agent's office. It would be easy to look up the address. So I walked out one day and there they were."

"As though it were a happy coincidence." I sounded bitter but I didn't care.

He shook his head, scowling. "The whole thing was an elaborately planned, deliberate lie."

"Welcome to my world."

He nudged me closer, weaving his arm through mine until we were linked together. I tried to ignore the fact that he smelled like heaven. He continued, "She begged my forgiveness and I told her the only way she could make it up to me was to face you and confess everything."

"I won't hold my breath."

"I wouldn't, either." He leaned his head against mine. "Look, I don't expect you to pardon me anytime soon for being such a dolt, but the truth is, I . . . I love you, Irish. I want to be with you. I want us to have a future together."

I sucked in a breath, unable to speak.

"I just hope you'll find a way to forgive me someday for being such a freaking idiot."

I sighed. "I've already forgiven you."

"Wait." He pressed his finger to my lips. "Give me a second. I want to savor this moment." He closed his eyes and took in the cool morning air. When he opened them, he said, "Thank you. You make me happy."

"I'm glad." I touched his cheek. "Life is too short to spend it being miserable."

"You can say that again."

"I'm sorry we were both played by Whitney," I said. "But hey, we'll get over it and be stronger for the experience."

His eyes narrowed in introspection. "You know, I've written diabolical characters, brazen killers, shameless thieves and liars, but I've never come up against someone like her."

"Scary, isn't she?"

"I don't know how you've put up with her crap all these years and still maintained an amazingly lovely heart. You're sort of like a pearl, aren't you? All that irritation makes you even more beautiful."

"Okay, now you're being ridiculous." I laughed and tried to pull away. "I need to get back to work."

"No, wait." He was laughing, too, and grabbed me around the waist. "I'm a writer. I know a cheesy metaphor when I hear one."

"Cheesy is the word for it."

"Let me try again. You're a delicate pearl that grows stronger and more courageous with each irritant you're forced to deal with."

"You got the delicate part right, anyway."

"And the irritation?"

I laughed again. "Oh, yeah. I get plenty of that."

He gazed at me, shaking his head. "I'm crazy about you."

"You're just crazy."

He kissed me then and I didn't care who was watching. I wrapped my arms around him, happy to be exactly where I wanted to be. It was about time.

"Finally!" someone shouted.

Mac and I both stepped back and I watched his teenaged niece Callie come racing across the grass.

"Shannon," she cried and launched herself into my arms, "I'm so happy to see you."

"Callie," I said, hugging her, "are you visiting for the holidays?"

"Yes. Uncle Mac stayed with us at Thanksgiving and I begged to come back here with him. So we have to go shopping, okay? Your hair looks great. Do you like mine? I'm growing it out."

"It looks beautiful," I said fondly. I had met Mac's niece when she visited him last year. I had hoped she would spend the summer here, but instead, her high-powered lawyer mother had sent her on a European tour. I hadn't realized how much I'd missed her until this moment. I gave her another hug. "I've really missed you, Callie."

"Oh, that's the nicest thing. I've missed you, too. You look so cool in your contractor outfit. Is that a leather tool belt? Uncle Mac, isn't that cool?"

He tried to hide a smile. "It's very cool."

She gave him a soft slap on the arm. "It took you long enough, you know. I had to sit in the car and watch. It was killing me."

"I had a lot of groveling to do," he said, gazing at me.

Callie looked beyond me at the imposing mansion. "Uncle Mac said this place is being fixed up for some families and you need volunteers."

"That's right."

"Can we help?"

"Absolutely," I said as the three of us linked arms and walked back to the house. "There's so much to get done before Christmas Eve."

"Why don't you have any Christmas lights up on your house?" she asked. "Do you have a tree yet?"

Because I didn't have much Christmas spirit before this moment, I thought, but those feelings were gone and I was brimming with holiday joy. "I'm planning to buy a tree and decorate the house this weekend. Do you want to help?"

"Yes! Can we help, Uncle Mac?"

He smiled at me. "Absolutely."

"Yay!" Callie clapped her hands together. "Oh, let's drink hot chocolate with marshmallows, okay?"

She was practically bouncing with excitement and I realized again how much I'd missed her. "I can't think of anything I'd rather do."

Callie stopped and stared at everyone who walked through the foyer. Two of my contractors strolled by talking about a load-bearing wall in one of the bedrooms. An electrician was busy testing the new GFCI outlets in the hall. Sean rushed past us carrying a stepladder.

"Wow," she whispered.

"It gets pretty busy around here," I said.

"Yeah. Hey, can I wear a tool belt, Uncle Mac?" she asked, glancing from me to Mac. "I think they're sexy."

I noticed Mac's look of alarm and laughed. "I'll see what I can do."

I decided to spend the morning with Mac and Callie and took them upstairs to apartment seven. This was a large, sunny room in the southeast corner with a balcony over-looking the back lawn and a view of the tall redwood and eucalyptus trees that lined one side of the property. The crew had spent all day yesterday pulling up the wood floor because most of the slats had sustained sig-nificant water damage from a leak in one of the big win-dows on the south side of the room.

Since the guys hadn't begun to work on all the hair-line cracks in the walls and ceiling, Mac and Callie were happy to do the job with me. Mac was an old hand at spackling, so I set him up to work on the ceiling cracks and concentrated on Callie. I showed her how to enlarge the thinner cracks slightly, using a small spackle knife. We did that in order to create enough of a crevice to hold the spackling compound.

After digging out a crack, I showed her how to use a soft, clean paintbrush to get rid of all the dust and debris in the trench.

Then, with our spackling knives, we scooped some compound out and applied it at an angle along the crack, using smooth, swift strokes, filling it completely and then feathering the edges with the knife so that it blended into the wall. It might take a few scoops to get the crack completely filled.

Once we'd gone around the room filling cracks and the compound was thoroughly dry, it was time to sand it down to a smooth finish. I had Callie put on a surgical mask and protective glasses to avoid getting the fine dust in her nose, mouth, and eyes.

I preferred to use a single piece of fine-grit sandpaper wrapped around a small wood block, rather than an electric sander. I wanted to control the pressure and feel the surface of the wall beneath my fingers. I showed her how too much sanding could create a slight depression, and if that occurred, we would have to add more spackle and go through the entire process again.

"Now, sometimes you can avoid sanding altogether," I said. "It's all in the way you apply the spackle and then scrape it with the wide edge." I demonstrated the technique and had her touch the wall.

"It's smooth."

"It's almost perfect," I said, then shrugged. "Frankly, even when it's this smooth, I'll still sand it a bit. You want the smoothest, glassiest surface possible when you finally paint."

"I've never painted a room before," she said. "I think I would like it."

"None of the rooms are ready to paint yet, but I'll set you up to do it when we reach that phase."

I looked up and smiled at Mac, who was spackling the ceiling. In general, when it came to spackling, ceilings weren't as much fun as walls because you were forced to use your muscles differently, stretching your arms up over your head instead of straight out in front of you. Your hands could get numb and you had to take breaks more often. It got old pretty fast, but that was the nature of the work.

"Isn't this fun, Uncle Mac?" Callie asked.

Mac grinned at his niece. "Most fun ever."

That night, I invited Mac and Callie to join me at Lizzie's for a few minutes, just to see the baby.

Lizzie opened the door and immediately gave Mac a big hug. "I'm so glad you're home."

"Me, too," he said. "I'm looking forward to the book signing this weekend."

"Thank you again for agreeing to do it," Lizzie said. "Judging from my customers' reactions, I think it's going to be standing room only."

"Music to my ears," he said with a grin.

"Mine, too."

She led the way into the house and that's when I saw all of my girlfriends standing around the kitchen island, sipping wine and munching on chips and dips.

"Are you having a party?" I asked.

Lizzie glanced around. "I might've invited a few people over."

"A few?" I repeated, laughing. A quick glance revealed at least eight of our friends, most chatting with Hal while a few sat on the couch to play with Angel, who was perched on the large coffee table in her bouncer.

Callie said, "I want to see the baby," and headed for the living room.

Mac and I joined the group at the kitchen island, where Hal poured two glasses of wine and handed them to us.

"Marigold and Lizzie were filling us in on the Potter situation," Jane said. "I still can't believe another murder happened in our town."

"I can believe it with Potter," Gus said cynically. Augustus Peratti was one of my oldest friends and also my auto mechanic. And he was dating Emily.

"Did you have dealings with him?" I asked.

"Didn't everybody?" Gus shook his head. "I hated that guy and he knew it. He tried to turn down a business loan."

"That jerk," I muttered. Gus had the most successful auto shop in the county, but Potter wouldn't care about that. He was always on a power trip. Always looking to screw up someone's life.

"Luckily my dad knows where the bodies are buried," Gus said. "He paid him a visit, and don't you know, that loan came through the next day."

"Good," Lizzie said. "I'm so glad he's dead." It took her a minute before she realized what she'd said and quickly began to protest. "I mean, I didn't kill him or anything."

I laughed. "Of course you didn't. I just wish I knew who did, because my father's currently in the hot seat."

"Your father wouldn't hurt a flea."

"No, he wouldn't, but there's circumstantial evidence that says otherwise." And I'd already said too much.

"No one in town liked Mr. Potter," Marigold said. "If your father is arrested, we'll all meet at the police station and protest."

"Thank you," I said, meeting her gaze. I could tell she was thinking of her aunt Daisy at that moment.

"What can we do to help?" Jane asked. "You know we can find out more information in a day than Eric can in a week."

"I'd rather you didn't say that to his face," I said, laughing. "But since you ask, I think Marigold's right. Everyone in town hated the man, so maybe we could all start asking around. Discreetly, of course. And if we could find out where certain people were the night Potter died, we might be able to narrow the suspect list. It would be easy enough to find out if anyone had reason to want him dead."

Hal snorted. "It's easy, because everyone in town had a grudge against him."

"Right," Gus said. "So all you've got to do is start a conversation with anyone and it'll wind its way around to the subject of Potter."

Lizzie blinked. Emily and I exchanged glances. Marigold and Jane looked at me and both of them rolled their eyes.

Emily, Jane, Marigold, Lizzie, and I had done some discreet detective work around town in the past, but this was the first time the guys had ever wanted to get involved. They were the ones who were always warning us to be careful.

Mac caught the exchanges and laughed. "Something's going on around here and I want in on it."

So after a quick check to make sure that Callie and

Marisa were happy to watch the baby, we gathered around the dining room table to discuss what to do.

"His secretary, Patrice, might know something," I said, staring at the impromptu list I'd made up. "Anybody know her well enough to start a conversation?"

"I know Patrice," Gus said. "Want me to approach her?"

Emily smiled. "She's sure to bare her soul if you do."

"Good idea," I said, chuckling as I made a note. Gus's reputation with the ladies around town was legendary—until he met Emily.

Marigold sat forward. "I'll talk to Daisy and try to get more information out of her. She's known Potter forever, although I never realized that until Shannon told me. But she might know someone who was particularly angry with him. Someone besides me, of course."

"Does anyone know any of the Santa Clauses?" I asked. "Not that I suspect them, but it couldn't hurt to talk to them."

"Steve Shore volunteers at the same soup kitchen where we donate our day-old bread and pastries," Emily said. "I'll talk to him."

Nobody knew the other Santas, so I volunteered to approach Slim and any of the others if they came around again.

"I'll talk to some of the other shopkeepers on the square," Lizzie said. "I know for a fact that most of them have been hassled by Potter once or twice in the past." She shook her head. "God, he was a jerk."

"Too true," Emily said.

"Yes, he was," Jane added quietly. "He and my uncle Jesse had a few run-ins over the years. I couldn't stand the man."

I glanced around and met Mac's gaze. He'd been quiet so far, but now his eyebrows were raised in concern.

"What is it?" I asked.

He gritted his teeth and looked around the table. "I'm not sure you realize that, based on tonight's conversation, each one of you could be considered a murder suspect."

Chapter Fifteen

Eight Shopping Days Until Christmas

Early the next morning, I walked into the Forester House foyer and found a bag hanging from the chandelier in the center of the room.

A bag. A plastic shopping bag. Dangling from one arm of the chandelier.

"What in the world?"

I had to admit, the sight gave me a chill. Sure, it was just an innocuous plastic bag, but it was weird. What was it doing there? I glanced around but knew I was alone in this part of the house. I'd seen the crime-scene guy's car and I figured he was working in the ballroom in the back of the house, so I doubted he would know anything about this. But I would find out for sure, as soon as I figured out what the heck was in the bag.

I walked down the hall to apartment one, found the stepladder, and dragged it out to the foyer. Climbing up, I removed the bag from the fixture. Back on the ground,

I hesitated to look inside, then mentally berated myself. What was I expecting, a snake? Of course not.

I took a quick peek and blinked. "What in the world?"

I held the bag over the red couch and let the contents spill out. There was a cellophane package containing three pairs of pink onesies, a pink pacifier, and a soft pink bunny. Obviously they were gifts for the baby.

And how strange was that?

"Very strange," I muttered. Except for the friends I'd seen last night and the baby's mother, whoever she was, nobody knew about Angel. Did the baby's father know about her? I wondered.

So how did this bag get into the house and onto the chandelier? Had the mother convinced one of my workers to hang it up there sometime in the night? Or had she snuck in here to do it herself? If so, how had she gotten inside the house? And why? The items were inexpensive and easily found at any store, so there was no urgency that I could see. It seemed an almost whimsical act, and that didn't track with her previous crime of essentially abandoning her baby in a truck.

Beyond all those questions, hanging this plastic shopping bag on the foyer chandelier where it was the first thing anyone would notice was just plain weird. Such an odd, seemingly random thing to do. And that's what convinced me to call Eric.

He arrived fifteen minutes later, clearly intrigued by the mystery of the plastic bag.

"I tried not to touch anything," I said. "Except for the bag itself."

"Good." He leaned over the couch and stared at the contents of the bag. Pulling a pen out of his pocket, he used it to nudge the plastic-wrapped onesies this way and that. "This might yield some prints."

"I hope so. Not that I want to get anyone in trouble, but the prints might lead us to Angel's mom."

"Charlie is in the ballroom," Eric muttered to himself.

"Yes, I saw his car out front. He got an early start."

He nodded. "I'll have him come process all of this stuff."

He used his phone to call Charlie, and a minute later the crime-scene tech walked down the hall to take care of the pink baby evidence. I still couldn't see how the contents of the plastic shopping bag had anything to do with the larger mystery of Mr. Potter's murder, but if it helped solve the puzzle of baby Angel, I would be very grateful.

Later that morning, I grabbed Wade and we walked over to the Foresters' garage to see what was inside. I hadn't seen April the Santa Slapper in three days, but I was still wondering about her. Was she just overly curious or had she been looking for something specific upstairs in the attic? Since everything had been moved into the garage, I wanted to hunt around to see if there was something in particular that might have drawn her to the house. She had to be too young to have known any of the Foresters, but maybe there was a family connection. Or maybe she was just an opportunist. Or a thief?

I didn't hold out much hope of finding anything important among the old furniture and furnishings inside the garage, but I was determined to give it a shot anyway. Frankly, April's presence here had been bugging me since the sound of that slap on Monday morning. If nothing else, it would be nice to expose her story and possibly vindicate Slim.

For an hour we searched through the furniture and trunks, but found nothing. Not to say there weren't some valuable items. I knew most of the furniture would get a good price in an antique store. But as far as we could tell there was nothing hiding inside, like a last will and testament or a deed to a gold mine.

After combing through everything, we still couldn't figure out what April might have been looking for, if anything. Maybe this was a wild-goose chase after all. Maybe she had just pretended to search around the attic, when she was actually looking for ways to avoid working. Who knew what she was really doing here? She was such an oddball.

That afternoon, I left the job site early to stop by Lizzie's and visit with Angel. The baby was just waking up from a nap.

"She's so lucky to have you taking care of her," I said to Lizzie as I watched her pull a tiny T-shirt over the baby's head. "You're so good with her."

"I'm the lucky one," Lizzie murmured.

"We're all lucky," I said. "But I feel so guilty for handing her over to you. I hope she hasn't caused too much havoc in your life."

She waved away my concerns. "I told you, we're having the time of our lives."

"I hope so."

She lifted the baby and held her out for me. "There. She has a clean diaper and is all ready to visit with you."

I cuddled the little one tightly. "Such a sweet little thing."

Lizzie patted Angel's back. "Let's make sure we find her a good home."

"I promise we will."

After a quick but happy half hour of holding the baby and talking to Lizzie, I took off for my appointment at Hennessey House with Jane. Her small hotel was quickly becoming known as the most fashionable inn along the northern California coast. It was a beautifully restored Victorian mansion with all the amenities and spectacular food, but I knew it was Jane's welcoming personality that truly made the place a hit with travelers.

"I appreciate you helping me with the interviews," I said as she led the way to a small, tasteful conference room at the end of the second floor hall. "But are you sure you're ready for this?"

"It's going to be fun," she insisted as we sat down at the table. The room was a tranquil shade of light, sage green and the furniture was lovingly refurbished and authentically Victorian. Jane poured us both a glass of water and we chatted about Angel and the progress made at Forester House. Amazingly we managed to avoid talking about Mr. Potter for ten blessed minutes until Jane's assistant walked in.

"The first interviewee is here," she announced.

"Please send him in," Jane said, exchanging a quick glance with me.

Ninety seconds later, the door opened and Santa Claus walked in.

"Ho ho ho!" he said, then stopped. "Wait. Shannon?"

I scrutinized his face, trying to see beyond the beard. "Steve? Is that you?"

"It's me," he said with a laugh, patting his belly. "I didn't know you'd be here."

"I work with Jane on the festival committee." I introduced him to Jane, then went through a brief explanation of Steve's and my connection through my dad and Forester House and the Santa Brigade. I glanced back at Steve. "I didn't think you'd be trying out for the parade since you work at the mall."

"The mall closes early on Christmas Eve so I'll have plenty of time to make it to the parade." He grinned. "If you choose me, that is. The entire Brigade is downstairs waiting to be interviewed."

I frowned. "Everyone's here?"

"How many is everyone?" Jane asked cautiously.

"There are ten of us," Steve said, his voice brimming with pride.

I saw the stunned look on Jane's face and decided we needed to talk. Turning to Santa Steve, I said, "I'm so glad you're available for the parade. Jane and I have a few things to discuss, and then I'll be in touch."

He gave me a hug and left the room. And that's when I laid out my brilliant plan to Jane.

From Jane's, I drove to the community center where our Thursday empowerment class took place. I was pleased to see that Lauren, Alyssa and Kailee's friend, was feeling better. She was still pale and a bit bloated—from the antibiotics, she explained—but it was good to see the happy threesome back together again. The DIY subject of the day was: how to build a brick wall. We had been given permission to build a small, decorative brick wall in the community garden. First I went over all the equipment needed, a spade, gloves, and a level being most important. Then I showed them how to mix cement using four parts sand to one part cement, plus a small amount of water. I pointed out the importance of staggering the joints with each new row, giving the brickwork more strength and support. Everyone had fun and we were laughing by the time we finished. And we had a beautiful, very impressive, very short brick wall to show for it.

I got home that night at seven o'clock feeling exhausted. My back and shoulders ached and I had to drag myself out of the truck and through the back gate. And that's where I found Mac preparing the grill. I simply had to stop and stare. I'd always thought the idea of someone's heart skipping a beat was a silly thing that songwriters wrote about. But my heart was jumping around like crazy. I pressed my hand to my chest to calm down.

"Hi," I said.

He grinned. "Hi. Feel like having dinner with me?"

"Very much." Funny. My exhaustion disappeared, just like that.

"Good. I bought steaks and potatoes."

"My favorite. I can make a salad, too."

"I love salad."

I laughed. "Let me put my stuff inside and get the potatoes going."

He followed me into the house. Robbie and Tiger were so excited, you'd think they'd never seen a human being before. Mac didn't seem to mind at all and sat down at the kitchen table to scratch Robbie's ears and let Tiger wind her way in and out and around his ankles.

"They're shameless," I said, giving the animals a stern look. "I can put them in the other room if they're bugging you."

He chuckled. "You know I love them."

"And they clearly love you," I said with a smile.

We talked about Callie and all the girlfriends she'd made during her trip here last spring. She was visiting one of them tonight, which was why Mac was free to spend the evening alone with me. I told him about the search through the Forester garage for something—anything—April might have been looking for. We laughed and wondered about the plastic bag of baby stuff I found hanging off the chandelier. I gave him the full story on how I'd found Potter with an ax in his neck. Being a writer and an aficionado of murder mysteries, he was fascinated, of course, and asked me a hundred questions about the murder scene.

As I set the table, I told him that my crew had finally finished the last bit of the work on his lighthouse mansion. I told him it was ready for him to move in, but he didn't seem to be in any hurry to move away from my garage apartment.

He opened a bottle of wine and we toasted to being together. It was the most perfect kind of night and I couldn't wait to do it again.

Seven Shopping Days Until Christmas

The next morning, Friday, I gathered all the contractors in the foyer and held an impromptu meeting. Each of them gave a rundown of what work had already been done and what was left to do in their apartments. Together we estimated the time each project would take to complete, and Wade and I readjusted our crews and volunteers accordingly. Despite Eric shutting us down the other day, I thought we were in good shape to finish on time, thanks to all of our incredible workers.

As we were wrapping up, the door opened and

Patrice, Mr. Potter's secretary, walked in carrying a huge pink box.

The *pinkness* threw me off and for a few seconds, I thought it might be another baby gift for Angel. But of course it wasn't.

She smiled brightly. "Good morning, everyone."

"Hi, Patrice." I walked over to greet her. "What a pleasant surprise. What are you doing here?"

"I'm sort of at loose ends at the bank." She set the box down on the red couch and opened the top. "I know that you and your crew had problems with Mr. Potter, but I'm hoping that this peace offering will help lighten any bad memories. There are muffins and pastries for everyone."

My crew needed no further arm twisting and swarmed the box like a horde of hungry hounds.

I pulled Patrice out of the way to avoid her being crushed by the mob.

"That was so thoughtful of you," I said, grinning at Wade as he walked off holding up a bear claw in victory. I glanced back at Patrice. "Are you taking a few days off work? This must be so hard for you to deal with."

She waved her hands in annoyance. "I've been crying for days and I'm sick of it. I want to get back to the real world and do some good. The pastries are my way of asking for forgiveness."

"Forgiveness? You don't need forgiveness from anyone, Patrice." I smiled a little guiltily. "I'll be the first to admit that Mr. Potter and I didn't get along very well, but that's got nothing to do with you. You're perfectly nice and my crew obviously adores you."

I swept a hand toward the men who were pushing and

shoving to get at the delectable pastries. We both watched in amazement for another minute until the last fellow walked away and the box was empty.

"Wow," I murmured. "Those went fast."

"I'm glad," she said, staring at the men as they headed off to different parts of the house. "That was fun to watch."

"It was."

"They're all so . . . uninhibited."

"When it comes to food, yes." I waited a moment, then felt awkward when she didn't make a move to leave. "Well, thank you again."

"I was wondering," she ventured shyly, still gazing around, not making eye contact. "Could I stay and work as a volunteer?"

I wasn't quite sure I'd heard her correctly. "You want to work here?"

"Well, yes." She wrung her hands. "The bank is still in charge of this project, so I talked to the president about my representing them as a volunteer. You know, since Mr. Potter is no longer . . . well." She touched her hair, trying to compose herself. "Our president was willing to let me help out here until Christmas."

Her hair was perfectly coiffed, of course. But I hadn't noticed her outfit until now. She wore a crisply tailored blouse tucked into brand-new denim jeans. I could tell she had ironed them because the crease was sharp as a knife. And her sneakers were as white and bright as her smile. It looked as though she had gone shopping for "casual clothes" for this very purpose. It was sort of endearing.

"I'll be happy to put you to work, if you're sure that's what you want."

"I'm sure. Honestly, I just don't want to be at the bank right now. Everything is in chaos. But I do want to keep busy."

I smiled. "Then you've come to the right place."

At noon, Lizzie surprised everyone by showing up at Forester House with baby Angel.

"I'm still not sure this is a good idea," she said, dropping her bags onto the red settee in the foyer. She placed the baby in her lightweight bouncer on a sturdy side table.

Angel was completely bundled up in another one of those sleeping bag suits, this one made of a pink, puffy, down material that looked cozy and warm. Which meant that Lizzie had gone shopping for the baby. It touched my heart and reminded me that I should buy a few items for Angel myself.

I helped Lizzie get situated on the couch. "You talked to Eric, right?"

"Yes, last night and again just a little while ago. He thinks it's a good idea to bring the baby out into the open."

"He thinks it might bring the mother out, too."

"I guess that makes sense." But she still looked worried.

I patted her arm. "I'm not worried, because I know you'll be watching Angel like a mama hawk."

"You'd better believe it."

"So nothing's going to happen to her."

As if to punctuate that thought, Eric drove up just then and parked his SUV on the side of the driveway. Apparently he planned to spend the rest of the afternoon close to the action. And the *action* I was talking about was baby Angel and anyone who came around to see her.

After a while, though, I realized that the real question was, who *hadn't* come around to see her. The baby was a huge hit with the entire crew, and for the rest of the afternoon it seemed like everyone in the house took a few minutes to come down to the foyer and get a peek at Angel. The baby loved the attention she got from both men and women.

Callie fell instantly in love with the little one. She sat down and kept Lizzie company for an hour, chatting about school and babies and television and every other possible subject in the universe. I had forgotten what a nonstop talker the teenager was. Luckily she was as charming as she was chatty, so Lizzie was happy to have her sit with her.

Heather Maxwell, minus her diamond charm bracelet, had finally returned to volunteer. She told me the police had returned her bracelet after keeping it in the crime lab for a few days in hopes of extracting the killer's hair or fibers.

Like Callie, Heather seemed mesmerized by the baby and made all sorts of excuses to walk downstairs and check on her every hour or so.

I was passing through the foyer on my way to apartment two, but simply had to stop and gaze at Lizzie and Angel and their current visitors, Callie and Heather. The two teenagers appeared to have bonded over their mutual baby love. I would have thought going googly over babies was a strictly female thing—if I hadn't already spotted several of my manly contractors also besotted by the tiny creature. The baby was a happy counterpoint to the gruesome murder that had occurred a few days earlier.

Hearing heavy footsteps on the stairs behind me, I turned to see three painters heading my way.

"Hey, Shannon," Freddie said, his white T-shirt spattered with a rainbow assortment of different paint colors. It was a uniform of sorts. "Glad we found you. Have you seen a five-gallon can of Le Petite Rose floating around?"

"It's missing from apartment eight," the second guy, Cliff, added.

I frowned at the word. "Missing?"

Freddie was more succinct. "Not missing. It's gone. Disappeared."

"Maybe Lou stowed it somewhere in a closet," I suggested, naming the contractor in charge of that room, "or someone else moved it out of the way."

"We already asked Lou and his crew. They're just as clueless as we are."

The third painter, Rick, a tall, scrawny fellow who looked young enough to get carded at the pub, scratched his neck, baffled. "We searched the closets, the bathroom, even checked the other apartments. Can't find it anywhere."

Le Petite Rose was the color I'd chosen for the walls in apartment eight because the space was being rented by two sisters. In reality, the color was a fairly basic taupe, but there was an underlying hue of rose that I thought would appeal to the older women.

I squeezed my eyes shut and mentally called up a picture of my schedule. I glanced at Freddie. "You're not ready to start painting until Monday, right?"

"Yeah. But we're getting through the job in apartment six faster than we expected, so I was hoping we might get started on apartment eight over the weekend."

"That would be great"—I gave them a weak smile—"if there was paint, right?"

Freddie grinned. "Right."

"Maybe the can will show up by then."

He gave me a dubious look. "Sure. Maybe."

"Look, if it doesn't show up by tomorrow, let me know and I'll send one of my guys to go buy another one."

"Thanks, Shannon."

The painters walked away and I sighed. A five-gallon container of that particular paint had cost us over one hundred twenty dollars, so I really hoped it showed up. Sometimes you just had to chock things like that up to the usual workplace pilfering. But seriously? It took a particularly slimy person to steal from a charitable organization like this one.

It also took someone with real muscle. Those big paint tubs weighed over forty pounds. Of course, almost every man working here could have lifted it and carried it out of the house. He would had to have done it after hours, because the sight of someone carrying one of those big tubs of paint out to his car would have been conspicuous enough to cause some of us to wonder what the heck was going on.

I made yet another mental note to search for the paint myself. But I had a feeling that unless the can magically reappeared soon, this was one mystery that would never be solved.

I worked late that evening, spackling and priming apartment six's bathroom so Wade could go home early and the painting crew could get started first thing

Monday morning. By the time I was finished, all of the volunteers and most of the workers had left for the day. After cleaning up my mess, I walked upstairs to the attic to start my usual end-of-the-day walkthrough of the house to make notes on the progress in all the rooms. I had finished with the rooms on the second floor and had come downstairs to start checking out apartment two, the large space at the back of the house that also contained the original kitchen, when I noticed that the door to the wine cellar was ajar. That wasn't a good thing. The reason the door was always locked was because there were still a lot of bottles of fine wine down there that would be sold for some serious money someday.

I crossed the kitchen to close it and heard an odd sound coming up from down below. I couldn't tell if it was coming from one of the heating vents or from something down in the cellar. But when I tried to shut the door, it wouldn't close. And that's when I saw that the lock had been jammed.

I knew for a fact that the door had been locked all week. So someone had done this today.

My shoulders trembled. The hairs on my arms stood on end as fear erupted inside me. My first, best inclination was to call the cops. And I would, in a minute.

I had been down in the cellar once before with Wade and Jason, the head of Holiday Homebuilders, when we'd first surveyed the house months ago. I knew the space was clean and well lighted, so there was no reason to be afraid. The fear came from knowing I was alone in the house and hearing noises I couldn't identify. I decided to do a quick check down there. My foot hit the first stone step—and I immediately questioned my own judgment. I mean, even if the cellar were spotless, it could still be dangerous.

Because . . . hello? Someone had obviously broken the lock. Were they still down there in the cellar? Were they doing something wrong? I had a feeling the answer was yes. Whoever "they" were.

I hustled my butt back up to the relative safety of the kitchen, pulled out my phone, and called Eric.

"I'm just a few blocks away," he said after hearing my concerns. "I can be there in five minutes."

"Good," I said, pacing around the kitchen. "Thanks."

"And Shannon?"

"Yes?"

"Don't go down there."

I frowned as I disconnected the call. How did he know I was planning to venture downstairs?

I guess he knew me pretty well.

An eternity later—but probably closer to five minutes—I heard the sound of a car pulling into the driveway. It had to be Eric, so I figured I was safe enough to venture down the thick stone steps. Halfway down, I stopped and stared across the small, dimly lit, cave-like room. There were six long rows with hundreds of vintage wine bottles lovingly stacked in open wooden crates. Each row represented a different wine region or style.

Right then, the pungent aroma of a heavy red wine hit me and I wondered who had broken into the bottles.

And there was that noise again. It was almost like a creaking door, except it sounded human.

"Uhhhh."

The sound was shiver-inducing.

"Hello?" I called. "Who's there?"

"Uhhhh."

That was a person! Right then, I heard the front door slam shut and scurried back to the top of the stairs.

"Shannon?" Eric called.

"Come to the kitchen, Eric," I shouted. "Someone's down there. They might be hurt."

He was there in seconds and ran to the stairs, jogging down to the stone floor of the cellar. I followed him, naturally, and while he headed left to explore the three rows on that side of the room, I turned right, going straight to the far corner, where the richest red wines were stored. That was what I was smelling.

I almost stumbled over the person stretched out on the stone floor.

"Over here," I cried, leaning over to get a closer look at the body. That's when the overpowering odor of the wine sent me staggering backward—right into Eric.

He steadied me and peered over my shoulder. "Do you know who it is?"

"It's Santa Claus," I said. "I'm not sure which one. And I'm sorry to say it, but he's dead drunk. I think he must've opened up one of the expensive bottles of wine. Can you smell it?"

I moved aside so Eric could look more closely. He aimed his flashlight downward and studied the figure for a moment. "He's not dead drunk, Shannon. He's still alive, but unconscious."

"But all that wine."

"He was hit in the head."

"Oh dear." I felt instantly remorseful for calling Santa a drunk. And I still couldn't tell which one of the many Santa Clauses it was. "With what?"

"With that," he said, focusing the light on a round object on the ground by his head.

"What is that?" I asked, straining my eyes to figure it out.

"It's a tape measure. A big one."

I gasped. It was Blake's heavy metal tape measure, the one he'd shown me a few days before. The one that weighed almost a pound.

"You know whose it is?"

"I do." I sniffed the air. "But why do I smell so much wine? Where's that coming from?"

Eric moved the light beam down to where Santa still clutched a broken bottle of vintage port. It had obviously hit the stone floor and its contents were pooling around Santa.

"Oh no," I whispered. "Poor Santa."

"Let's get out of here," he said and hustled me upstairs to call an ambulance.

Chapter Sixteen

It turned out that the injured Santa Claus in question was Slim Daley. On the way to the hospital, he had slipped into a coma. That was all Eric would tell me when I texted him later on. I called the nurse's station to check on Slim the next morning and all they would tell me was that he remained in critical but stable condition. I assumed that meant he was still in a coma. And that meant that Slim couldn't tell the police who had attacked him.

Six Shopping Days Until Christmas

On Saturday morning, I dashed over to Forester House to check on the contractors who had insisted on working over the weekend. I was secretly thrilled that some of them would get a head start going into next week, including my dad and his crew who were there to help the other guys. I decided not to mention Slim's injuries to anyone until we had more information. I was glad I didn't say anything, because the house seemed to buzz with a lighter energy. Maybe because it was the weekend. Or maybe because the dark cloud of Mr. Potter's death was beginning to dissipate. Either way, I was looking forward to Monday and seeing the progress they'd made.

That afternoon was Mac's book signing at Lizzie and Hal's shop. It was a huge success, with people lined up and down the sidewalk, waiting for their chance to meet Mac and get a signed copy of his latest blockbuster hit. I'd never seen Lizzie happier, and Mac was thrilled by the turnout, too. Afterward, we all went out for burgers and fries at the pub and Callie called it the most excellent ending to a perfect day.

Five Shopping Days Until Christmas

On Sunday morning, Mac and Callie helped me buy a Christmas tree. The sky was clear and blue but the air was frigid as we picked out the biggest, fattest tree we could find. It was a perfect day for hot chocolate, just as Callie had hoped for, and we all decorated the tree with the hundreds of ornaments and doodads I'd kept for years. Many of them had belonged to my mother and those were extra special to me. Callie and Mac bought me an angel for the top of the tree and I knew I would treasure it forever.

That afternoon Mac went above and beyond the call of duty by climbing up the ladder to string lights along the eaves, circling the entire front side of the house. Callie applied stenciled reindeer and snowflakes to my windows and decorated a wreath with more ornaments. We hung the wreath on the door and then spent the rest of the afternoon making a big pot of chicken vegetable soup. We laughed and talked and napped and read books in my living room. It was another perfect day that I hoped would never end.

And I knew I was in dangerous territory.

Four Shopping Days Until Christmas

Monday morning, I arrived at the mansion as the sun was rising. When I walked into the foyer, I found Santa Steve waiting for me. He wore civilian clothes: blue jeans, work shirt, and a heavy corduroy jacket.

"Are you working here today?" I asked.

"I am." He gave me a hug, then gazed into my eyes. "I heard you found him."

"Yes, I did," I said, knowing he was referring to Slim. "I'm so sorry."

"Do you know what happened?"

"I—I don't. The police whisked me out of there fast." I smiled weakly, abruptly wary. Eric had warned me before not to discuss crime scenes and evidence. I didn't suspect Steve, of course, but now that two attacks had occurred on the site, I was becoming more and more suspicious of everyone around me. After all, Steve had mentioned his own run-ins with Mr. Potter, and now Slim had been attacked. Steve and Slim appeared to be friends, but who knew the real story?

More guilt flooded me for doubting Steve, so I made my excuses and hurried off to get some work done. From here on, it would be best if I just kept my mouth closed and my thoughts to myself.

Despite the assault on Slim, I was relieved that Eric had given us the all-clear to go back to work in the ball-room and the butler's pantry. The downside was that he'd had to cut off all access to apartment two—where the door to the wine cellar was located—for at least a day. I understood the need to close it off, but we were nearing the end of our time here and I was growing concerned. Nevertheless, the apartment two team obligingly split up to help out the crews in the other apartments who needed some extra hands.

I headed for the ballroom and met Dad and Phil on the way.

"It'll be good to get back to our original project," Phil said cheerfully. "As soon as Bud and Pete get here, I'm going to have them pick up where we left off with the drywall."

"Sounds good. How about you, Dad?"

"I'm looking forward to getting my toolbox back," Dad said resolutely. "And then I'll get started pulling up the tiles in the bathroom."

I threaded my arm through his. "You okay with this?"

"Sure. Look, I'll admit it's unsettling. We still don't know who killed Potter, so that's worrisome."

"I'll say." Did we have a killer working in the house? The thought was definitely unsettling.

"As far as my tools go, well, my ax is gone and a few of the screwdrivers were tossed around, but as far as I know, none of my other tools were touched. So I'm going to reclaim them as my own and we'll finish this job with time to spare. And make you proud."

"You already do," I said, and planted a loud kiss on his cheek.

As we entered the ballroom, we stopped and looked

around. It looked pretty much the same as when we left it. But we all knew it wasn't the same.

Finally, Phil broke the silence. "What are you working on today, Shannon?"

"I'm going to get started on the butler's-pantry cabinets."

"That's a beautiful piece of craftsmanship," Dad said, with an approving nod. "You'll do it up right."

"Thanks, Dad." He had taught me carpentry at an early age and I still loved working with wood. I didn't get the chance very often, but I enjoyed it whenever I did. "It'll probably take me up until the very last day to complete it. But it's got to be done and I'm just happy to work with all that lovely wood."

I carried my small toolbox into the hall and stopped when I realized where I was standing: directly on the spot where Mr. Potter had fallen and died. The wood floor had been scrubbed clean by a team of hazmat workers from a company who handled biological waste. It was weird to be told by the cops that when blood was spilled during a crime, you could be left with a biohazard site.

I took a few gulps of air and quickly switched my view to the U-shaped butler's pantry. All three walls of the room were covered in gorgeous wood cabinets and drawers. There was a generous, four-foot-wide area inside the space in which a butler could work and move around.

Traditionally a butler's pantry had been used to store the most valuable silver and crystal under lock and key. It had held all the serving dishes and often doubled as the butler's office, where he kept his logs and house accounts close at hand.

I stood in the hall, studying the cabinetry. Straight

ahead were elegantly designed glass-fronted cabinets. This was where the Forester family would have stored all of the fancy dishware and serving dishes for both formal and family dinners. On the right side of the room were rows of plain wood cabinets that would have held all sorts of silver pieces: platters, teapots, coffeepots, water pitchers, bowls, vases, and the like. These were not kept in the glass cabinets because it was thought that sunshine, and light in general, would cause their surfaces to tarnish more quickly.

On the left side of the space was a sink and a marble counter where dishes were washed and water pitchers were filled. The thick marble counter ran across all three sides of the room and beneath it were rows of wide drawers that held linens and silverware and serving pieces. Smaller drawers held specialty items, barware, and such.

A small crystal chandelier hung down from the center of the ceiling. It was a beautiful, compact room and I imagined the Foresters' butler had been the envy of his peers.

But the pale buttercream paint was beginning to peel off some of the lower drawers. The paint had been tested for lead and found to be loaded with the dangerous metal. Most paints in the 1890s were at least fifty percent lead based, and there was no way I would allow it to remain in this house, particularly in an apartment where a six-year-old girl would be living.

Plainly put, it would be malpractice for me to do nothing.

For some reason, the upper cabinets had suffered no peeling or other damage. The first time I saw this room, I had decided the quickest way to fix it would be to strip the paint from the lower cabinets and simply cover them in a clear varnish. The natural wood would be a lovely contrast to the buttercream cabinets hanging over the marble counters.

"No time like the present," I murmured, and went out to my truck to get more tools and stripping supplies.

I ran into Patrice on the back veranda. "Do you need any help?" she asked. "I've finished scraping the caulk off the windows in apartment seven."

I smiled. "I would love to have you help but I don't think you'd like what I'm doing."

"Why not?"

"I'm working in the butler's pantry," I said gently.

"Oh, but I can . . . oh no." Her eyes widened and began to tear up. "Oh dear."

I handed her a tissue from my tool belt. "I'm sorry."

"No, don't worry." She dabbed her eyes with the tissue and sniffled. "I appreciate you trying to look out for me. You're right, I'd rather not go into that room if you don't mind."

"Not at all," I said. "Let me text Wade and see who else needs help."

"Thank you, Shannon." She gave me a watery smile. "I've really enjoyed getting to know you."

"I've enjoyed it, too," I said, a little surprised that I'd become friends with this old-fashioned Southern lady.

"Maybe when we're through with this project, we can go to lunch."

I smiled at her. "I would like that very much."

I started by taking pictures of the pantry from every angle. Then I began removing each knob, hinge, and door pull on the bottom set of cabinets. A few days from now, when I was finished with this job, the photos would be a reminder of how to reassemble all of the hardware I'd removed.

I planned to assign a volunteer to clean all the brass hardware. It would mostly consist of dipping them in a solution and rubbing them until they were bright and pretty again. They could even do the work outside on the veranda.

I wouldn't have that luxury, which was too bad, because the chemicals found in wood strippers were highly toxic to my lungs as well as dangerous to clothing and skin. In preparation, I laid down two layers of tarp to protect the wood floor and opened both hallway windows. Not to be overly cautious, but I had a respirator mask, splash-proof goggles, heavy-duty plastic gloves, and a hazmat jumpsuit I'd bought online. Somewhat apropos attire, I thought, given what had happened in here. By the time I was dressed and ready to start the work, I looked like an astronaut gearing up for a walk in space.

I wasn't sure how quickly the old paint would react to the stripper's harsh chemicals, but I was pleased to see it blister and sizzle almost as soon as I applied the first coat. On the flat surfaces, I scraped off the sludgy paint with a small putty knife. On the ridges and crevices and corners, though, I had to use a small, wiry scrub brush to get into all those tight spots and remove the paint. After as much of the paint as possible was wiped away, I applied a second coat of stripper and repeated the process.

Once I finished stripping a larger section, I applied mineral spirits to that area to get rid of any remaining stripper residue. Otherwise, I would risk a bad chemical reaction between any of the excess stripper and the new finish.

After that, probably sometime late tomorrow, I would sand it by hand until it was smooth and beautiful. Then I would apply two coats of a simple marine-grade varnish to show off the wood grain and protect the surface of the cabinets. And voilà!

It would be fabulous when I was finished, but for now the job was slow and repetitive, mainly because there were so many drawers to deal with. The results would be worth it in the end, though.

I removed my respirator while I prepped the second row of small drawers. First I opened each drawer to make sure that any old paint still covering the edge of the inner box would be removed as well. One drawer stuck and I pulled it a few times, but it still wouldn't budge. I reattached the hardware and it was still tight, but it opened finally. I realized the drawer had been jammed in at an angle and just needed to be straightened. After that, it was easy to open and close. I noticed a crumpled piece of paper inside the drawer, so I removed it, shoving it into my tool belt to toss out later.

I slipped on my respirator, goggles, and gloves, and repeated the lengthy process all over again on the new set of drawers.

All day long, I continued to take breaks to walk outside and breathe. Even with the respirator and the windows wide-open to let in the cold air, my head got a little foggy once in a while.

I strolled around the ballroom, enjoying the beauty of the room. I couldn't wait to see it furnished and ready for Sophie and Molly. I wondered idly where they could put a Christmas tree. That's when I realized: "We need Christmas trees."

"What, honey?" Dad said, walking into the room from the bathroom, where he was starting to lay down the new tile.

"We need to buy Christmas trees for all the apartments," I said. "The families won't be able to afford them."

"They're moving in on Christmas Eve. It makes sense."

"This is something Jason's people can do." I reached into my bag for my phone.

"That's my girl. Delegate."

I laughed. "It's more fun than I thought it would be. Anyway, he's handling the decorators, so I think he should ask them to include Christmas trees."

"With all the decorations."

"Absolutely."

Three Shopping Days Until Christmas

The next day, after checking in with each of my contractors to see how their rooms were shaping up, I climbed up to the attic to touch base with Blake. I hadn't been up here in a few days and it reminded me that I hadn't seen April around lately. And that realization reminded me that I hadn't followed up on the Santa-pinching accusation, either. Frankly, I just didn't believe her, and since she wasn't around to bug me about it, I was satisfied to let things lie for the time being.

I found Blake in one of the new rooms he and his crew had created. There were five micro-apartments up here now and each room was approximately five hundred square feet. They were small but typical single apartments with a main area that would have a pull-out couch for sleeping. There was an electric wall fireplace, a kitchenette with room for a small table and chairs, and a bathroom and closet area. Each room had a big window and three of the rooms even had their own tiny terraces, thanks to a series of deeply set dormer windows the original architect had created at the top of the house.

"I can't believe this was one big, dark attic space seven days ago. It looks better and better every time I come up here."

"I think so, too," he said, running his hand along the smooth plaster wall. "I was really pleased with the way they all worked out."

"I know we won't finish up here before Christmas, but we might make it by New Year's."

"That's my goal," Blake said.

We moved on to the next micro-apartment and I couldn't get over how comfortable the small space felt. "I'm so glad you're on the team. I'm really impressed with your work."

"Thank you, but I only joined up because I was so impressed by your work."

We both smiled. "Aren't we lucky?"

"Yup." He opened the door to the next room. "This one's my favorite. If I didn't have three kids, I would try to rent this one myself."

"I didn't know you had three kids, Blake."

"Yeah," he said, grinning. "Three little monsters."

"That's so sweet."

"No, it's not. They're terrors." He frowned as he glanced around. "Yeah, I definitely need to rent this place. I could use some peace and quiet once in a while."

I chuckled as he walked over to show off the new double-paned mini sliding glass door he'd installed. I called it a mini door because it had to fit into the space of the old window, which was large enough, but not quite the size of a door.

Still, you could use it to walk out onto the reinforced terrace, so I did, stepping outside to enjoy the view. "This space is going to be awesome for some single person."

"Or for me," he muttered.

I laughed. "Good luck convincing your wife about that."

He scowled. "I can't tell her or she'll want a room here, too."

I was still laughing when I noticed the large garage on the other side of the back lawn. It reminded me again of April, so I turned to Blake. "Did you ever see April around here again? You know, the woman who was up here last week."

"Yeah, I remember. Haven't seen her in a while. She sort of disappeared."

"Yes, she did." Interesting, I thought as I stepped back inside. "Let's take a look at the next room."

As she had done for the past few days, Patrice walked into the foyer that morning carrying a large box of pastries. By now the crew was completely infatuated with her because, along with supplying us with our daily sugar rush, Patrice was a good worker and happy to help out.

Lizzie showed up with the baby again that afternoon and held court in the foyer. It seemed that everyone on the crew was taking time to stop by and say hello and admire the little darling. We had all fallen in love with Angel Baby, as some of the guys called her.

Callie and Mac showed up for work each day, too, and I was overjoyed to see them. It felt so comfortable to have Mac around, I could barely remember when he wasn't here. Or maybe I just didn't want to remember.

The work was going well and the rooms were beginning to shine. But more quirky things were happening this week. Another paint can went missing and several of the guys complained about lost or possibly stolen tools. Evidently, we had a petty thief in our midst.

But there were some happy incidents, too, which were even more puzzling, frankly. The crew in apartment eight reported that they couldn't finish up their drywall job the night before, then came in the next morning to find that it had been completed. I went around to every single person in the house and asked them if they had done the work. No one fessed up.

At the end of the following day, one of the painters told me that he'd had a bad toothache earlier and ran off to the dentist at lunch. When he returned three hours later, his room was completely painted. And again, no one would admit to doing the work.

So along with the petty thief, we apparently had a shy but Good Samaritan in our midst. Or maybe it was all the work of mischievous Christmas elves.

New baby clothes and formula and baby binkies and baubles kept showing up in odd places around the house, too. A day after I found the items hanging from a chandelier in the foyer, one of the guys found a brand-new, infant-sized, lacey pink dress with matching tights and baby shoes hanging on a shelf in the library. Later that same afternoon, Callie thought it would be fun to take the elegant house elevator up to the second floor. When she stepped inside, she found a baby animal mobile hanging from the ceiling light.

So far, the unknown gift giver hadn't revealed herself.

Christmas decorations were starting to show up, as well. Yesterday morning I walked into the house and saw that someone had twisted red-and-gold garland around the foyer chandelier. The sparkly garland was also intertwined along the banister, weaving in and out of the balusters and culminating in a big bow around the newel post at the top of the stairs. Bunches of mistletoe began to appear in different places: over the front door; above the steps of the central stairway; just inside the library on the second floor. Everyone was on alert in case a new sprig showed up in an unexpected spot in the house.

Yesterday, Spencer had come to work wearing a hideously tacky Christmas sweater his mother had knitted for him. Everyone mocked him unmercifully, but this morning, three more crew members wore silly Christmas sweaters.

I imagined that by Christmas Eve it would reach epidemic proportions, with everyone in the house showing up wearing their worst nightmare of a holiday sweater.

Each contractor and their crew had added their own decorations to their apartment. One of the guys had run a string of lights around the windows of the tower. Blake had dragged a full-sized Christmas tree all the way up to the attic. Everyone in the house took turns running upstairs to add a silly decoration to the tree. The volunteers were starting to show up with fudge and cookies and candies and cakes to share with everyone. The spirit of Christmas was alive and well at Forester House. And unlike a week ago, I was now right in the thick of it, filled with the joy of the season.

It was ten o'clock that night and I was trying to finish the final row of drawers in the butler's pantry before going home. I took a break to go stand by the open window to suck in some fresh air, and that's when I saw a flash of light coming from the six-car garage at the end of the driveway.

I'd grown smart enough in my old age to resist the urge to run over there to investigate on my own. Okay, that was a lie. I was determined to go check things out. But first, I called Eric. When he answered, I said, "You're probably getting tired of hearing from me."

"Never," he insisted. "Except for the part where you keep giving me bad news."

"Yeah, I'm not sure where this falls, but there's someone sneaking around inside the garage over here."

"You're still working?"

"Yes. I had something to finish."

"Anyone else around?"

"Nope. I'm it."

"I'll be there in ten minutes. Stay put."

"I will."

I dashed around turning off the lights in the pantry and the ballroom and then waited and watched until Eric arrived.

But before he could get here, I saw someone sneak out the side door of the garage carrying some kind of a suitcase or a small trunk. I knew Eric would be here any minute, but he was going to be too late.

I moved quietly across the ballroom floor and opened one of the sets of French doors. The grounds were dark and I tried to make out the silhouette of the person creeping down the driveway. I followed them—just as Eric's SUV swung into the drive. His headlights illuminated the person, who took a quick detour into the thickly wooded area lining the property.

Eric jumped out of the car.

"They're getting away!" I shouted, pointing toward the woods, and took off running after the thief.

"Get back here!" Eric shouted, but it was too late. I was fifty feet into the woods before I knew it and unable to see a thing. I stood perfectly still and tried to acclimate my vision to the darkness while regretting that whole "take off into the woods without thinking" idea. What if they had a gun? Or a knife? I couldn't see or hear a thing. They could sneak up and knock me out before I even realized they were close by. Although, when I took a second to think about it, I knew it would be impossible to sneak up on anyone, since the ground was covered in dried, dead leaves that crackled and snapped with every step.

And now that I was standing still, I could feel the cold wetness of the woods seeping into my bones. That settled it. I turned to scamper back to my truck.

A sudden loud scream caused me to halt instantly. It had come from only a few yards away. The scream was followed by wild thrashing among the brush and bushes.

Was the thief tangling with some forest beast?

"Who's there?" I said.

"Get back to the driveway," Eric commanded.

"All right, all right," I muttered, secretly thrilled to

know he was close by. I raced back to the open area of the driveway and waited.

Seconds later, the forest beast—Eric—emerged from the grove, pulling the person along beside him. The moon came out from behind a cloud and I could see that the angry, struggling person was a woman, and she was still carrying the suitcase.

The woman was April.

Eric took her to police headquarters for questioning and as soon as I cleaned up the butler's pantry and closed up the house, I raced over to find out what was happening. I arrived just in time to see Eric releasing her instead of arresting her.

As she walked out smirking, I turned to the police chief. "Are you kidding? I saw her steal the suitcase."

I could tell he was disgusted. "It's an old, empty suitcase that's falling apart, Shannon. There's nothing inside it. She claimed she was just on a lark, trying to find some silly tchotchke to memorialize her time at Forester House."

"That is the biggest bunch of baloney I've ever heard."

He scowled. "I agree. But I had to let her go."

"She's up to something, Eric."

"You're probably right, but it doesn't matter at the moment. Go home, Shannon."

I knew he was right. Besides, I was tired and just wanted to go to sleep, so I nodded and left the station. But I was more determined than ever to figure out exactly what game April was playing.

Chapter Seventeen

Two Shopping Days Until Christmas

Two days before Christmas, the house was buzzing with activity and excitement. Crews of carpenters, plumbers, electricians, and decorators were racing in and out of every room trying to complete their jobs in anticipation of the big Christmas Eve celebration with the families.

Most of the apartments were fully decorated now with the designers adding their very last touches and flourishes to each of the rooms. Dad and his crew had finished the designer closet for the ballroom apartment and it looked fabulous. Everyone in the house had stopped by to check it out and express their jealousy. I couldn't blame them. I was jealous, too. But I was thrilled for Sophie and Molly, our new tenants. They were going to love it here.

Jason from Holiday Homebuilders had come through with fresh Christmas trees for each of the apartments. When he realized that two of the new families were Jewish, he asked the designers to find some pretty blue and white decorations and a menorah and some candles for those apartments. That worked for us and I knew the tenants would appreciate it, too.

I had one more coat of varnish to apply to the butler's-pantry cabinets and I would be finished. While the second coat dried, I walked around, checking on volunteers and crew. The painters were adding a new coat of paint to the grand-stairway balusters, so I decided to take a shortcut through apartment two's kitchen, into the sunroom, and up the old servants' stairs. The lovely old sunroom, with its art deco–style furniture and view of the woods, would be accessible to everyone once they all moved in. The stairs would be, too, although they were steep and narrow. A week ago, they had also been rickety with a few rotted-out boards, but now they'd been fortified with all new wood steps and balusters. They had received a new coat of light paint to brighten up the area, making the staircase strong and safe enough to hold any of the new tenants.

At the bottom of the stairs I glanced up—and jumped back a step. "What are you two doing here?"

Alyssa shrieked and Kailee elbowed her to be quiet. I guess I shocked them as badly as they shocked me.

"Hi, Shannon," Kailee said, obviously trying to be cool.

"It's so dark in here," I said, glancing around. "What's going on? Oh, are those Christmas decorations?"

"Yeah," Kailee said, elbowing her friend again.

"Yeah," Alyssa said quickly. "Christmas. That's it."

My two high school students were draping items over the banister. And they were lying through their teeth while they did it.

I walked up the steps to get a closer look at the decorations. But instead of finding garlands and silver bells, there were baby clothes, pajamas, and a blanket adorning the railing. I stared at the baby items, then up at the girls.

"You two?" I shook my head in shock and disbelief. "You've been leaving these things around the house?"

Alyssa hung her head but petite Kailee stood her ground, resembling an adorably defiant elf. "So what? There's no law against it."

I decided to go after the weak link. "Alyssa, do you know who the mother of the baby is?"

Her eyes widened and she exchanged a quick glance with Kailee.

"You won't get into trouble," I rushed to add. "I promise. But baby Angel is going to be given up for adoption. I really can't keep her."

"But you're our first choice," Alyssa cried.

"Thank you, sweetheart. I'm honored, I really am. But I'm just not able to take care of a tiny baby right now. So she'll be put up for adoption and I think the mother would like to know where she's going. I know I would. Wouldn't Angel's mom love to be a part of her life?"

"She would be, if you're the mom," Alyssa said, and got another elbow from Kailee, who shushed her.

"Stop hitting me," Alyssa said, rubbing her arm. "We might as well tell her the truth."

"Yes, you might as well," I said, folding my arms across my chest. "Come on, girls. You know you can trust me."

Kailee huffed out a heavy sigh. "Fine. It's Lauren."

I was pretty sure my mouth was hanging open in astonishment. Lauren was one of my favorite students at the empowerment center. She was sweet and smart and pretty. A little overweight, maybe—or so I'd thought—but that hadn't kept her from being a great worker, a good team player, and a role model.

Apparently all that extra girth was actually baby weight. She'd hidden it well, even telling me she was bloated from antibiotics the other day. And clearly her friends had conspired to help her cover up her condition.

"Lauren admires you," Kailee said. "She didn't want you to know it was her baby because she thought you'd think she was stupid for getting pregnant in the first place."

"She was wrong," I said, "but I understand her feelings."

Alyssa said, "We thought that if we gave the baby to you, we could see her once in a while and keep up with her life."

"And you would be a perfect mom," Kailee added.

"Why do you think that?" I asked, genuinely interested.

"Because you're the best teacher we've ever had," Alyssa said. "You're smart and patient and you don't yell."

"And you bring snacks," Kailee added.

"Let's go downstairs and talk about this."

As we walked down the steps, Kailee explained that the three girls had decided to buy the baby clothes and supplies to help me out.

"Babies are expensive," Kailee explained. "Lauren didn't want you to go broke."

"That was very thoughtful. But why did you put things all over the house."

"Oh, that," Alyssa said.

Kailee shrugged. "It made us laugh. When we told Lauren that we hung the bag from the chandelier, she cracked up. So we kept trying to come up with funny places to put things. She's had a pretty hard time of it, so we wanted to brighten up her day with our stories, you know?"

"You're lucky no one around here saw you."

"We usually snuck in late in the afternoon and hid until everyone was gone."

Hearing their strategy caused sudden chills to spring to life along my spine, then creep up my neck and across my shoulders. I hustled the girls out the kitchen door and into the side yard. I glanced in every direction to make sure we were alone. "I have to ask, were you girls here the night Mr. Potter died?"

Kailee looked horrified. "No way!"

"Ew, no," Alyssa said. "That's so gross."

My entire system relaxed, knowing the girls weren't in any danger from the killer. "Just checking."

"We didn't start bringing presents over until after we put the baby in your truck," Kailee explained.

The baby arrived late afternoon of the second day of renovations, I thought. So the girls really were safe. "Okay, good to know. Now, when can I visit with Lauren? I want to make sure she's happy."

One Shopping Day Until Christmas

After another night of tossing and turning, I woke up on Christmas Eve morning knowing exactly what to do about the baby. I just hoped that Child Protective Services would agree, because I felt really good about the decision.

I rushed to get dressed, excited about the day's festivities and anxious to get to the work site. The families would be moving into Forester House later this afternoon and the Christmas Festival and parade around the town square afterward promised to be a wonderful finale for the entire building project.

If only we had a murder suspect behind bars.

I stopped on the way to work to buy a treat for Patrice. I'd been thinking about doing something all week and this was the last day I'd be able to get her something. She had been so sweet to everyone and was such a hard worker. Everyone had managed to warm up to her after being so put off by her boss.

I parked in front of my friend Emily Rose's tea shop and ran inside.

"Shannon!" she cried, coming out to give me a hug. "I haven't seen you in days. Not since we first saw the baby at Lizzie's house."

"I know. The holiday project has taken up every minute of the day and I've barely had time to breathe."

"'Tis the season," she said jovially, her soft Scottish brogue coming through. "Now, what can I get you?"

I gave her my order and she slipped around the counter. Opening the glass case, she removed the most perfect cupcake and placed it in a pastel green bakery box.

Handing me the box, Emily said, "I'm so disappointed I couldn't get over there to volunteer. We are busier than ever this year. The town is overrun with tourists and I haven't been able to take an hour off since Thanksgiving."

"It's a good problem to have," I said, smiling.

"Absolutely." The tourists loved Emily's tea shop, along with all the other beautiful stores on the town square. Many of the tourists also came for the Christmas

Festival, too. And the beach, of course, and the pier and marina and the redwoods and everything else that Lighthouse Cove had to offer, including the lighthouse.

It was probably harsh to think so, but I was glad Mr. Potter was gone, so that none of our shopkeepers would have to live in fear of his wrath anymore.

"Will you be at the parade?" I asked.

"Wouldn't miss it. I'll look for you."

"Okay." Which reminded me: I would have to leave work early to get to the square and officially start the parade.

"Let's get together next week with all the girls," she said.

"Perfect. And I'll give you all the gory details about finding Mr. Potter."

"Yes, I want to hear everything. But ugh, you poor thing, finding the body." She shuddered and rubbed her arms. "The police haven't arrested anyone?"

"No." I made a face. "I thought one of the volunteers was a good suspect, but Eric let her go." *And April hasn't been seen since*, I thought. What a weird woman.

"Someone I know?" she asked.

I shook my head. "A stranger."

"A stranger volunteered for our annual town event? How odd."

I nodded slowly. "I always thought the same thing."

Twenty minutes later, I walked into Forester House and felt instantly comfortable with my surroundings. And why not, after ten days of concentrated work on the place? It was shiny and new now, and yet it retained the dignity and grandeur of its past. It had been alive and standing for nearly 150 years, through good times and bad, I thought. It had seen births and deaths, wars and floods, sadness and triumph, and still remained standing.

I greeted crew members and contractors on my way to apartment three. The ballroom. I was going to miss this place. Today I would do a final walk-through, inspecting each apartment with its contractor and crew so that if there were any last-minute changes or fixes, they could do them on the spot. After two o'clock, the new tenants would start moving in.

At three o'clock, the organizers had scheduled the official opening of the Forester House Apartments for the tenants, workers, and anyone in town who wanted to attend. In the foyer there would be a huge cake along with a champagne toast. Jason had assured me that apple juice would be available for the children and anyone else who didn't want to start imbibing so early.

Then, at five o'clock, the Christmas parade would begin, culminating at six o'clock in the town square, where gift boutiques and food stalls and games were set up for everyone's pleasure.

I couldn't believe that Jane and I and our stalwart committee were about to pull off another grand event.

Of course, we hadn't pulled it off just yet.

"Don't count your chickens," I muttered, then laughed at myself for ever doubting that the Christmas parade would go off without a hitch.

I stepped inside apartment three and marveled at the changes that had been made in the last two days. Thanks to the quick work of the decorators, it was furnished and looked like a home now, albeit with all the rooms contained inside this one large one. An old-fashioned

modesty screen and a healthy ficus tree created a border
between the bedroom and the living room area. A set of
open bookshelves cleverly separated the mother's space
from her daughter's. A sturdy wicker table and chairs
indicated the dining room, along with a small hutch that
held a few pretty vases and serving pieces. The decorator had set up the dining room adjacent to the door leading to the butler's pantry and kitchenette, which had
been installed in the closed-off hallway.

"It's so pretty," I said. A beautifully decorated Christmas tree had been positioned on the opposite side of the
room from the elegant fireplace. Two side chairs brack-
eted the tree. A comfy couch and an easy chair had
been arranged in the center of the large room, facing the
fireplace, a perfect spot to relax and read a book. A
small stack of wood in a brass basket had been placed
on one side of the hearth.

We had converted the fireplace to gas and it would
turn on with one switch near the mantel. My father, as
the official head contractor for apartment three, would
give Sophie and Molly their official tour of the space.
Dad would also demonstrate to Sophie how to use the
fireplace as well as the other features of the apartment.

Wondering if my father and his crew would be doing
any actual work this morning, I set my backpack and the
cupcake down on the wicker dining table. I imagined
there were a few odds and ends to take care of, but for
the most part, apartment three looked spiffed up and
ready for its new residents.

I took the cupcake out of the box because I wanted
Patrice to see how beautiful it was. Checking my phone
for the time, I wondered when Dad would show up. I'd
also told Mac where I would be working this morning.

In the meantime, I headed for the butler's pantry to make sure everything was in perfect order in there.

I happened to glance out the French doors and saw April rounding the corner of the house.

"Hey!" I started to cross to the doors, but I heard a loud bump come from the butler's-pantry area. I jolted at the sound, then felt silly. But after so many surprises this week, who could blame me for jumping at every sound?

"Dad? Is that you?" Instead of chasing after April, I walked quickly over to the pantry door and opened it. "I was just wondering where you . . ."

But it wasn't my father. It was Patrice, opening and shutting all the cupboards and drawers in the butler's pantry.

"Patrice, are you looking for something? Can I help?"

"Nobody can help," she muttered, and continued opening and closing drawers.

Had my father asked her to come in here and check on the drawers? She was so good about helping out, she'd probably gone around asking everyone if they had anything for her to do.

"They're in pretty good working order," I said, testing one of the drawers nearest me. "Thank you for checking, though."

She didn't say anything, just kept opening, then slamming drawers. I watched her working, still not sure why Dad had asked her to do this.

"Hey, Patrice," I said. "Do you happen to know that woman April who was working here as a volunteer?"

She looked up and glared at me. "She's Mr. Potter's niece. They're two of a kind."

Potter's *niece*? They were two of a kind? Did that

mean that April was as despicable as her uncle? Could April have *killed* her uncle?

I started to leave the pantry to go after April, but Patrice was growing more and more upset as she continued opening and slamming drawers.

"Is something wrong?" I asked. "Did you lose something? Can I help you find it?"

She grumbled but didn't answer.

"By the way," I said gently, "I just refinished those drawers. If you could be a little more careful opening and closing them, I would appreciate it."

Christmas was a difficult time for some people, I thought as I walked back into the ballroom. Seeing the cupcake, I wondered if something sweet would help calm her down. I picked up the big, sugary, frosted beauty and called to her. "I brought you a Christmas treat, Patrice. You've done so much for everyone, I thought you deserved a little something for yourself."

Before the sentence was out of my mouth, Patrice screamed and came rushing out of the room.

"This might cheer you up," I said, offering it to her. "It's a Christmas cupcake."

She stopped and shook, looking absolutely beside herself. With another jungle screech, she rushed toward me.

"What are you—?" I dropped the cupcake on the table and held up my hands to defend myself. Had she breathed in too much of the varnish in the pantry? "What's wrong with you?"

"You!" She shrieked and started slapping my face and shoulders.

"Stop it!" I cried, holding her off by smacking her hands away before they could strike me. "What're you doing?"

"Where is it?" she screamed. "What did you do with it?"

"Calm down, Patrice. What did you lose?"

She managed to break through my defenses and slammed her hand against my ear. She hit me so hard that my ear was literally ringing.

"I said stop it!" I grabbed her hands but couldn't hold on to her.

It was like she was possessed.

I broke away and circled around to the other side of the dining table. She came after me and I moved farther around. We did a little dance as she tried to figure out which way I was going to run.

"You said you fixed the drawers," she said.

"I did."

"What did you do with it?" Her voice was no longer soft and southern but rough and demanding. I got a good look at her eyes, saw the deep-seated rage there, and realized she was angry enough to kill me if she got the chance.

"What did I do with what?" I shouted. Then it hit me. "Oh my God, you killed him. It wasn't April. It was you."

"April?" She looked confused for a second, then blinked, clearly too far gone to have a conversation about anything. But I pushed ahead anyway, if only to keep her from attacking me again.

"You killed Mr. Potter. Why?"

She bared her teeth at me and actually growled. The sweet southern belle had been transformed into a raging bull.

"Not that I blame you," I added quickly. "In fact, some people would probably thank you, because he was despicable. But why are you trying to hurt me?"

She didn't answer and I could see her eyes watching me, waiting for me to take off running.

Was she angry with me for interrupting her frantic search for . . . whatever she was looking for? Had she hidden something in the pantry after she killed Potter? But what could it be? Money? Tickets to Tahiti? What?

All I could do was try to distract her, continue asking questions. Anything to keep her away from me. "Why did you kill him, Patrice?"

"Shut up!" she cried.

"You're right, it's a dumb question. He was awful. I don't know how you worked with him for so many years." I continued moving my feet, ready to take off for the doors if she stopped paying attention.

I watched her eyes as she watched me. She was breathing heavily and I wondered if I could make it past her to the front door in time to escape. I was younger and stronger and probably faster than she was, but her berserk energy might level the field.

I wondered where my father was. And where was Mac? If I could hold her off for another few minutes, they might show up and grab her or at least distract her.

I saw her expression change and knew she was ready to charge me. I had to take a chance.

I took off running for the door and she was behind me in a second, grabbing my shirt and dragging me backward. I wriggled to break loose, but at the moment she had the advantage, especially because I had my back to her. It was awkward and dangerous. She was clearly capable of anything. I couldn't see her, wouldn't know if she was getting ready to strangle me or hit me over the head with whatever she might grab hold of. I had to get free.

I continued pulling and her grunts and groans grew

louder from the exertion of fighting me. I hoped she was slowing down. I should have been able to tackle her easily, but she had rage and insanity-driven energy on her side.

As she stretched out her free arm to reach something near the fireplace, I was able to twist free. I turned and saw her lifting a fireplace tool and tried to slap it out of her hand. She'd grabbed the broom in her haste, thank goodness, and not the poker. The tool was too heavy and awkward and it fell on the marble hearth with a clang.

I ran to the other side of the room, hoping to escape through the French doors. I only made it as far as the dining table before she grabbed hold of my long hair and pulled.

I screamed and tried to maneuver around to shove her hand away. That's when I saw the giant candy cane nutcracker in her other hand. It was something the decorator had placed on the bookshelf and Patrice must have yanked it off while I was running to this side of the room. The thing was big and heavy, and she wielded it like a weapon. I kept screaming, hoping someone would hear me, as she lifted the thing up to bludgeon me. The front door flew open and Mac, his face turned white with shock, ran into the room shouting.

Patrice whipped around and the momentary distraction allowed me to grab her arm and shake the nutcracker out of her hand. The thing crashed on the clean hardwood floor and I had the fleeting thought that I might have to repair the dent. If I lived that long.

Patrice went scrambling for the nutcracker.

"No!" Mac shouted again, already halfway across the room. I thought I heard my father's voice yelling, too, but in that moment, all I could see was Patrice rushing at me to bash my head in with the nutcracker.

I needed my tool belt, my hammer, a wrench, anything. I looked around but remembered I'd left everything in my backpack. I couldn't think, could only grab the one thing available to me on the table.

The cupcake.

Patrice came at me and I shoved the cupcake, frosting first, right into her face.

She shrieked and her arms thrashed around in her attempt to hit me with that stupid nutcracker, but she couldn't see anything with frosting in her eyes. I clutched her arm and twisted. The nutcracker fell from her hand, and I shoved her away from me as hard as I could. She stumbled backward, her arms windmilling in an attempt to regain her balance. But she kept going, falling, almost in slow motion, and I watched in horror as she tumbled into the Christmas tree, toppling it over.

She was stunned for a long moment, then tried to move. But she was stuck on her back like an ungainly turtle, unable to right herself. She tried pushing up, tried turning over, all the while wiping green frosting off her face.

"Help me," she cried.

"No," I muttered, and fell into Mac's arms.

"Eric's on his way," Dad said, standing watch at the French doors. "I told him to come around the back."

"Thanks, Dad."

While waiting for the police, Mac had pulled Patrice up from the fallen Christmas tree and led her to a side chair. He pulled the other chair over and sat down.

After handing her his handkerchief to help her wipe off the frosting, he used his charm and skill to cajole her into confessing everything.

It turned out that Patrice and Potter had been having an affair for years while the bank executive was skimming money from the bank.

"He always promised that we would run away together," she sobbed. "But last week I caught him with another woman. An *older* woman! She looks exactly like me—in ten years!"

"Was he with her at the Lobster Pot?" I asked, apropos of almost nothing, except that Lizzie had claimed to have seen the two of them together. I wanted to make sure my friend hadn't gone bonkers.

Patrice looked almost frightened by my supernatural ability to know such a thing. "Yes! How did you know?"

I shrugged, thinking, *There's one point for Lizzie.*

"I was so angry," she said. "He was cheating on me, after all I did for him. And with an old bag. It made me sick."

"Did you argue in here?" Dad asked.

She glanced around, slowly recognizing where she was. "Yes. He came in here to hide the bracelet in your tool chest."

"How did he steal the bracelet from Heather?"

"That was April's doing. She's his niece and Potter hired her to do some dirty tricks around here. She was only here to cause mischief. Mr. Potter had a good laugh when she told him that she'd accused that Santa Claus person of assaulting her. And all along, she swore she would steal something from the garage, just for a kick."

"But why?"

"Peter was furious with the bank's board of directors for donating this property to that stupid charity. He had planned to sell it off in parcels and pocket the money."

"Peter Potter was a slimeball," I muttered.

She ignored me. "He considered sabotage his only recourse and brought April to town to help."

"Because they're two of a kind."

"Yes." She gazed at Dad and I thought she might have looked contrite for a moment. "He said it was icing on the cake to be able to ruin the project *and* damage Jack Hammer's reputation at the same time."

"What a sweetheart," I said through my teeth, not missing the subtle irony of her face covered in icing.

"He was," she sniffled, "to me."

"For a few years anyway."

"Twenty years," she wailed. "The best years of my life."

"There, there," Mac said, patting her hand solicitously in order to get her to continue spilling her guts.

"So you were in here," I prompted, "watching Potter hide the diamond charm bracelet in Dad's tool chest. And then what happened?"

"What else could I do?" she asked, glancing at all of us. "I confronted him. I had put up with him for twenty years and now he thought he'd cut me out of the deal? Not likely!"

"And what did he say?" Mac asked.

"He laughed at me," she snarled. "He pulled a piece of paper out of his pocket and waved it at me. Taunting me. Assuring me I would never get my greedy little fingers on it." She waved her hand toward the butler's pantry. "And then he strutted away like the arrogant bully he's always been."

"But there's no exit that way," I reminded her.

She sniffed. "He didn't know that and neither did I."

"Were you angry?" Mac asked. He was in his element asking her probing questions as though he were interviewing an expert for one of his stories. It made me smile despite the miserable events that had just taken place.

As Mac spoke, I watched Eric slip into the room and figured he would put a stop to the conversation immediately. But to my surprise, he just stood by the door, watching and listening.

"I was beside myself with rage," Patrice admitted. "I wanted to kill him."

Mac sat close to the edge of his seat. "What did you do next?"

"I needed a weapon. I don't know if I meant to kill him. I just wanted to get his attention. How dare he betray me after all these years?"

Patrice seemed to be enjoying Mac's interest in her story. Maybe that's why Eric was allowing him to continue questioning her.

"He was not a good person," Mac said, encouraging her.

"No," she agreed. "He'd pushed me to my limit. I looked around and saw that Jack's tool chest was still open. I—I grabbed the first thing on top. It was some sort of ax. I tore the cover off and went running after him and I was surprised to find him just inside the hallway. I thought he would be long gone by then. But the hallway ended after a few feet. It must've concerned him that he found himself cornered."

I thought about it. Potter probably didn't want to face Patrice's wrath, so he was trying to figure out the best way to leave the house. Maybe he opened the window.

Patrice sighed. "I didn't even think about it, just thrust the ax as hard as I could into his back. I didn't think it would do anything to him. He's quite large, you know, and I'm not very strong. But it landed in his neck."

"What happened then?"

"He . . . stumbled and fell. I was scared to death he would fall on top of me, so I scooted around and got out of his way. As he fell, he grabbed the door and it closed behind him. He just stared at me for a moment, then he fell forward, on his face. He squirmed a few times, then stopped. I still didn't think he was dead. I thought maybe he had fainted or something. I took a chance and went through his pockets, looking for that piece of paper. But then I heard footsteps upstairs and knew I had to get out of there."

Footsteps upstairs? Who else was in the house that night? One of the contractors, I supposed, but I would have to figure that out later, because Patrice was still talking.

"I couldn't budge the door. His feet were in the way and I couldn't move him."

She took a deep breath. "I had to climb over him to reach the window. It was already open, so I pushed out the screen and jumped down. And ran."

"You were afraid," Mac said.

"Yes. Terrified. Mainly because I knew he would wake up and come after me."

"What did you do when you found out he was dead?" I asked.

She closed her eyes and breathed slowly. "I was so relieved at first, but then I knew I had to be on guard." She opened her eyes and looked at me. "I had to find a way to get information. I decided to try and ingratiate myself around here so that I could keep tabs on the investigation."

"You certainly did ingratiate yourself," I said, thinking of those dozens of pastries she'd brought every day. She had to know that construction workers were easily led around by their stomachs, but still. "I've got to ask, Patrice: why were you tearing into the butler's pantry this morning?"

Her eyes seemed to glaze over, and for a moment she stared at nothing in particular. I wondered if she was drifting back to insanity land.

"Patrice?"

Finally she murmured, "I knew he must have hidden it in there somewhere."

Mac leaned forward and touched her hand. "What did he hide, Patrice?"

She blinked and looked up at him. "The numbers. To the Swiss bank accounts."

So Potter really had been stealing money from the bank. I met Eric's gaze. He stood with his arms folded tightly across his chest and his jaw clenched. I could tell by that look that he knew he'd discovered the answers to more than one crime today.

"I had to find them," she continued. "But then I couldn't get into the pantry. It was sealed off for days and there was always someone around to make sure no one got in there."

"And then I started working in there."

She glared at me. "Every time I came around, you were there. But I had to keep trying because it was the only place he could've hidden the numbers. I finally got in there this morning. But I couldn't find them." She glanced up at me. "I know you have them."

"I don't."

Her eyes narrowed in on me. I knew she would have come at me with fists flying if there weren't a bunch of men watching her every move.

At that moment, I saw Tommy slide into the room and stand next to Eric. I figured Eric had texted him. Maybe they were ready to take her off to jail, but I had a few more questions first.

"Why did you try to kill Santa Claus?"

Mac's eyes widened and he turned to Patrice. She was breathing more heavily, getting angry all over again. Mac leaned over and touched her arm calmly. "Tell me about Santa Claus, Patrice."

She stared at him and smiled. She must have enjoyed his voice a lot more than mine, and that was okay. I understood and I didn't care, as long as she answered the darned question.

"He was working late that night," she murmured. "Said he was looking over his new apartment upstairs. He must've seen me sneaking out of the house, because when I started working here, he came around looking for me. He told me he saw me that night."

So it was Slim's footsteps that she heard. That answered that question. But I had more.

"Did he try to blackmail you?" I asked.

"No. He tried to convince me that I'd done the right thing. He hated Potter for driving him out of business. He told me that if I ever wanted to talk about it, he was a good listener. He said I could trust him to keep quiet, but I knew I couldn't."

So Potter had driven Slim out of business. Another mark against him.

"How did you know about the wine cellar?" I asked.

She waved her hand in the air blithely. "Oh, Peter used to go down there and steal a bottle every so often."

"So you lured Santa downstairs?" Mac asked.

"No, of course not," she said, smiling coyly. "I simply asked him to carry something up from the cellar for me."

She'd tried to kill him, simply because he had tried to be a friend to her. "You know he's in a coma and expected to recover."

"That's what I've heard," she said darkly. "I had planned to visit him in the hospital one of these nights."

And do what? I wondered. *Finish the job?*

I shuddered and glanced at Eric, who looked as though he'd heard enough. He crossed the room and stood next to Patrice. "Would you stand up for me, please?"

She stood slowly, meeting each of our gazes directly. Eric took hold of her arm and started to lead her out of the room. I was glad she was going to jail, not for killing Potter, but for attacking me so viciously. All for a stupid piece of paper.

I gasped, realizing at that very moment what she'd been talking about. "Wait!"

I ran to my backpack, pulled out my tool belt, and found the crumpled piece of paper from the pantry drawer. I held it out for her to see. "Is this the paper you were looking for?"

Her eyes widened. She screamed and lunged at me. I let out a little shriek and scrambled backward, out of range of her fingernails.

"That's enough," Eric commanded. He grabbed her arm and yanked her back next to him. Tommy took her other arm and the two of them dragged her away.

When the door shut behind them, I slid into my chair and tried to catch my breath. It took a while for me to breathe a little easier. Mac sat on the arm of my chair and wrapped his arm around my shoulders.

"Never a dull moment with you, Irish."

I smiled. It was true, I suppose. Lizzie had said something similar a few nights ago, and she was right. I did lead the most interesting life. Right then, though, I would have been perfectly happy to have a touch more boredom.

My dad and his guys set the Christmas tree back upright, rehung the displaced ornaments, and swept the fallen pine needles off the floor. I spent an hour erasing all traces of Patrice from the ballroom. None of the pantry drawers were damaged, but I found bits of green frosting all over the dining area. The injury done to the wood floor from the nutcracker was minimal and wouldn't be noticed by anyone but me. Nevertheless, when the time was right, I planned to get back in here to pump it full of wood filler, sand it, and refinish it, just to get rid of the bad Patrice vibe.

Everything in the room was back in order when the door to apartment three opened and a little girl peeked inside.

"Mommy, is this our new house?"

"Yes, honey. We can go inside."

"Come on in," Dad said. "Welcome to your new home."

"Thank you," Sophie said. She introduced herself and her daughter, Molly.

"Mommy, there's a Christmas tree," Molly whispered. "Can we pretend it's ours?"

"It is yours, Molly," I said. "Everything in here is yours, and I hope you love it as much as we've loved fixing it up for you."

Molly was mesmerized by the sparkling ornaments

while Sophie's eyes teared up. She managed a shaky smile. "Thank you. Thank you all so much. You have no idea what this means."

But of course we did.

Mac and Dad and I left Sophie and Molly to explore their new home. Wandering out to the foyer, we found Callie chatting with another new tenant. I could hear other new tenants walking around upstairs as the different contractors went from room to room, showing off the library and the laundry room and other common areas. There was some crying and a lot of laughing, and I'll admit I might have shed a tear or two myself. I was determined to savor every joyful moment after experiencing the terror of Patrice only an hour before.

Slowly but surely everyone made their way to the foyer. Jason gave a heartfelt speech welcoming everyone and thanking the crew for the fantastic job we'd done. I couldn't have agreed more.

I raised my glass and Mac clinked his to mine. Then we both touched Callie's glass of apple juice.

"Merry Christmas, sweetie," I said.

Callie grinned. "Merry Christmas, Shannon."

I moved around the room clinking glasses with Lizzie and Hal and Marigold and Daisy. Jane was there, too, and every single one of my contractors and all the crew members. I tried to clink my glass with each one of theirs, thanking them for their help and wishing them Merry Christmas.

Jane found me in the corner by the fireplace talking to Zach about his wife's new plan. "She wants to adopt."

"That's a great idea," I said.

"But, wow, Shannon," Zach said, "it's going to cost us thousands of dollars."

"Well, I suppose giving birth can be expensive."

"Yeah, but most of the money will go to lawyers and intermediaries." He shrugged, then grinned. "Still, it's worth it. We really want to have a family."

I gave him a quick hug. "I'm so happy you've made a decision."

"Thanks. Julie's really happy, too."

Jane coughed lightly to interrupt the conversation. "I'm sorry, but we've got to be going. The parade starts soon."

I turned to Zach. "Will you be there?"

"Sure," he said easily. "I'm meeting Julie at the dog-shelter booth. That's always our favorite place."

"Mine, too," I said, squeezing his hand. "And don't miss our doggy Christmas fashion show. It promises to be the hit of the festival."

He chuckled. "I wouldn't miss it for the world."

The floats were lined up and ready to go. I did a last-minute check of the first float to make sure that Santa Claus was comfortable and warm and had enough candy to toss out to the crowd.

I checked the Paper Moon float and Santa gave me a jolly thumbs-up.

I moved to the next float, sponsored by Emily's tea shop. Santa Claus sat at an oversized tea table with three little girls in frilly dresses, ready to partake of afternoon tea. Naturally, they wore long underwear underneath those pretty frocks. Santa assured me that he had everything he needed and was all set to go.

The float after that was from Hansen's Hardware. The Santa Claus here had a big red tool chest by his feet, filled with chocolate Christmas trees and gummy stars to toss to the parade-goers.

I gazed down the line of colorful floats, each decorated to the max in Christmas lights and garland and oversized ornaments, and smiled. Yes, each float had its very own Santa Claus on board. It really was the best solution of all. After all, how could I possibly choose only one Santa Claus when they were all so special in their own way?

It promised to be the best parade ever.

Jane stood at the front of the line, blew her whistle three times, and shouted, "Start your engines! The parade is ready to begin."

The float cars revved their engines and the parade began to move at glacial speed.

"We did it," I said, bouncing up and down and hugging Jane.

"The night is still young," she said, laughing. "But yes, we did it again."

"And naturally, it's the coldest freaking night ever," I said, shivering as I zipped up my down jacket.

"I know," Jane said. "I'm freezing."

But I felt warm inside as I watched the Cozy Café float lead the way toward Main Street and the town square.

I walked along with the float and waved at the parade-goers lining the streets around the town square.

Without warning, something wet fell on my head. "Oh no," I shouted to Jane. "I hope it's not going to rain." But I realized she couldn't hear me over the roar of the crowd.

I patted my hair but didn't feel any raindrops, so I

ignored it, until something else fell on my head. That's when I looked up and saw white bits falling from the sky. For the briefest of seconds, I wondered if some pillow stuffing had broken loose somewhere.

"It's snowing!" someone shouted.

I laughed and looked around for Jane. She was walking next to the float behind me. She wore the biggest smile as she gazed up at the snow-filled sky.

For a brief moment, the crowd was silent as everyone took in the wonder of the rare snowfall.

"Can you believe it?" Jane said.

"No. I don't remember it ever snowing before."

"Once in 1957," old Mr. Hansen said, his voice cracking in the night air. "Now that was a cold one."

The doggy fashion show was a hit, as expected. More animals found forever homes and children walked around with snowflakes painted on their faces. It was another successful festival, and Jane and I couldn't have been happier. The cold wasn't even discussed, because it had brought a beautiful snowy night.

Callie and Mac found me at the side of the stage. Both of them were loaded down with bags of Christmas gifts from all the different booths. I hoped there was a box of fudge somewhere in one of those bags.

"Are you ready to go home?" Mac asked.

"I have one more thing to do. It's special. Would you like to come with me?"

"Sure," Callie said.

We strolled across the street to Lizzie's store. The snow was still falling and it was a beautiful sight to see it scattered on the peaked roofs of the Victorian shops around the square. We walked into Paper Moon and saw everyone gathered around the front counter.

I moved closer and understood why. The baby was sitting in her bouncy seat, giggling and burbling with joy at all the happy faces gazing at her.

The store was warm and cozy and the scent of Christmas pines filled the air, accented by the wonderfully pulpy smell of books and handmade paper.

"Shannon!" someone called.

I glanced in that direction and cried, "Lauren!" I rushed over and gave her a hug. "I'm so glad you came. Did you see the baby?"

She nodded, sniffling, and I knew she had been crying. "She's so beautiful."

"Yes, she is." I stroked her hair. "And so are you."

"Thank you, Shannon. I knew you would know what to do."

I just hoped I wouldn't let her down.

Zach and Julie walked in, hand in hand, and I went to greet them.

"What's going on, Shannon?" Zach asked. "Julie said you wanted us to meet you here."

"I want to introduce you to someone." I led them over to Lauren and her girlfriends and introduced everyone.

"Lauren just had a baby," I explained.

"The baby's right here," Lauren said, grabbing Julie's hand. "Come say hello."

Julie flashed Zach a look of alarm, but then followed Lauren over to the counter. "Isn't she pretty?"

Only then did Julie realize there was a baby on the counter. "Oh, she's beautiful. You're so lucky."

"I know," Lauren said. "I love her so much. Enough to know that the right thing to do is give her up for adoption. And I think I've found the perfect parents for her."

Julie let loose a sob. "I'm so happy for you."

Zach was by her side in an instant. "It's okay, honey." He glanced around, caught my eye. "We should go."

"No, not yet," Lauren said, wrapping her hand around his arm. "Stay. Please. I want you."

Frowning at her words, Zach gave Julie a quick look, then said, "Okay."

"Good," Lauren said, looking from Zach to Julie. "You're perfect."

Zach looked thoroughly confused now. "I'm . . . we're . . . what're you talking about?"

"Don't you know?" Lauren frowned. "But . . . aren't you looking for a baby to adopt?"

Julie gasped, suddenly realizing what the teenager was trying to say. With a loud sob, she dissolved into tears. "Yes. Yes, we are."

"Angel is a good little baby and she's extremely healthy," Lauren explained, sounding very official and grown-up. I couldn't have been prouder of her. "She cries once in a while, but all children do that."

And some shriek like demon kittens, I thought fondly, quickly brushing that memory away.

"Will you be Angel's new mommy and daddy?" she asked. "And will you mind terribly if I can be her honorary aunt?"

Clearly in shock, Julie and Zach gazed around the room, looking at each one of us. "Is this for real?" Zach asked.

I was sobbing along with Lizzie and everyone else,

but managed to say, "Yes, it's for real if you want it to be."

Lauren reached for the baby and pulled her out of her chair. "Don't you want to hold her?"

Julie nodded warily, as if afraid to believe the baby wasn't a figment of her imagination. Lauren handed Angel to her and she hugged her lightly against her chest, swaying slightly to the Christmas carol playing in the background.

Mac grabbed my hand and squeezed it. Callie came around and hugged me.

Zach touched Angel's back as he gazed at Julie. "What do you want to do, honey?"

Julie looked down at the baby and back up at her husband. "I want Angel."

He laughed joyfully. "So do I, sweetheart." And then he wrapped the two of them gently in his arms.

Everyone cheered and laughed and cried, and Angel cooed adorably, kicking her feet in joy.

"Look, it's still snowing," Callie said, pointing at the window.

"It's a Christmas miracle," I whispered, and Mac hugged me a little tighter.

It was indeed a miracle for Angel and Julie and Zach. And for me and Mac and Callie and everyone in Lighthouse Cove. The best Christmas miracle ever.